"It's not enough, is it?"

Kelley's voice was quiet. "You work and work, and there's still something…hollow about it."

"No, damn it. It isn't enough," Sam said. "But I don't know what else to do."

Suddenly he seemed to forget what they were speaking about and pulled her onto his lap.

Sam Cotter kept the world at arm's length most of the time by making it clear—with his slouch, his blunt speech, his flint-hard glare—that he didn't give a damn what anybody might think or say about him. Even when he smiled, his expression hovered halfway between warning and mockery.

But Sam had another smile, one he rarely used. It was slow, surprised looking. Tender. And infinitely sexy, because it was a window into the real Sam Cotter, with none of the usual barriers and barbed wire in the way.

It was one of the most beautiful things Kelley had ever seen.

And against all expectations, she was seeing it now.

Dear Reader,

Wow! What a month we've got for you. Take *Maddy Lawrence's Big Adventure*, Linda Turner's newest. Like most of us, Maddy's lived a pretty calm life, maybe even too calm. But all that's about to change, because now Ace Mackenzie is on the job. Don't miss this wonderful book.

We've got some great miniseries this month, too. *The One Worth Waiting For* is the latest of Alicia Scott's THE GUINESS GANG, while Cathryn Clare continues ASSIGNMENT: ROMANCE with *The Honeymoon Assignment*. Plus Sandy Steen is back with the suspenseful—and sexy—*Hunting Houston*. Then there's Beverly Bird's *Undercover Cowboy,* which successfully mixes romance and danger for a powerhouse read. Finally, try Lee Karr's *Child of the Night* if you enjoy a book where things are never quite what they seem.

Then come back again next month, because you won't want to miss some of the best romantic reading around—only in Silhouette Intimate Moments.

Enjoy!

Leslie Wainger
Senior Editor and Editorial Coordinator

Please address questions and book requests to:
Silhouette Reader Service
U.S.: 3010 Walden Ave., P.O. Box 1325, Buffalo, NY 14269
Canadian: P.O. Box 609, Fort Erie, Ont. L2A 5X3

THE HONEYMOON ASSIGNMENT

CATHRYN CLARE

Published by Silhouette Books

America's Publisher of Contemporary Romance

SILHOUETTE BOOKS

ISBN 0-373-07714-9

THE HONEYMOON ASSIGNMENT

Printed in U.S.A.

Books by Cathryn Clare

CATHRYN CLARE

is a transplanted Canadian who followed true love south of the border when she married an American. She says, "I was one of those annoying children who always knew exactly what they were going to be when they grew up," and she has proved herself right with a full-time career as a writer since 1987.

"Being a writer has its hazards. So many things that I see—a car at the side of the road, two people having an argument, a hat someone left in a restaurant—make me want to sit down and finish the stories suggested to me. It can be very hard to concentrate on real life sometimes! But the good part of being a writer is that every story, no matter how it starts out, can be a way to show the incredible power that love has in our lives."

**For Deborah Voss,
with love.**

Prologue

Everything was going just right. Sam Cotter squinted into the sudden glare of the warehouse lights and watched the night guard push the button that would open the big loading door.

"You know what you're going to do, right?" He barely whispered the words to the woman at his side. Kelley Landis was tall—five-nine to Sam's six foot one. He didn't even have to lean over to say the soft words at her ear.

She nodded, her concentration fixed on the guard they had been hired to watch. "Keep the camcorder rolling while the driver pays off the guard," she whispered back. Sam could see the video camera's strap already looped around Kelley's slender wrist.

"Good." He squeezed her shoulder, and immediately drew his hand back again. Even that brief touch was enough to send his senses spinning. He thought about waking up next to Kelley this morning, about putting his hand on her warm, still-flat stomach, trying to believe it was really true that there was a new life growing there who was partly his doing.

It still seemed impossible that in three more days he would be married to Kelley Landis, and that a few months after that he would be the father of a child. It was enough to make a man believe in fairy tales and happy endings.

It was also enough to distract him powerfully from the job he was supposed to be doing, he told himself.

What he was supposed to be doing was straightforward enough. The case had been tricky at first, but Sam's hunch about the truck driver—about the guy's pent-up look and the defensive way he talked to people—had finally cracked it open. It had been a good illustration of one of the rules Sam was drumming into Kelley as he taught her the ropes of the investigation business: a good detective listens to instinct, as well as to fact.

Unfortunately his instincts kept drawing him closer to Kelley now. And it was an undeniable fact that he kept finding himself fantasizing about getting her back to his apartment later tonight and undressing her piece by piece, kissing every silken inch of her that he uncovered....

He shook his head and stepped slightly away from his bride-to-be. "There's the truck," he said, keeping his rough whisper as low as he could. "Let's get to work, sweetheart."

The quiet whir of the camcorder and the click of the shutter on Sam's camera were masked by the engine of the big truck backing slowly into the warehouse. They'd picked a spot where the overhead lights wouldn't reflect off their lenses, and they'd already verified that the bales on the loading dock were full of VCRs whose serial numbers had mysteriously been sanded off. A few clear shots of the truck driver paying off the night guard would wrap up another successful case for Cotter Investigations.

"This is a cream puff," Sam murmured.

And then, suddenly, it wasn't.

"Looks like they're arguing." Kelley still had the camcorder to her eye. Sam couldn't tell if she was talking to him or just putting the comment onto the tape, for the record.

The voices of the two men were raised, but Sam and Kelley were too far away to hear what they were saying. "Keep filming," he whispered. "I'm going to get closer, see if I can figure out what's going on."

He edged along the warehouse wall, keeping to the shadows. He wished he didn't feel so uneasy about leaving Kelley on her own. *You're just out of shape for working with partners,* he told himself. *Hell, you've never really been in shape.* Sam Cotter had roamed the world strictly on his own for a lot of years, and he still hadn't gotten used to the idea that he wasn't alone anymore.

He could hear words from the argument between the guard and the driver now. The driver was saying something about being double-crossed. That didn't bode well. Sam moved through the darkness at the end of the warehouse as quickly as he could. If the situation blew up, taking Cotter Investigations' case with it, he wanted to know why.

"...been double-dipping on the side...."

"Hey, man, if you'd pay me what they're worth..."

The two men were shouting now. And Sam was close enough to hear the driver's fist connecting with the guard's chin as the bigger man landed a solid punch. The guard went down in a heap, but got back up almost immediately, fists flying.

Sam glanced back to where Kelley stood. She was lost in the shadows, and he couldn't see her face. But he sent her a silent message: *Keep filming. Don't let this get to you.* And he hoped like hell she would have the sense to realize that this wasn't a situation where her peacemaking skills could do any good.

She'd grown up in a family of four brothers, stuck in the middle between two older hellions and a pair of rowdy twins. She'd become a diplomat early on, not afraid to wade into a fight, never giving up until she'd effected a truce.

And she was good at it. On the very first case Sam had taken her out on, he'd watched in amazement as she'd coaxed a sulky runaway into sitting down and listening to her parents. It had been Sam's expertise that had traced the girl in the first place, but it had taken Kelley's quiet skill to get the two sides talking.

There were times, though, when diplomacy wasn't what was needed. And this was shaping up to be one of them.

"Stay put, damn it," Sam muttered. He looked back at the struggling men. There was blood on the guard's face now, and he seemed to be regretting getting into the fight. He kept trying to shield his head, but the driver—bigger, stronger and clearly out of control—was managing to land blow after blow.

Sam caught a sudden glint from where Kelley stood. She'd lowered the camcorder, he thought. He could almost *hear* her trying to figure out if there was anything she could do to help.

"There's nothing you can do." He said the words through clenched teeth. He knew he should be capturing what he could of the fight on film, but he was too concerned for Kelley—for her generous heart, her inexperience in this often harsh business, her belief that she could fix things when they went wrong.

He could hear the guard begging the driver to stop now. The desperate cries touched even Sam's toughened-up heart. He could just imagine what they were doing to Kelley's.

He had to get back to her. She didn't know this business nearly well enough to handle what might happen if she barged into this. Sam growled a curse as he slung the camera over his shoulder and started back toward the woman he loved.

He didn't get there in time. He saw her shadowy figure stooping—putting the camcorder down, he thought—and watched with a terrible sinking sensation as she strode out into the light, long-legged, determined.

"Damn it, Kelly—"

He didn't care that his shout attracted the attention of the two fighting men. He and Kelley could still make their escape through the back warehouse door they'd left open, if only—

She wasn't going to give them the chance. He watched her pull her private investigator's license out of the back pocket of her jeans, holding it up, putting all the authority she could into her voice.

"Hold it!" she called, moving quickly now. "You're both in deep trouble, and killing each other isn't going to help."

Sam groaned and reached for his revolver. There was no good way out of this now. He sprinted back through the shadows, hoping at least for the element of surprise, and tried not to groan again when he saw what he'd been most afraid of: the metallic glint of light off the barrel of the gun in the driver's shaky hand.

Suddenly everything was going very, very wrong.

Chapter 1

Three years later

"That's everything but the last case." Wiley Cotter paused and looked down at the single file folder remaining on his desk. "Want to go across the street and get a beer while we talk about this one?"

Sam and Wiley had been at this for hours, reviewing all the current cases being handled by Cotter Investigations. Until just this moment, Wiley had been his usual thorough, no-nonsense self. He'd thrown dates and figures at Sam with the relentless accuracy of a machine gun, summing up everything Sam would need to know to take over the organization his brother had started.

But now Wiley's manner had changed. And Sam didn't like it.

"No, I don't want to go across the street and get a beer," he said. "What have you got up your sleeve?"

Wiley didn't answer right away. It wasn't like him to hesitate like this, even with one of his brothers. Usually he kept his thoughts to himself as well as any high-stakes poker player. But it was clear now that he was trying to find the right words for whatever he wanted to say, and his uncharacteristic pause was starting to make Sam uneasy.

Wiley had done a lot of uncharacteristic things lately. He'd fallen in love, for one thing—or rather, he'd fallen *back* in love with a woman he'd lost a long time ago. Sam still wasn't used to the new light in Wiley's dark eyes, or the new openness in his style. He wasn't used to the idea that Wiley was leaving the investigation business, turning the agency over to Sam and riding off into the sunset to be with the lady he loved.

Actually, Wiley was only riding as far as the restaurant across the street. He and Rae-Anne had bought the little barbecue joint and were in the process of renovating it so that it would be ready to run when Wiley left Cotter Investigations next month.

In the midst of all the sudden changes in the Cotter brothers' routines, Sam was glad his big brother was sticking close to home. He liked having Wiley around. He liked Rae-Anne. And he liked barbecue. Having his brother and sister-in-law serving up good food right across the street was definitely an attractive idea.

But he *didn't* like the way Wiley was looking across the desk at him now. There was concern in those intelligent dark eyes, as if Wiley had bad news to break.

"Come on, Wiley," Sam said impatiently. "Cough it up."

"All right." Wiley finally opened the file folder in front of him. "But I think you're going to wish you'd taken me up on that offer of beer."

At first Sam couldn't see any reason for his brother's warning. The case seemed straightforward, if a little ticklish.

Counterfeit bills had been turning up in a Gulf Coast resort town, and the millionaire developer who was trying to sell vacation homes in the community wanted it investigated before any adverse publicity could affect the place's reputation.

Cotter Investigations had handled similar cases with success in the past. The only real mystery to Sam was why Wiley hadn't called him in in the first place, since Sam was the agency's expert in financial crime.

And then Wiley hit him with it.

"The only problem," he said, "is that the place is designed for couples, not singles. The client is insisting we send a pair of agents, so nobody gets suspicious."

"So send Sherrill to pose as my wife, or girlfriend, or whatever."

Sam didn't have a wife, or a girlfriend, or whatever. And Wiley knew perfectly well why that was.

"Sherrill's going on vacation."

"Vacation?" Sam snorted. "Sherrill never takes vacations."

"That's what she pointed out to me. She said she figured it was time she tried one, just to see what all the fuss was about."

Sherrill Goldwin, the younger of Cotter Investigations' two female employees, was smart, savvy and as tough as boot leather. She and Sam got along well, in a light-handed, bantering way.

It was more than he could say for his relationship with Cotter Investigations' *other* female employee.

"She'll probably hate it," he said. "She'll be bored as hell. Call her up. Maybe she'll be willing to—"

"She's already gone. She's in Costa Rica." Wiley was looking more and more apologetic. "And I couldn't call her up even if I wanted to. She didn't leave a number."

"Then we can wait till she gets back."

Wiley shook his head. "Nope," he said, "we can't. Our client was only able to stall his bank for a week. Normally the procedure is to hand over all counterfeit money to the Treasury Department, as you know perfectly well. This guy's got a lot of clout in the town of Cairo, so his bank manager cut him some slack. But we've only got a week to get in there, wrap things up and get out again. And that means—"

Sam had seen it coming now.

"No," he said bluntly. "Don't even suggest it."

"Sam—"

"Forget it. I am *not* spending a week in some resort cabin with Kelley Landis. Are you out of your mind, Wiley?"

He could feel the tension rising in his voice as he spoke. It was crowding into other parts of him, too, making his long legs suddenly feel restless and confined in the small space of Wiley's private office.

He shoved his chair back and got to his feet, glaring down at his older brother. It wasn't easy to meet Wiley's steady, sympathetic gaze, but it was a hell of a lot easier than letting his mind wander to images of Kelley's face, her eyes, her tall, graceful form.

It was bad enough that he occasionally had to encounter her here at work. It was worse yet that he'd never been able to banish her from his dreams, and from his waking thoughts on the nights when he couldn't sleep, couldn't dream, couldn't do anything but relive their brief shared past uselessly, endlessly.

It was impossible to imagine doing what Wiley was asking him to do now.

"This is an important client, Sam. Could be a big thing for the agency."

Sam started to say he didn't care, but the words wouldn't come out. He *did* care about Cotter Investigations. And he cared about Wiley. Wiley had scraped Sam up and helped put him back together when Sam had resigned himself to being alone in the world. He owed his brother for bringing him together with the only family he had, and for finding him a job he loved.

There weren't many professions where an ex-drifter with a short fuse and a loner's streak a mile wide could fit in. Sam didn't want to lose the life he'd built here in Austin. But still—

"Can't you do it yourself, if it's so all-fired important?" he demanded. "You've got three weeks before you quit."

"I can't, Sam." Wiley sighed and ran a hand through the dark hair that was starting to show faint streaks of gray. "You know I can't. It took Rae-Anne and me a long time to find each other again, and even then it was a near thing. I can't turn around and leave her now, not when we've just gotten back together. And especially not when this assignment means shacking up with another woman for a week."

He flashed Sam a faint grin. "Hell, I'm not even sure I *could* pretend to be married to somebody else at this point. I'm too damn happy thinking of getting married to Rae-Anne."

This was getting worse and worse. Sam moved toward the doorway that led out into the larger office area beyond Wiley's private office and reached up to grasp the door-frame with one hand. He leaned stiffly against his left arm, closing his eyes as he faced away from Wiley's too-knowing gaze.

And the instant he'd done it, he could picture her.

She had a dancer's grace, a dancer's confidence in the way she moved and turned and tilted her head. Sam had always felt like a rodeo bull next to her—big and awkward and always careening out of control.

And yet whenever he'd held her in his arms, some of her calmness had seemed to find its way into his own body, softening his rough edges, giving him a kind of peace he'd never known anywhere else.

Her eyes were as blue as the sea on a sunny day. In his imagination, her baby-fine ash blond hair always looked as though a breeze had just ruffled it, curling its softness into a halo around her fine-boned face.

He should open his eyes, he knew. In another two seconds—

It was already too late.

This happened every single time he let himself think about Kelley Landis. He would let himself be drawn into the remembered calm of her eyes, and then he would see that smile of hers starting deep down in those blue depths, swimming up at him with seductive intimacy. Waking or sleeping, dreaming or fully conscious, there was nothing in the world he could do to keep his whole body from responding to it.

The tightening in his loins now was only the first sign that he was letting his futile memories get the better of him. In a moment his blood would start to feel warmer in his veins, and he would breathe a little more freely, and then, if he let himself go on picturing that sweet and sultry smile—

"Hell."

He slammed his open palm against the doorframe and forced his eyes open. He had no right to be thinking about Kelley this way. He was no longer the lover she'd favored with that slow, enticing smile. He was the man who'd nearly wrecked her life three years ago, and he didn't blame her for avoiding him whenever possible. He couldn't imagine she would tolerate being assigned to spend a week with him on her own.

"It's out of the question," he told Wiley firmly.

"Is it?" Wiley leaned back in his swivel chair, clunking the heels of his expensive cowboy boots onto his desk. "You're not the boss yet, little brother. But you will be soon. How are you planning to handle being around Kelley then?"

That stopped him.

Sam had asked himself the same question a dozen times. He didn't have a good answer for it yet.

Wiley was nodding, as though Sam's silence *was* an answer. "You two aren't going to be able to go on playing hide-and-seek around the office the way you have been for the past three years," he said bluntly.

"Throwing us together on a fake honeymoon is a bit extreme, don't you think? A bit like tossing a kid into the deep end of the pool to find out if he can swim?"

"Sorry, Sam." Wiley sounded sincere. "The case is urgent, and I've got nobody else to send. And you're going to have to work something out with Kelley sooner or later, unless one of you intends to quit the firm."

"I sure as hell don't intend to quit."

"Well, neither does Kelley. She's worked damn hard to get where she is. She gets along with everybody here—everybody except you. And she's already agreed to take on the counterfeiting case. She's home packing right now."

"She's *what?*"

"I called her this afternoon as soon as I got off the phone with the client. She'll be ready to go as soon as you are."

Sam looked hard at his older brother. Beneath the concern, beneath the professionalism, right at the back of Wiley's watchful expression, Sam wondered if he was catching a glimpse of something like satisfaction.

"You'd better not even remotely be thinking about matchmaking, big brother," he warned. "If you and Rae-Anne have been putting your heads together about this—"

Wiley snorted and let his boot heels clunk back down onto the floor. "Matchmaking?" he said. "Don't kid yourself. I'd sooner wrestle a pair of alligators with my hands cuffed. This is a business decision, pure and simple."

Nothing was either pure or simple for Sam where Kelley Landis was concerned. And his reaction to Wiley's words now just proved it.

He should be following Wiley's lead and forcing himself to think of this as just another assignment, nothing more.

He should be admitting to himself that Wiley was right: Sam was going to take over at Cotter Investigations, so he was going to have to find a way to work with Kelley Landis, and the sooner the better.

But he wasn't thinking about those things. He was picturing eyes as blue and inviting as a summer sea, and feeling—

Disappointed.

And excited.

And scared.

It was crazy to feel disappointed simply because Wiley was pointing out that this was nothing more than a business matter. It was even crazier to be excited at the prospect. It *was* a case, nothing more, and they needed to get started on it pronto or lose a potentially lucrative account.

As for the part of him that was scared...

"How did Kelley react to the idea of spending a week with me?"

The question came out almost involuntarily. This was disturbing in itself. Sam, like his brothers Wiley and Jack, an FBI agent, had had long years of practice at keeping his thoughts to himself. But despite this long-ingrained habit, even the mention of Kelley's name seemed to be enough to toss all his usual rules right out the window.

"She said she obviously wasn't thrilled, but she could see the reasons for it. She said she wouldn't let her feelings get in the way of doing her job."

Sam wasn't quite ready for the sharp sting that rippled through him. It seemed to settle in his right shoulder, the one that had been torn apart and rebuilt after the accident at the warehouse. Unconsciously he reached up his other hand to cover the part of him that hurt.

He could vividly recall warning himself, just minutes before all hell had broken loose back at that warehouse, that

he'd let his mind be distracted from the job he was supposed to be doing. He still hadn't come to terms with how
much his own lapse had cost Kelley, or himself. The lingering pain in his shoulder was the least of it.

And here he was on the verge of doing exactly the same
thing all over again. And Kelley, damn the woman, seemed
to be able to muster all the professionalism she needed with
no effort at all. Sam forced himself back into the small inner office and sat down, silently cursing the confused tangle
of memories snarling around him.

There was no way of knowing whether Kelley had sorted
out her own memories or whether she was just masking her
feelings. It didn't matter—the point was, she had faced the
inevitable with far more grace than Sam himself was
showing.

Well, grace was one of the things he'd loved about her,
after all.

One of so many things...

"All right," he said gruffly to Wiley, who'd been waiting through Sam's silence. "Let's get this over with. I need
names, bank account numbers, employment histories,
everything you can give me. And I *don't* want to talk any
more about Kelley Landis, if it's all the same to you."

Wiley's quick shrug assured him that the subject was
closed. But that faint look of concern lingered on his face
as they got back to work. Wiley already knew, it was clear,
what Sam was just figuring out: that this could very well
seem like the longest week of his entire life.

He was refusing to meet her eyes.

There was nothing very startling about that. Over the
past three years Sam had made an art form out of avoiding
her. And Kelley hadn't exactly gone out of her way to be
around him, either. But still—

"I wasn't counting, but it seemed like you said about
twenty words on the trip down here," she said as they set

their suitcases down in the middle of the living room floor. "If we want people to believe we're really honeymooners, maybe we should start talking to each other."

No one had ever hurt her the way Sam Cotter had. And he'd done it without a single angry word—almost without a word at all. He'd simply withdrawn from their love as though it had never happened, retreating into some lonely place inside himself that Kelley couldn't reach.

His first comment to her when they'd met in Austin this morning had echoed with the coldness of that solitary place. "This wasn't my idea," he'd told her bluntly, as he hoisted her suitcase into his old black pickup truck. The bitterness in his voice had made Kelley flinch.

She'd spent the rest of the three-hour trip telling herself that the coming week was going to be a golden opportunity to get Sam Cotter out of her system once and for all. By the time they finally arrived at the Windspray Community, she felt a little more in control of herself and the situation.

But she still couldn't get Sam to look her in the eye.

"You're right." He was stalking around the cottage now, looking into the bedroom, the open kitchen and dining area, the spacious deck that surrounded the building on three sides.

"I mean, we need to agree on some kind of cover story," Kelley went on, glancing into the bedroom as Sam came out of it. She didn't know which was more disturbing, the realization that the queen-size bed was the only place to sleep, or the familiar clunking of Sam's boot heels as he made his way around the cottage.

She'd always found his long-legged gait one of the sexiest things about him. Something in the slow rhythm of his heels thudding on the floor seemed to find its way into her bloodstream, making it hard to breathe calmly.

Sam was opening the cupboards now, inspecting the fully stocked kitchen with professional detachment. "I've already come up with a story," he said. "We'll say I'm a financial analyst in Austin, and you're a bank loan officer. It's always better to—"

"Use a cover story that's close to the truth. Believe it or not, I actually do remember some of what you taught me, Sam."

Her mocking tone seemed to surprise him. He glanced over his shoulder at her, stopping just short of meeting her gaze.

Sam *was* a financial analyst of a kind. He seemed to have a natural genius for sniffing out scams involving money. It was his specialty at Cotter Investigations. And Kelley really had been a loan officer at an Austin bank, before she'd gotten intrigued by an inquiry the Cotter brothers had conducted in her department, and had decided to switch occupations.

"So when did we get married, if anybody asks?" It was hard work to keep her voice light, but she managed it.

"Saturday." It was Tuesday now, a warm but blustery early November day.

"Big wedding?"

"Nope." Sam shook his head, then pushed back the unruly dark brown hair that still—no matter what he did with it—always got in his eyes. "Registry office. Just our immediate families—your parents, your brothers, my brothers."

That was exactly how they'd planned to be married, three years before. Apparently Sam was untouched by that fact, if in fact he even remembered it.

Kelley nodded, trying to match his tone in spite of the quiet hurt that kept pushing at her. "And Harold and Helen Price are friends of friends, which is why we chose this place for our honeymoon," she finished.

"Right."

Harold and Helen Price were Wiley's clients, a wealthy couple straight out of Houston's upper crust. Kelley had seen their names in the society columns for years, and had known, even before she'd read Wiley's case notes, that Harold had largely retired from the oil business to launch various investment projects of his own.

The Windspray Community, in the tiny Gulf Coast town of Cairo, was the latest, and, according to Wiley, the most ambitious of Harold's schemes. Sam and Kelley were staying in one of the dozen or so luxury cottages that curved around a secluded road at the tip of a westerly-facing point. A health club and restaurant occupied the main building at the entrance to the community, and there was a new pier with boat slips and fishing facilities around the tip of the point.

"Cairo's practically a ghost town," Wiley had told her, "but the Windspray Community could turn that around, if things go the way Harold plans."

The problem was that Harold hadn't planned on a recession, or on having half his newly built resort homes sit empty. He hadn't been happy about the news that a phony twenty-dollar bill, then a second one, had turned up in the Windspray bank deposit.

"Harold's getting ready to do a big publicity blitz, trying to sell the rest of his cottages," Wiley had said. "He wants people to think of Cairo as the new hot Gulf Coast vacation spot, not as the place where somebody's printing funny money."

Enter Cotter Investigations, Kelley thought. Enter Sam Cotter and Kelley Landis, trying their best to pretend they were blissful honeymooners spending a week on the coast.

"Anything else we should get straight before we meet Harold and Helen Price?" she asked.

Every long step Sam took drew her eyes to the faded, familiar crease lines in his jeans. When he paused to stare out toward the beach, hooking his thumbs into his belt loops, Kelley had to close her eyes against a wave of memory that suddenly crashed right through her, sweeping her into the remembered sensations of Sam's hips leaning close against her, and his hands—those beautiful hands, so sure and strong—touching her skin.

Apparently he wasn't sharing her thoughts. His face, when he turned toward her, was set and hard.

"Yeah," he said. "There is one more thing." His gaze flickered to hers for the merest instant, then moved away. "I don't want you getting any ideas about us being partners again. We may be stuck working together, but this case is mine to run. You're only here as a part of the cover. Have you got that?"

It was as if he'd thrown something heavy at her without warning. Kelley half laughed, then realized she was having a hard time getting her breath back.

"If you think I'm incompetent, Sam, why not just come out and say so?"

He seemed suddenly fascinated by the sliding glass doors leading onto the deck. His gaze was riveted there, unmoving.

"I don't think you're incompetent," he said. "You're just—less experienced at this kind of case than I am."

And it was her inexperience that had cost them their love—and their child—three years ago. He might as well be saying it out loud. She saw it written in the taut set of his jaw, and in his stance, hands on his hips, feet planted wide as if braced to defend himself, dark brows lowered over turbulent blue eyes that still refused to meet her own.

Three years ago she'd sat at the foot of Sam Cotter's hospital bed racked by a sympathy he didn't seem to want and a grief he didn't seem to share. He'd been wearing the same expression then—the one that said *None of this means a damn thing to me.* The disdain in his face now made Kelley want to wrap her arms around herself, holding in everything she felt but couldn't make Sam understand.

But she made herself stand still, hands at her sides. There was nothing—nothing in the world, she told herself—that could induce her to open her heart up to Sam Cotter a second time. She'd survived his indifference once before, and she could do it again.

She'd survived the first time by pulling the pieces of her professional pride around her, working as hard as she knew how to become the best investigator she could. And she refused to let Sam take that away from her.

"This isn't like the last time, Sam," she said. "I'm not as green as I was. I've—"

"I don't want to talk about the last time."

And he finally swung his eyes around to meet hers.

She hadn't expected the pain in those dark blue depths. Sam's eyes could be as cold as gunmetal when he wanted to keep someone at a distance, and it was clear that that was what he was trying to do now. But underneath the steeliness of his glare, at the very back of the blue eyes that had once looked at her with such love, Kelley could see a half-buried anguish that shocked her.

Sam's rejection of her had been so abrupt, so total. And over the past three years he'd barely bothered to glance in her direction. Then why—

She shook her head. She couldn't—wouldn't—respond to whatever pain Sam might still be dealing with. Coping with her own feelings was more than enough at the moment. She refused to let herself be drawn back into the walking enigma that was Sam Cotter.

Fortunately he'd already torn his gaze away again and was frowning out at the Gulf of Mexico. Kelley forced her thoughts away from the defiant slope of his hips as he leaned against the counter. She knew she should be coming up with an answer to his ridiculous edict about letting him handle this investigation on his own, not letting her mind wander to all the things she'd once found so irresistible about him.

"So am I supposed to sit around like some kind of Barbie doll, being decorative while you solve the case?" she asked.

"You can do whatever you like. Hell, it's a nice spot. Relax. Take the week off. Enjoy yourself."

"It's funny—Wiley didn't mention anything to me about taking the week off. He seemed to expect me to earn my paycheck as usual."

"You will be. You'll be providing cover for me."

"While you do all the work."

"That's right."

Kelley lifted her hands in the air. "Well, thanks, Sam. You do wonders for my professional self-esteem."

His eyes flashed dangerously at her, a sudden beam of light out of a dark sky. "I'm not interested in your self-esteem, sweetheart." His voice grated over the words. "I want you out of the way, that's all."

Kelley closed her eyes and reminded herself of all the overtime hours she'd put in over the past three years, studying every aspect of the investigator's trade. She was searching for the right words to remind Sam of that fact when she heard a soft knock at the living room door.

She turned quickly and saw a thickly built man with a curly head of red hair peering through the screen. "Sorry to bother you folks," he said. "Maintenance sent me around to install that phone you wanted. But I can come back if—"

"It's fine. Come on in." Kelley moved to open the door, shooting Sam a pointed look as she walked past him.

He glared back at her, and Kelley felt the little click of connection between them that had always meant they were thinking the same thing. She'd almost forgotten how perfectly they'd sometimes seen into each other's minds.

In this case, the thoughts they were sharing weren't happy ones. Not only had they been caught arguing, but they'd been snuck up on. The redheaded handyman had gotten to within a dozen feet of them, and Kelley had been so busy reminding herself of her own competence, and Sam so bent on convincing her that he could handle things on his own, that neither one of them had heard a damn thing.

It wasn't the most promising beginning to what was clearly going to be a very difficult week.

Chapter 2

"Sam—"

It was hard work keeping up with Sam's long strides as they crossed the beach. Kelley found herself half jogging, and finally tugged at the sleeve of his blue shirt to slow him down.

"Sam, listen to me."

They were on their way to Harold and Helen Price's house, one of several big vacation homes that lined the sheltered side of the point. The Windspray Community's handyman, who'd introduced himself cordially as Steve Cormier, had mentioned that Harold and Helen were keeping an eye out for Sam and Kelley's arrival.

"They seemed concerned about you," he added. "Anxious that you get your phone installed and all that. They're like that with everybody here—real hospitable folks."

Jittery clients was more like it, Kelley thought. She'd seen it before: people waited until the last possible moment to call in an investigator and then they wanted instant results.

The handyman's words had seemed to deepen Sam's funk. He was digging into the soft sand with every step now, as though the beach itself was getting in his way.

He stopped at the touch of Kelley's hand on his sleeve, and frowned down at her. "We've already gotten off to a bad start," he said. "I'm just trying to get things on track again."

"By making it look as though we can't stand to be anywhere near each other?" Kelley gestured toward the Windspray cottages to their right. "I know there aren't going to be people in most of these places until the weekend rolls around, but the few who *are* here could very well be looking out and wondering about us. We're new here, so we're bound to be a curiosity."

"Damn." The steady sea breeze tugged Sam's dark brown hair into chaos again. He pushed it impatiently out of his eyes as he glanced from the cottages to Kelley's face.

"You know I'm right," she persisted.

"Don't rub it in." He adjusted his stance in the fine shifting sand and moved his hand to massage the back of his neck, as though it felt stiff. "When this case is done, I'm going to shellac Wiley's hide for getting me into it in the first place."

"Getting *us* into it, you mean," she reminded him. "I'm not a whole lot happier than you about having to put on a public display of affection."

Her words seemed to surprise him. "I suppose that's what it amounts to," he said slowly. "A public display..."

"Well, if we do it in private, it hardly counts, does it?" She was starting to be exasperated with him, and that was good. Out of all the things Sam Cotter was capable of making her feel, irritation was probably the easiest to cope with.

"You're right." He looked toward the cottages, hesitating before he spoke again. "You got any ideas about how to make this work?" he asked finally.

So that I'm-in-charge act *was* partly a charade, Kelley thought. She wasn't sure if it was reassuring or unsettling to know that.

"Well, we could hold hands, for starters." She reached for his free hand before he could argue about it.

At first they stood stiffly, like teenagers on a first date. The breeze off the Gulf whipped steadily around them, singing through the tufts of beach grass at their feet and making it hard to stand still. Kelley had braided her hair before leaving her apartment this morning, but the wind kept tugging the fine strands loose. She had a feeling her appearance was as disordered as her thoughts by this time.

She was about to suggest that they start walking again when Sam's grip changed. His palm had been awkward and reluctant against her hand when she'd first touched him, but now, slowly, he threaded his fingers through hers, lacing them together with the strength and certainty she remembered so well.

And she was swept into the familiar feel of him before she could even think of resisting it. She looked up at him quickly, startled by the dark fire in his blue eyes.

"If we're going to do this, we might as well make it look real."

His voice was even rougher than usual, half-lost in the whistling of the ocean breeze. Kelley didn't answer right away. She was feeling lost, too, caught up in the shock of the way his skin felt against hers. He'd touched her exactly this way in the days when he'd loved her. Surely—

Surely the turbulent look in his eyes meant that he was disconcerted, as she was. Surely she wasn't the only one fighting off old memories, old desires.

"If you're as professional as you say you are, then none of this should affect you, right?" he was saying. "If I kissed you, for example, it wouldn't bother you."

His words were as blunt and uncompromising as ever. But the ragged sound at the back of them made Kelley hesitate before answering. "I'm not sure we need to take it that far," she hedged.

"Why not?"

His blue glare was challenging her, probing past the calm expression she was trying so hard to hold on to. Could he feel the accelerating pulse rate in the palm of her hand, see the badly mixed feelings in her eyes? Damn it, she'd thought she was ready for this, but maybe she'd been wrong.

She'd forgotten how overbearing Sam could be. He was pushing her now, not giving her room to think. He was doing it on purpose, she knew. Whenever anything threatened to touch him too deeply, his first reaction was to bully his way out of it.

Whenever anything touched him... The thought steadied her a little. Deep down, Sam must be as shaken by this as she was, if he was reacting this way.

And the best defense against his bullying had always been to meet him halfway. She lifted her chin and said, "You're right. After all, this is just a job, right?"

"Right. And since you're so sure we've got an attentive audience out there—"

He didn't finish the sentence. And Kelley didn't have time to react before he'd dragged her against his chest, surrounding her with his arms and covering her mouth with his own.

He didn't just kiss her, he overran her. He crowded into every part of her, as big and rough and sexy as ever. His familiar deep growl resonated low in her body. She could feel his fingers splayed out against her back, digging into the light fabric of her white shirt, crushing the two of them together.

She gasped at the taut slickness of his tongue alongside hers as the kiss tangled them up. He raised one hand, threading his fingers into her hair, ravaging what was left of the careful braid she'd labored over this morning.

She'd wanted to appear poised, collected, in control of herself and the situation, putting the past firmly behind her, where it belonged.

And in under thirty seconds Sam Cotter had managed to rip all of that away, and to arouse her as suddenly, as completely, as devastatingly as he ever had.

She didn't want to let herself remember how hungry Sam could make her, or the way he'd always made her wilder than she'd thought possible. But it was all racing back in on her now as he demolished the self-control she'd built up so slowly.

She raised her hands to his shoulders without meaning to. She touched his strong neck, his high cheekbones, that satiny dark brown hair that refused to get the message about staying combed back.

It was falling forward again now. The feel of it between her fingertips shot through her like pure adrenaline.

She met his kisses hungrily, aching for more, suddenly aware that she'd been starving for this man for what felt like forever. There was nothing gentle in the way either of them was moving. Sam held her as though she was a captive who'd threatened to escape him. His thighs were rock solid against hers, his mouth possessive, demanding.

And Kelley was turning to liquid in his arms. For the first few confused seconds, she'd had some idea of resisting him, of letting him know he was pushing her too hard, too fast. She'd been envisioning a polite peck on the cheek, for heaven's sake, not full-scale plunder.

But her own longings were undoing her. Sam had always been able to sear the core of her with a single touch.

He called up responses from Kelley that she hadn't known she had in her until the first time they'd made love. And once that erotic secret had come out in the open, it had been impossible to hide it away again.

So she met every suggestive thrust of his tongue with an answering caress of her own, letting herself ease into his embrace until her whole body fit along the length of his— soft curve meeting solid muscle.

They'd always fit together this way, she thought, in a rush of remembered sensation. As though the gentle slope of her hip had been made to slide into the hard angle of his thigh. As though the sinewy strength of his arms belonged around her, clamped tight to the subtle bend of her waist.

It was impossible to hide her own pleasure, impossible to miss the shudder that ran through Sam's long body when she moved against the ridge under the zipper of his jeans. He was as aroused as she was, and the thought made her light-headed and reckless. And the whole time, in the midst of her crazily tumbling emotions, she could hear a voice saying, *I want this to go on, and on, and on . . .*

It didn't. Sam broke away abruptly, with a harsh exclamation that sounded half angry, half astonished. They were both breathing hard, and Kelley wondered if her own eyes looked as dark and wild as Sam's.

Then he glanced down, toward her belly, and Kelley was rocked by something just as strong as the passion that still gripped her. Sam's eyes hadn't lingered, but even that quick look was enough to tell her what he was thinking. It was something she was amazed she could have forgotten herself.

The last time they'd let their feelings for each other distract them from their work, they'd lost the future they'd longed for. Their love. Their trust. And the brand-new life of their child.

They'd been together now for under four hours and already they seemed to be in danger of letting the same thing happen all over again. It was enough to slow Kelley's breathing, if not quite enough to calm the ache she felt when she met Sam's still-roiling eyes.

She could see him hauling in a slow, deep breath as he reached his hand for hers again. She took it reluctantly, suddenly resenting whatever curious eyes might be watching them across this windswept beach. What had just happened between her and Sam had been so intense, so private, that she hated the idea of being seen by anyone else.

Sam's caustic words seemed to echo her thoughts. "If that was playacting, you should have headed for Hollywood instead of Austin, lady," he said. "You still sure you're not in any danger of losing your head this time around?"

She wanted to ask him exactly the same question, but she wasn't at all confident her voice would work if she tried it.

"Four units sold out of fourteen, and we're going to have to lower the price another notch if things don't start moving soon." Harold Price extended the pitcher of margaritas toward Sam, who shook his head to decline a second drink. "The very last thing we need down here at this point is a scandal. I hope you people are as discreet as I hear you are."

Sam had been taking notes during the conversation, jotting things down in the angular scribble that Kelley had always insisted looked more like crabs' tracks than written words. He glanced up now, carefully avoiding Kelley's eyes and trying like hell not to think of the way their kiss had nearly shaken loose any notion that he was supposed to be working on a case.

"Cotter Investigations is as discreet as they come," he assured Harold Price.

"I'm sure you are," Helen Price put in. "The firm came very highly recommended."

Helen was clearly the peacemaker of the pair. Sam had already pegged Harold as "old Texan"—gracious, affable, but with a telltale gleam in his crackling blue eyes that meant he would shoot you down in a second if he thought you were in his way.

Helen was his opposite, a gentle, sixtyish woman with soft brown hair and a thoughtful, slightly distracted expression. The two of them clearly knew each other inside out, and Sam had found himself wondering, as he'd listened to them talk about the Windspray development, what it must be like to spend forty or so years loving and trusting the same person.

It wasn't something he was ever likely to find out for himself. He shelved the question and concentrated instead on the inquiry. Wiley's briefing had been thorough, as always, but Sam liked to take his own notes, as well. He'd spent too many years alone to really trust anyone else's judgments, even his own brother's.

"The first counterfeit bill showed up in the Windspray deposit after Labor Day, is that right?" Kelley was asking.

Harold nodded assertively, the way he did everything. "The bank manager flagged the account, and when the second bill showed up at the end of last week, he called me in. A week's grace was all I could squeeze out of him."

"You were lucky to get a week," Sam said. "The Treasury Department isn't too pleased to have counterfeit bills going unreported."

"Most of the businesses around here—including the local bank—are hoping for Windspray to succeed," Harold said. "Cairo's like a damn ghost town, in case you hadn't noticed that already. Not like it was when I was a boy."

"Harold's family has owned property here for generations," Helen put in.

"We have a stake in the area," Harold added. "That's why I want this handled quickly and discreetly. I don't just want it solved, I want it buried. I don't want anybody to know a thing about it. I just want you two to uncover the counterfeiter and hand him—or her—over to the feds on a platter.''

''Is there a reason you say 'her'?''

Kelley had asked the question a split second before Sam had picked up the comment. *Always go after anything a witness tacks on to a comment* was one of the rules Sam had taught her when she'd first come to work for Cotter Investigations. And her gentle voice made the question sound more natural than Sam's blunter manner would have.

But that didn't change the fact that he'd told her in no uncertain terms to let *him* handle this case. It was hard enough just being around each other. If they tried to work together, too—

He glared at her from across the room, wondering how the hell she managed to look so dazzling in a pair of plain blue jeans and that loose white shirt. Was it her coloring, fair as the white beach they'd just crossed, smooth as the breeze that had whirled her hair into a honey blond halo around her face? Or was it the serenity she seemed to gather around herself like a cloak, the elegance that had always driven him half-crazy?

She met his eyes briefly, but that calm, sea blue gaze of hers told him nothing before she turned it toward Harold Price, waiting for the answer to her question.

''Wiley Cotter asked me to get together the names of all the people who were at Windspray when both bad bills showed up,'' Harold said. ''There were a couple of women on the list—one guest and one of the health club staff. That's all.''

Sam already had a copy of the list, and enough information to narrow down his first avenue of inquiry. He got to his feet, closing the small notebook he always carried in the back pocket of his jeans.

"We'll get started on this right away," he said, using the term *we* only because it was easier that way. "We'll report as soon as we have anything to tell you."

Harold and Helen got up, too, and followed Sam to the door that led out of the big screened porch at the front of the old house. "Actually, we'd like to hear from you at least once a day, whether you've got anything to report or not," Harold said.

This was the part of his job Sam liked least. He was about to tell Harold Price that no investigator worth his fee had spare time for holding his clients' hands, but once again Kelley got in ahead of him.

"Of course we'll check in every day," she was saying, as though there was no question of doing it any other way. "And our phone is being hooked up down at the cottage right now, so you can call us if you think of anything we should know, or if you have questions."

Great, Sam thought. Not only had she ignored his warning about staying out of the investigation, but she was acting as though Harold and Helen were also welcome to tag along whenever they wanted to. Maybe they should just issue invitations to the whole Windspray Community while they were at it.

He knew he was being unreasonable, but he still hadn't gotten over the bolt of fear that had gone through him when he'd realized, out on the sand dunes with Kelley in his arms, how easily this woman could make him forget everything except her own sweet presence. He needed to get his thoughts straight, and he knew it wasn't going to be easy.

He stayed silent while Harold and Helen walked with them to the beach road that led back to the Windspray cottages. Kelley was drawing Helen out on the subject of the property, which had apparently been in the Price family for several generations before Harold had decided to develop it.

"You must love it here," Kelley said, looking toward the cove where several tall sailboats bobbed on the water, their riggings clanking faintly in the breeze.

"Oh, we do," Helen said. "It's always been such a wonderful escape from Houston. And the light is so marvelous here, of course."

"Helen's a painter," Harold added. "A damn good one. You'll see her work in the Windspray restaurant."

There was obvious pride in his voice. Sam wondered again what it must be like to have someone in your corner for you, not just for the short term, but over a lifetime.

It was as much of a mystery to him as the identity of the criminal he'd come here to catch. And the thought of it— the contrast between his own solitary life and Harold and Helen's obviously vital partnership—made his voice rougher than usual when he and Kelley were finally alone on the sandy road back to their cottage.

"Looks like I didn't make my point clear enough," he told her.

She walked without looking at him, gazing out at the ocean view ahead of her. "Oh, you made it perfectly clear," she said. "I just don't buy it, that's all."

"I don't want to spend the whole week arguing about this, Kelley."

"Good. Neither do I." Her voice was as gentle as ever, but he could hear the determination in it. "Did it ever occur to you, Sam, that you cause as many problems as you solve by insisting on doing everything your own way?"

"What are you talking about?"

"I'm talking about what happened just now with Harold and Helen. Those people are paying good money to hire Cotter Investigations, and they're entitled to know what's going on."

"And I'll tell them—as soon as there's anything to tell."

"No." She shook her head firmly. Her strides had gotten longer, matching his own, and Sam found himself caught up in amazement at how she could look so graceful and so angry at the same time.

"Do you have any idea how much time Wiley spends spreading oil on the waters whenever you're assigned to a case?" she was asking. "You get results, Sam—nobody does it better—but you also tend to offend people along the way. Important people, like the Prices."

"Who says they're so important? Just because they get into the Houston society pages—"

"They're important because they're our clients." She frowned at him, then reached out an open hand. "Come on. We're almost back to the Windspray road."

He took her hand quickly this time, hoping that their angry words would be enough to cancel out the sweet sensation of her warm, smooth palm against his. He didn't want her to see how it shook him to touch her even casually.

"Wiley's never said anything about this," he muttered.

"He's tried. I've heard him. You just don't listen. You're like a bull in a ring sometimes, Sam. All you care about is tossing the rider off your back. And you don't care who you happen to kick while you're doing it."

He heard her voice waver slightly and looked hard at her. But her eyes were still looking straight ahead, and her face had settled into the expression—beautiful, serene but slightly masklike—that she'd worn whenever they'd encountered each other in the office over the past three years.

"Maybe he tossed us together on this job so you could get used to my style again," he told her. "In three more weeks I'm going to be taking over the company, in case you'd forgotten."

He felt her fingers tighten around his and heard her frustrated sigh. His own annoyance should have canceled out any gentle feelings he might have had toward Kelley, he told himself. But the pressure of her fingertips was connecting far too intimately with parts of himself that their earlier kiss had awakened, places that he'd almost forgotten about in the years since he'd last felt Kelley's smooth, soft skin.

Her words were anything but soft.

"And maybe Wiley tossed us together because he thought it was time you figured out how to work with other people again," she said. "Maybe he hoped I would tell you exactly what I'm telling you now. Did you ever think of that?"

He hadn't. It was so surprising that Sam suddenly stopped walking, tugging Kelley to a standstill along with him.

"Wiley wouldn't do that," he said.

"Wouldn't he?"

He didn't like the edge to her tone, or the glint in her blue eyes. He didn't like what she was suggesting, because somewhere, deep down inside, he had to wonder whether some of it might actually be true. Wiley *had* muttered things, over the years, about wishing Sam would check in with the office more often when he was working on a case.

Sam had sloughed off the comments, the way he'd sloughed off all the bad report cards he'd gotten as a kid. *Sam is bright with numbers, but needs to work at getting along better with others.* That was just his way, he'd always told himself.

And it was still his way. But somehow it was harder to defend when he was holding on to Kelley's hand like this. It was as if something of her softness had managed to get inside his own tough skin, making him think all kinds of things he had no business thinking.

He growled something inarticulate and let go of her. His free hand was halfway to his back pocket when her honey-eyed voice stopped him short a second time.

"I thought you quit again," she said.

Sam glowered at her. "I did, damn it," he said. "But you're enough to drive a man back into any number of bad habits."

"If you try to smoke in the cottage, you're going to have another fight on your hands." Her voice sounded more confident now, as if she knew she'd scored a point. It didn't do anything to improve Sam's temper.

"Don't worry," he growled. "I'm not completely uncivilized, no matter what you and Wiley may think."

There was a leftover pack of cigarettes in the cab of his truck. Sam headed that way now, leaving Kelley at the edge of the gravel road that looped around the Windspray Community.

At the moment he didn't care if it looked as though the supposedly happy honeymoon couple had just had an unhoneymoonlike tiff. He needed a break, a chance to air out his own thoughts and untangle himself from the slow, seductive magic of Kelley's voice, her eyes, her presence.

"Five hours," he muttered to himself as he stalked toward the parking lot. "Five hours with her and you're already a basket case."

It was beginning to occur to him that he was already in far deeper with this woman than he'd ever wanted to be again.

"What does your husband do?" Susan Gustaffson asked.

Kelley took a sip from the water bottle next to the step machine and glanced at the petite blond woman beside her. Susan and her husband owned one of the Windspray cottages, and their names were on Harold's list of people who'd been at the community when the phony bills were passed. Meeting Susan at the community's health club was a piece of good luck that Kelley was determined to make the most of.

"Sam's a free-lance financial analyst," she said, using the cover story she and Sam had worked out.

"When did you get married?"

Kelley glanced down at the small gold band on the fourth finger of her left hand. Sam wore a matching one, provided by Wiley. It had felt strange, slipping the rings on in Sam's truck yesterday afternoon. The quick, meaningless gesture was so very different from the joyful ceremony they'd planned three years before.

She managed a quick smile at Susan Gustaffson, though, before the other woman could wonder why a new bride was looking so pensively at her wedding ring. "Last weekend," she said.

"And what kind of work do *you* do, Kelley?"

"I'm a loan officer, in a bank up in Austin."

And that was enough answers, Kelley thought. "How about you?" she asked. "And *your* husband?"

"I'm a stockbroker, with a firm in Houston. And Jon is a commercial artist."

"Really? Does he work with computers?"

"Oh, sure. Everybody in the design field has them now."

Kelley made a mental note next to Jon Gustaffson's name. Computer technology was taking over counterfeiting, too, making it much easier for anybody with the right equipment to turn out a passable forged bill.

"I always think of artists as struggling," she said. "Or is that only when they don't have the sense to marry stockbrokers?"

Susan smiled. "There's good money in Jon's business," she said. "He works for some pretty fancy companies. He's got a real state-of-the-art setup, so he can do whatever anybody is looking for."

Including creating a phony greenback? The combination of Susan's financial savvy and Jon's design skill definitely made the couple worth looking into. She hoped Sam would agree, and that this case wasn't going to turn into one argument after another.

Her lingering resentment at Sam made her move a little faster on the stair machine, outpacing Susan's slower gait. By the time the two women had finished their workout, Kelley was breathing hard but feeling purged of some of the troublesome longings that had been shooting around inside her all afternoon.

She still couldn't seem to stop picturing Sam's steely blue eyes and rich dark hair. But at least her whole body wasn't aching for him the way it had been when he'd suddenly walked off and left her after their visit to Harold and Helen. *It's just leftover lust,* she told herself as she headed for the shower. *Nothing a good workout can't cure.*

"Do you sail?" Susan Gustaffson asked as they were getting dressed in the locker room.

"I've sailed a few times. Why?"

"Harold and Helen have this gorgeous boat. We've been out on it a few times. They'll probably invite you, too, while you're here. Other than that, there's not a whole lot to do except put your feet up and relax."

"What about in town?"

"Cairo?" Susan laughed. "It's a cute little place, but it's the original one-horse town. Not even a movie theater. The local gun club has a target range on the other side of the peninsula, if you're into shooting guns."

"Sounds like you two spend a fair bit of time down here," Kelley commented.

"Well, we try to. It's just an hour from Houston, and we always feel so relaxed when we've been out of the city. Actually—" she smiled suddenly, a satisfied and very private smile that made Kelley look sharply at her "—we've been trying to get pregnant, and we just found out this week that we've succeeded. We decided to take the week off and come down here to celebrate."

Kelley's mouth suddenly felt dry as she offered her congratulations. She had to work hard to keep her hand from straying to her own belly in an immediate, sympathetic response.

I don't want one of our prime suspects to be pregnant, she thought. *I don't want one single thing to remind me of that brief time when I was pregnant myself.*

She pulled her comb through her fine blond hair, tugging impatiently on the tangles in it as though it might be a way to pull all those useless, painful thoughts out of her head.

There was no way to avoid thinking about the child she'd lost. She thought about it every day of her life, even after three years. And Sam's quick glance, flickering toward her stomach out on the beach this afternoon, told her he hadn't forgotten about the baby, either.

But the news of Susan Gustaffson's pregnancy wasn't going to make things any easier. Kelley forced herself to ask all the expected questions about the due date and maternity leave, but as soon as she could do it tactfully, she turned the conversation back to Windspray business.

"How well do you know the other residents?" she asked.

"Pretty well. They're a nice bunch of people. You'll meet more of them this weekend. Some of them are just renting, of course, while Harold tries to sell the rest of the units. Did you say you knew Harold and Helen?"

"They're friends of friends."

Susan nodded. "And Wayland?" she asked.

"Who's Wayland?"

"Harold and Helen's son."

Wiley hadn't mentioned anything about a son. Neither had Harold and Helen when they'd met with Sam and Kelley earlier.

"Actually, I'm a little surprised he wasn't around when you arrived," Susan went on. "He likes to check out the new guests and residents." She snorted. "Somebody probably should have told him that a community for couples isn't exactly the best place to go looking for romance, but—well, that's Wayland. He thinks he's irresistible to women.''

''Does he live here?''

''He does now. He moved in at the end of the summer. I think his most recent wife got tired of him freeloading and kicked him out.''

The first counterfeit bill had shown up just after Labor Day weekend. Kelley could feel the familiar little buzz of excitement that happened whenever two unconnected facts in an inquiry suddenly came together.

''Does he live at Harold and Helen's place?'' she asked.

Susan shook her head. ''Living with Mom and Dad isn't nearly hip enough for Wayland,'' she said. ''No, he talked his way into one of the cottages that hasn't sold yet. He lives in the one closest to the pier. I'm sure you'll meet him before long. Just don't encourage him and you'll be all right.''

In fact, Wayland Price put in an appearance before Kelley and Susan Gustaffson had left the health club. As they reached the front door, a man with slick black hair and dark sunglasses was on his way in.

''Right on schedule,'' Susan murmured. ''We can avoid him if you like.''

''That's okay,'' Kelley said. ''I'm interested in meeting all the neighbors.''

She was particularly interested in a freeloading son who had shown up at about the same time as the first phony bill. Putting up with a man who believed he was irresistible seemed like a small price to pay for getting acquainted with Wayland Price.

An hour later she was seriously reconsidering that thought.

Chapter 3

Sam had found only one cigarette in his truck, so he'd driven into town to buy more. The trip to Cairo hadn't taken long. The town hadn't exactly been a metropolis to begin with, and now half its downtown buildings were either boarded up or had given way to grassy vacant lots.

Here and there Sam had seen signs that people were hoping Harold Price's resort development would jump-start the local economy. There was a fancy little restaurant a block up from the beach, and a sign in an empty storefront announced the opening of a craft boutique in time for Christmas.

In general, though, Cairo seemed like a place down on its luck, waiting for somebody to work a magic trick that would restore the little seaside town to some kind of prosperity. No wonder the local bank manager had given Harold a week's grace with the counterfeiting problem, Sam thought. Harold was clearly a potential savior for the place, and it was in the town's best interests to make sure that the Windspray development was a success.

With a single pack of cigarettes in his back pocket—he *was* supposed to be quitting, after all—Sam headed back to the Windspray Community. Maybe, with the help of some nicotine in his bloodstream, he'd be able to face Kelley Landis a little more calmly than he'd managed to do so far.

But she wasn't at the cottage when he got there.

"Kelley?"

It was unsettling to be calling her name this way, almost as unsettling as his sense that she wasn't anywhere near the airy three-room cottage. Sam slid open the doors that led to the screened porch on the west side of the building and to the open deck on the east. But Kelley wasn't around.

"Damn."

Sam shook his head and swore again as he went back inside. He changed his city boots for sneakers and his long-sleeved shirt for a weathered red T-shirt, then sat himself on the porch swing just off the kitchen and smoked and tried to sort out his thoughts.

Sam had worked out his own philosophy about life at a very early age. It had to do with keeping one step ahead of everybody around you and not being left in the dark. It was what had made him a very good investigator once he'd joined up with his brother Wiley about eight years ago.

The trouble was that his philosophy wasn't just an intellectual exercise. Sam *hated* being left behind. The fear of it was his own personal demon, one that had driven him hard for a long time now.

It didn't matter that he knew perfectly well where that fear had come from. Understanding it hadn't done anything to calm it down. Having Kelley disappear on him like this made him crazy, just as crazy as he'd been all those years ago when he'd watched his father trying to walk away from the Cotter family home.

He'd gone after his dad, and it had shaped the way his whole life had turned out, for better and worse. And in spite of his own worry about all the things Kelley Landis could do to him with a single look, a single touch, he knew he needed to go after her now.

He finally found her in the restaurant, with another man.

The restaurant and health club occupied a big low building near the entrance to the Windspray Community. The dining area looked out toward the Gulf, and Sam's eyes were too dazzled by the afternoon sun on the water to make out the faces of the few people sitting at tables near the big plate-glass windows.

But he heard Kelley's voice, low and clear. He couldn't hear what she was saying, but he would have known that honeyed sound anywhere in the world.

And then, as his eyes adjusted to the light, he saw who she was laughing with.

The guy looked thirtyish, Kelley's own age, a little younger than Sam's thirty-six. But unlike Sam, whose lean and rangy body was pretty much the one he'd grown into twenty years ago, the stranger obviously spent a lot of time at the gym toning his muscles and trimming his physique. Sleek black hair and a dazzlingly white smile went with the rest of the impression. Whoever Kelley's companion was, he clearly spent a lot of time checking his appearance in the mirror.

In his old T-shirt and jeans, Sam suddenly felt scruffy by comparison. It didn't do anything to improve his mood. And neither did the unexpected sting of jealousy he felt.

The black-haired man had turned to say something to a waiter as Sam approached, so only Kelley noticed him heading their way. And the moment her eyes met his, she shot him a wide, welcoming smile that almost stopped him in his tracks.

Was she really glad to see him, as the sudden warmth in her face seemed to say? Or was she just acting, for the benefit of the people around them? Sam cursed under his breath, angered all over again by the way Kelley's presence was making this case so much more complicated than it needed to be.

Well, if he had to play the jealous husband, at least he was in the right frame of mind for it. Without waiting to be invited, he slid onto the bench next to Kelley.

"Hi, honey," he said, draping an arm across her shoulders. "I was wondering where you'd gotten to."

The way she eased into the shelter of his arm almost undid him. Damn it, she felt so *right* there. Suddenly it was hard to remember that it had been three long years since they'd been lovers.

The look in her eye was almost as startling. There had always been moments, especially when they'd been working together, when Sam had been able to meet Kelley's eyes and know exactly what she was thinking.

This was one of those moments. She was glad to be rescued, he realized, as he caught the quick, grateful flash of her gaze. And yet she hadn't walked out on this guy. There was some reason why she was putting up with his company.

Was she investigating on her own, nosing around in what Sam had plainly told her was none of her business? He frowned at her, trying to figure out what was going on, but by then the man across the table had finished his conversation with the waiter and turned his attention to Sam and Kelley.

The guy looked disappointed, and Sam didn't blame him. Basking in Kelley's undivided attention was a treat Sam himself would have fought for at one time. "Sam Cotter," he said, reaching across the table to shake the other man's manicured hand. "And you are—?"

"This is Wayland Price," Kelley put in. "Harold and Helen's son. He's been telling me all about spending his childhood summers here in Cairo."

Sam hadn't known that Harold and Helen had a son, much less that the man lived at Windspray. His frown deepened.

"Pleased to meet you," he said to Wayland, aware that he sounded anything but pleased. "I was beginning to wonder what had become of my wife." It took an effort to get the words "my wife" out, and he hoped Wayland would chalk the grimness of Sam's tone up to simple possessiveness.

Fortunately that seemed to be the message Wayland was getting. And the guy was smooth, Sam had to hand it to him. He took in the situation in a glance and widened his perfect smile to include Sam, too.

"I've been trying to convince Kelley to come out for a sail on my parents' boat one evening this week," he said. "It's a great way to see the sunset. Stop by my cottage anytime if you decide you want to do it—I'm always looking for excuses to get out on the water."

After a few minutes of polite chat, Wayland seemed anxious to leave, and Sam and Kelley followed him out of the restaurant. Kelley let her breath out in a sigh of relief as she watched his slickly combed black head disappearing into the white sports car parked beside the building.

"I thought I was going to be stuck with him all evening," she said. "Thanks for bailing me out, Sam."

So he'd been right. But still—

"If you're as competent as you say you are, you could have found a way to walk out on your own," he told her.

"Not without offending him." Her smile had dimmed visibly at his tone. "Wayland thinks he's God's gift, in case you hadn't figured that out for yourself. But I wanted to hear what he had to say."

"Why?"

"Because he was at Windspray when both those bad bills were passed. In fact, the first one showed up right after he arrived." She looked closely at Sam, pushing one loose strand of hair back from her face. "You didn't know that, did you?"

Sam's voice was tight. "He wasn't on the list Harold Price gave to Wiley."

Kelley nodded. "It apparently didn't occur to Harold to list his own son as a possible suspect," she said.

Sam didn't know which was worse, the feeling that he didn't have all the cards he needed to play his hand, or the realization that Kelley had gotten a step ahead of him already.

She was literally ahead of him now, too, climbing the grassy hill in the center of the circle of cottages. The little knoll gave a view of the beach and the ocean, and Kelley paused for a moment before starting down the other side toward their own cottage. Sam was frowning again as he caught up with her.

"Wayland said this all used to be wild," she said, lifting her chin toward the windswept dunes between the cottages and the water. "He sounded a bit sorry that his father had developed it, although I think he likes having a rent-free oceanfront place to live."

"He lives at Windspray?"

She nodded. "According to Susan, it suits his life-style to hang around down here."

"Susan who?"

God, he hated having to grope for answers like this. It wasn't made any easier by the intelligent gleam in Kelley's blue eyes. Was it possible that she was doing this on purpose, pointing out to him that there were things he didn't know?

"Susan Gustaffson," she told him matter-of-factly. "She and her husband Jon have the cottage two doors down—"

"I know that." And he knew the Gustaffsons' names were on the list Wiley had given him, too.

"I ran into Susan at the health club. She's a friendly type, so I stuck with her for a while. I got some good leads out of our conversation."

Sam clenched his jaw. "You're not going to stay out of this, are you?" he demanded roughly.

"Can you think of a good way to stop me?"

Short of roping her to a chair, he couldn't. And even then she would probably find a way to wriggle free. In that quiet way of hers, Kelley was the most persistent woman he'd ever known.

He closed his eyes for a moment. Three years ago, her persistence had launched her into a situation that had nearly cost her her life. And Sam had been powerless to stop her then, too. He didn't like the feeling that where Kelley Landis was concerned, his own stubborn strength simply wasn't enough.

"You should be happy to have me along," she told him as she led the way down the far side of the grassy slope. "Wayland may be a bit slimy where women are concerned, but at least he likes talking to them. Somehow I can't see him sitting down and chatting with you for an hour at a stretch."

"It was more like two."

He thought she shuddered slightly. "It only seemed like more," she said. "But that's not the point. The point is that I can move this investigation forward. I can help wrap it up sooner. We both want that. And you know I'm right about this. Why go on fighting about it?"

She sounded so calm, so reasonable. Her steady pace didn't falter as she crossed the backyard of their cottage and headed toward the shallow wooden steps that led up to the deck.

It was only in Sam's imagination that she was staggering, dragged along by a frenzied swindler with a loaded gun in his hand. The memory of it slammed into him as it did every time he let himself picture that nightmarish scene at the warehouse.

Kelley had reached the first step now, but Sam reached out for her, taking her elbow and turning her abruptly to face him.

"I'm fighting about it because every single time I've tried to do anything with a partner in my life, things have blown up in my face, that's why." He knew he sounded harsh, but he didn't care, as long as she listened.

Her face was thoughtful, watching him. He could practically feel the intelligence and concern in her eyes. The serenity of her blue gaze felt like a balm for everything that had ever hurt him in his life.

Except that it wasn't. He'd tried to trust that serenity once, tried to accept the sweet comfort Kelley had offered him. And it had ended in heartache for both of them.

He let go of her elbow and waited for her answer. With luck, she would be recalling that scene at the warehouse, too, and realizing that he had good reasons for acting this way.

"Every time you've worked with a partner..." She was repeating his words, puzzled, it seemed. "I didn't know there were other times."

He didn't want to talk about that. Damn it, he didn't really want to talk about any of this.

But Kelley was pushing him. "Sam?" she asked, looking up at him with that open blue gaze that always made him want to shake her, or kiss her.

He couldn't do either one. The first was out of character for the role he was supposed to be playing, and the second was just plain dangerous. "It doesn't matter," he growled. "Let's focus on the problem at hand, all right? If I can't concentrate on what I'm supposed to be doing—"

The slam of a screen door startled both of them, and they turned to see Steve Cormier, the red-haired maintenance man who had installed their phone earlier in the day. Sam cursed under his breath, realizing that the guy must have been inside their cottage all along.

Could he have heard their argument? Sam tried to push all of his own confused emotions out of the way, wondering if they'd said anything that might give away their real reason for being here.

"Just testing your phone line," Cormier was saying. "Couldn't get it to work earlier. Seems to be okay now."

"Good." Sam could see by Kelley's expression that she, too, was backtracking through their conversation, wondering what the handyman might have overheard.

"You married, Steve?" he asked abruptly.

The redheaded man looked surprised. "Never had the pleasure," he replied.

"Good." Sam reached one arm out for Kelley in what he hoped looked like a fond but weary gesture. "Smart man. Kelley and I have been living together, perfectly happy, for years. And then we decide to get married, and all of a sudden we're arguing all the time. We came down here to get away from it all and end up talking about nothing but financial investigations at work, like we're still in Austin."

The handyman grinned. "A week of sea air'll fix that," he assured them. "I won't be bothering you folks again, now that the phone's fixed. Although it sounds like you might be smarter to unplug it, if you're really trying to have a honeymoon."

If you're really trying to have a honeymoon. The words nagged at Sam all evening. Did Steve Cormier suspect that Sam and Kelley weren't the vacationing newlyweds they claimed to be? Cormier had happened to be around twice today while they were arguing about how to conduct their investigation.

Or had he just "happened" to be around? All of Sam's cautious instincts were operating by now, and he insisted on thoroughly checking over the cottage—twice—before he risked lifting his voice above a gravelly whisper again.

"Looking for bugs?" Kelley's voice was low, too, as she watched him feeling along the baseboards behind the living room sofa and chairs.

Sam nodded.

"Cormier's on that list of possible suspects, isn't he?"

Sam nodded again. He still wasn't sharing this case with her, he told himself firmly. It was just that this was easier than launching back into all the arguments that still hung in the air between them like a string of summer thunderstorms.

When he'd satisfied himself that the handyman hadn't planted any listening devices in their cottage, Sam felt freer to talk again. But by then Kelley seemed to have run out of things to say. The evening was nearly silent, punctuated only by a brief debate about who was spending the night where.

It ended with Sam sleeping on the couch, at his own insistence, and Kelley settling into the big bed alone, just one thin wall away from him. The thought of her there, warm and silky among the smooth white sheets, was enough to keep Sam tossing restlessly in the living room until well after midnight. When he finally did get to sleep, his dreams were even more disturbing than his waking thoughts had been.

It turned out that that was a very good thing.

He wasn't sure exactly what woke him, or whether he'd really been asleep at all. Kelley's soft voice seemed to come out of the distance, so muffled that at first he wasn't sure he'd heard it.

"Sam..."

It didn't sound like her. There was none of the sweet richness in her tone to match the sleeping fantasies he'd just been having about her.

But *something* had wakened him just now. Sam dragged a hand across his eyes and propped himself up on his good arm, listening hard.

Not far off, at the end of the sandy point, he could hear the sound of surf pounding the sand. No birds were singing at this late hour, and there wasn't enough wind to stir the low shrubs around the edge of their deck.

He *must* have been dreaming, Sam thought. His unconscious mind must have drifted back to those days when Kelley had said his name with such intimacy, such longing. And so he was starting to hear that same sound—soft, blurred by sleep—in his own dreams.

He shifted his long body on the sofa and had his head halfway to the pillow when he heard it again.

"Sam?"

It was even fainter this time. Faint, and frightened. And it was definitely coming from Kelley's bedroom. Sam was on his feet in a flash, clicking on the lamp on the table, heading into the bedroom without stopping to think.

The smell of gas met him like a slap in the face as he pulled the door open. His senses recognized it as propane, but he didn't stop to put a name to it, not yet.

Damn it, he roared silently at himself as he launched himself toward the bed. He'd thought she would be safe here, in this quiet, secluded place, with him sleeping in the next room! He'd been sure that by excluding her from the case, he'd be protecting her from anything that might go wrong. But now—

She'd tossed the covers aside and lay at the very edge of the bed, as though she'd tried to get up and found herself too groggy to move. Sam's lungs were screaming for air, but he fought against the urge to breathe as he scooped Kelley's nearly unconscious body into his arms and lifted her free of the sheets.

Her nightgown was thin, leaving most of her long legs exposed to his view. Her head fell onto his shoulder, seeming to nestle comfortably against him. She felt soft and familiar, as if he'd last held her like this just hours ago, not years.

He couldn't think about that now. The only thing that mattered was getting her out into fresh air, into safety.

He carried her out to the back deck and gently set her down outside the bedroom door. Then he sprinted to where the gas leak had to be—the propane tanks that stood at the back kitchen window, not far from the bedroom door.

He cranked the shutoff valve viciously, already searching for signs that the tanks had been tampered with. In spite of the darkness, it didn't take long to spot it: someone had monkeyed with the valve, adding an extra fitting so that a length of hose could be run not just to the stove inside, but along the doorsill and under the bedroom door, as well.

"Damn it!" Sam saw Kelley's head move at his explosive words, as though the anger in them had penetrated her fog. He slammed a hand against the wood siding of the cottage and went back to where she sat, head in her hands.

If she was sitting up on her own, she was still okay, Sam told himself. He told her the same thing, taking her hands, rubbing them briskly between his own, reassuring her that with a few more breaths of fresh air she would start coming around.

And the whole time he was silently cursing himself, and Wiley for getting him into this, and whoever had rigged the valve on the propane tank. What if Kelley hadn't moaned his name? What if she hadn't wakened at all? What if . . .

He could barely force himself to look at the awful possibility. What if someone had managed to kill Kelley Landis while he'd been sleeping on the living room sofa not ten yards away from her?

He spit out a string of expletives and stood up abruptly. Kelley was lifting her head now, starting to ask dazedly what had happened.

Sam didn't want to tell her.

He was still searching for the right words—*I want you out of here before the sun comes up* was as close as he got—when the nightmare became even worse.

Sam was no stranger to gunfire, but the sound that split the night air was oddly muffled. At first he couldn't imagine what it was. He saw Kelley turn confusedly toward the dark hill behind the cottage where the noise had seemed to come from. "What—" she started to ask.

By then Sam had figured it out. He'd heard the sharp ping against the cottage wall, too damn close to them for comfort. And he'd seen the doorframe splinter under the impact of the bullet.

Someone was shooting at them.

Someone was serious about wanting them dead.

He could picture the two of them, illuminated in the faint light from the lamp he'd been fool enough to switch on: Sam in a light-colored T-shirt and boxer shorts, and Kelley in her pure white nightgown. They were both easy targets.

The second shot went wide, zinging past the corner of the building and toward the front yard. By then Sam had Kelley clasped to his side and was propelling her through the still-open cottage door and into the living room. He eased her down onto the carpeted floor and joined her there a moment later when he'd turned off the lamp.

"Do you have your gun?" He whispered the question urgently, and felt her nod.

"In my suitcase. Sam—"

He was starting to snake his way into the bedroom, but the surprising strength of her hand on his arm stopped him.

"Don't leave me."

The whispered words were like an echo out of the depths of his own secret fears. *Don't leave me...* How could he turn his back on her, even for a moment, even when it was for her own safety, when she was looking up at him with such confusion in her face, such pleading in her tone?

"I have to, sweetheart. I have to get that gun."

"Your shoulder—"

Sam couldn't bite back a groan. Was she going to touch *all* his sore spots at once?

"You're hurt." She was struggling to sit upright now, moving against him with a gentle determination that left Sam only too aware of how thin their two layers of clothing were. "The fender slammed right into you. I saw it—"

She stopped, and the confusion in her eyes deepened. Sam hauled in a long breath and wished his heart would stop pounding against his rib cage.

Kelley was disoriented, drifting in time. That was obvious as her puzzled gaze met his.

But it didn't help to know that she was mixing this up with another dark, dangerous night they had shared, one that had left Sam's right shoulder in pieces and their unborn child dead.

He gritted his teeth now, fighting as hard as he could against the soft concern in her voice as she added, "Can you shoot? Are you all right?"

"Yes, I'm all right." He couldn't keep the harsh sound out of his voice, no matter how hard he tried. "I can't *aim* worth a damn, but I can pull a trigger. If nothing else, it'll let that bastard know we're armed."

Damn it, he was starting to lose his grip on reality, too. It wasn't propane that had blurred his thinking, but the agonizing memory of the last time he'd held Kelley like this, supporting her while they waited desperately for help to come.

Help had come too late, three years ago.

And this time Sam was determined not to rely on anyone's help but his own. "Hang on," he said now as he squeezed her tightly in his arms and then let her go. "And don't move, not even an inch. I'll be right back."

The air from the open door and window had cleared almost all the propane out of the bedroom. Sam could breathe normally as he groped his way to Kelley's suitcase and found the weapon and ammunition that Wiley insisted all Cotter Investigations agents carry with them on assignments.

Sam had ignored the rule, as he ignored any rule that didn't suit him. What was the use of carrying a weapon when his right shoulder was too banged up for him to aim it properly?

That had been his reasoning until tonight. Now, all of a sudden, being armed seemed like a very good idea. And Kelley, thank God, was more of a team player than Sam was. The weight of her pistol in his palm was a blessed relief.

Relief came to an abrupt halt when he heard her shaky voice speaking to him from the bedroom door. "It's in the closet."

"I figured that out, damn it! And I said to stay put!"

"Sam—"

He'd expected an argument. He heard a plea.

She was staying close to floor level, as Sam was. Her eyes were wide open now, and in the dim light he could see she was aware that the shooter could be right outside the building, choosing which entrance to come in by. The open, airy cottage, so appealing in the morning sunlight, suddenly felt hideously exposed. There were too many doors, too many dark windows for a killer to look in through.

"Sam—please don't leave me alone again . . ."

He heard her fighting her own fears, and losing.

Sam had heard Kelley Landis sounding frightened exactly one time before this. That night in the warehouse, she'd called his name with the same rising panic in her voice. And a moment later she'd been dragged into the cab of a truck with a gun at her head.

Sam knew he should be thinking, planning, getting a jump on whatever the hell was going on around them. But he'd only gotten as far as loading the five-round magazine into Kelley's pistol when the soft quaver of her voice got to him. If she was going to fall apart, Sam suddenly wanted it to be in his arms and nowhere else.

He didn't have to issue an invitation. She was already on her way across the darkened bedroom floor. Sam was half kneeling by the bed, and Kelley moved closer to him, the way she always did in his dreams, silently, almost magically.

In his dreams it was passion that made her quiver. Nothing had ever excited him like the way she let go of all that feminine elegance of hers and turned into a wild woman. In spite of the danger around them—in spite of everything—Sam felt himself responding to the deep tremors that he could feel running through her body.

But he knew it wasn't passion she was feeling. It was terror, pure and simple. He closed his arms tightly around her and pulled her against his chest, kissing her soft hair and the rapidly beating pulse at her temple.

"It's okay, sweetheart," he said. "I've got you. It's all right."

He didn't blame her for being scared. She must have half-wakened in the haze of the propane that had seeped with deadly silence into her room. And before she'd had time to start thinking clearly again, someone had started shooting at them. The marvel was not that she was shaking, but that she wasn't shaking any harder than this.

Her arms were wrapped around his waist. Sam could smell the faint perfume of her skin, scented with sea air now. She was clinging to him as if she was cold, but her body felt warm. And soft. And more enticing than any woman had a right to be.

He had a feeling she was near tears, and resisting them as hard as she could. "Cry if you want to," he whispered at her ear. "Hell, I'd cry myself if I wasn't such a tough guy. This case was supposed to be a desk job, not a damn shooting gallery."

"Sam, what's happening?" She was whispering, too. He was right about the tears, he thought. He could hear them at the edge of her voice. He leaned a little lower and tilted her face up toward his. Her mouth—the mouth that could look so poised, or so seductive—was trembling slightly.

He knew he shouldn't be doing this. But there was nothing he could do to stop himself.

He was trembling, too, as he answered her. "What's happening," he said gruffly, "is that somebody around here has already figured out the questions we're asking aren't just because we're curious."

"They must have thought—" She glanced up toward the big bed where she'd been sleeping alone. If they'd been real honeymooners, they would have been there together. "They must have been trying to kill both of us," she whispered.

He barely heard her, because he was barely listening any more. The way Kelley tilted her head brought her sweet mouth to within inches of Sam's. She was half sitting across his thighs, and some unmistakable signals were starting to blitz through his body.

It would be crazy to kiss her now, he thought. She wanted comfort, nothing more. And he was supposed to be protecting her, protecting both of them.

But her softly upturned face was so hauntingly beautiful in the faint predawn light. He'd kissed her temple just a few minutes ago, and nothing earth-shattering had happened to either of them. Surely—

He dropped his head lower and let his lips graze the angle of her chin. And then her cheekbone—that elegant, aristocratic line that drove him half-crazy whenever he looked at her. And then her jawline. The skin there was unimaginably smooth and soft.

"Sam—"

He didn't know what the sound in her voice meant now. He only knew that the ache in it connected intimately to parts of himself that only Kelley Landis had ever known how to reach.

He took her mouth with his, blindly, urgently. His own harsh moan of need shocked him. When he felt her lips parting to welcome him, he couldn't think of any good reason for being here except to recapture—somehow—everything that he and Kelley had lost.

Lost...

The word echoed in his ears. He kissed her as though he could erase the lonely sound of it. How could this be anything but right, when their bodies were responding to each other as though they'd last made love hours ago, instead of years?

His free hand moved over her waist and up across her breasts. Through the thin fabric of her nightgown he could feel their tight centers, aroused and explicit against his palm. He groaned again as Kelley's mouth invited him even deeper, into depths he didn't think he could ever get tired of exploring.

He thought of the other depths of her body, and the warm explosiveness of her lovemaking, and the way she'd rocked him all night long, leaving both of them exhausted and amazed. Those memories found their way into his kiss now. He raised his other hand to cup her face, wanting to pull them as close as a man and a woman could be, wanting this to go on until the hunger in both of them was eased.

His hand stopped just short of her face.

He was holding a loaded gun, for God's sake.

Suddenly the danger outside seemed to have invaded this darkened room. He was doing the same thing he'd done before: forgetting himself at the worst possible moment. He felt the shock of it like a fist hitting him in the small of his back.

He broke off the kiss abruptly. "I must be out of my mind," he said. His voice barely worked, but he could see in Kelley's startled eyes that he'd gotten the point across.

Maybe he *was* out of his mind. Maybe his own tormented memories had driven him there. Whatever the reason, he realized he'd been on the verge of losing himself in Kelley's sweet kisses while in one hand he held a loaded weapon, and while somewhere, possibly just outside the cottage, was someone who had just tried—twice—to kill them.

Gently, with muscles that shook almost as much now as Kelley's had when he'd taken her in his arms, he extricated himself from the embrace. "I'm sorry, sweetheart," he said. "There's just no way—"

He couldn't come up with the right words. He'd never been able to make words say what he was really feeling. There were people who thought he could be cruel—hell, Kelley was probably one of them—when in fact the plain truth was that Sam Cotter was scared to death of all the things he felt sometimes. And he had no idea how to say that out loud.

Settling for distance seemed safer most of the time. It seemed a whole lot safer right now.

"I'm going to get to the phone," he said, glad he'd had the foresight to insist that it be installed as soon as they arrived. "A call about a prowler ought to bring the local patrol car by, and that should be enough to scare off our friend with the gun."

"And then what?"

Sam refused to let himself be drawn into the soft mix of fear and curiosity and lingering desire that he heard in Kelley's voice. "And then we keep our heads down until daylight," he said, "at which point we start figuring out what the hell is going on around here."

Chapter 4

"Well, shoot," Wiley said.

Sam grimaced and stubbed out his second cigarette of the day against the metal shelf under the phone. He'd come into Cairo to buy a stronger brand—he figured he deserved it, after the night he'd had—and had decided to call Wiley while he was there. The anonymity of the beachside phone booth was a bonus, even though the wind whistling across the sand made it hard to hear his brother's deep voice.

The last words had come through loud and clear, though. "*Shoot?*" Sam echoed. "That all you have to say? Somebody tries to take out two of your best agents and you just say, 'Ah, shucks'?"

"What do you want me to say? I'm not thrilled about it, obviously. On the other hand, it means you're doing your job. You've got somebody worried, and that means there's something there to find out. All you have to do is—"

Sam cut short this little lecture, which he'd heard before. "Aren't you missing the point here, big brother?" he asked.

"The point being?"

"That I was right about it being a bad idea to have Kelley along on this case."

The pause on the line seemed very long. Sam's eyes traveled restlessly over the big fishing pier that jutted out into the Gulf, and the massive stones of the breakwaters that sat at both ends of the town beach. Cairo was a pretty spot, he thought, but a bit too exposed to the ocean for his own taste.

"Why?" Wiley asked finally.

"*Why?*" Sam's frustration came to a sudden boil. "Because she's in danger, that's why. Because somebody tried to kill her—to kill both of us—last night. If you'd been listening—"

It was Wiley's turn to jump in. His voice was still even, but Sam recognized the slight edge in it that meant Wiley's patience, like his own, was getting short.

"Sam," he said, "you and Kelley are both professional investigators. I don't expect my agents to put their lives on the line every single moment of every single case, but I also don't expect them to run away at the first sign of trouble."

"I never said anything about running—"

"No," Wiley cut in again. "And neither has Kelley. Has she?"

Reluctantly, Sam had to admit she hadn't. In fact, she'd been disconcertingly businesslike this morning. It was almost as though their adventures of the night before had caused some mental gear-shifting inside her. She'd spoken briskly to him over breakfast, outlining her plans for the day, and had apologized briefly for falling apart on him. She'd been confused, she said. Disoriented by the effects of the propane. It wouldn't happen again, she promised.

"Where is she now?" Wiley was asking.

"At Harold and Helen Price's, filling them in on what happened last night."

"Good." Wiley sounded grimly satisfied, and Sam couldn't help wondering if Kelley had been right yesterday. Was it possible that his big brother was trying to teach Sam some kind of backhanded lesson here?

If he was, Wiley was keeping it to himself. "What about the rest of the day?" he was asking.

"The Prices and their son and a couple of the people on Harold's list are going on some kind of sailing trip. We're invited."

"Better yet." Wiley sounded pleased to hear the news, although he knew Sam hated boats and everything that went with them. "You can tell Kelley from me," he added, "that she knows she can call it quits any time she thinks things have gotten out of hand. And that goes for you too, little brother."

As if he'd leave Kelley here on her own! Sam almost laughed at the thought, except that he was too annoyed to laugh. He hung up wondering if Wiley would be so cavalier if it was his beloved Rae-Anne that somebody was shooting at.

Of course, Wiley was in love with Rae-Anne. Openly, admittedly, head over heels in love. Whereas Sam wasn't in love with Kelley Landis. Not anymore.

He didn't stop to dwell on that thought as he lit another cigarette and stalked back to where he'd parked his truck.

"Honey, I want to talk to you."

Susan Gustaffson joined Kelley at the railing of the big white sailboat, tilting the rim of her baseball cap down so that it shaded her eyes from the early-afternoon sun.

"Sure." Kelley shifted her position to make room for the other woman, feeling the deck under her feet rising and falling as the boat cut through the waves.

Harold and Helen's sailboat was a beauty, a forty-five-footer with room for six in the sleeping quarters below and plenty of space for the seven people who occupied the deck now. She and Sam, along with Susan and Jon Gustaffson and the three Prices, were taking a lunchtime cruise along the coast east of Cairo, heading for a secluded bay that Helen said was perfect for picnicking.

And for information gathering, Kelley hoped. She'd accepted the Prices' offer because it seemed like a good opportunity to see both the Gustaffsons and Wayland. The first part of the trip had been occupied in touring the boat and watching as Harold—a former World Cup crew member, his wife proudly pointed out—expertly piloted the big craft out of the boat slip in Cairo and onto the open water.

Now, as they neared their destination, Kelley was glad to see Susan Gustaffson approaching—at least until she heard what Susan had on her mind.

"I'm a little worried about you, Kelley," the petite blond woman said. "I mean, I asked that gorgeous husband of yours if he was enjoying his honeymoon and he looked at me like I'd asked if he enjoyed rattlesnake handling. Honey, are the two of you having problems?"

Good going, Sam, Kelley thought grimly. She glanced over to where he stood now, leaning against the railing in the cockpit. Trust him to find the part of the boat that pitched and rolled most dramatically, and then plant himself there like grim death.

And trust him to look gorgeous, too, just as Susan had said. He should have been nondescript in those beat-up navy cotton shorts and half-unbuttoned white shirt, especially compared to Wayland Price in his slick white outfit and Jon Gustaffson, who wore a bright red swimsuit and matching windbreaker.

But there was something impossible to ignore about Sam, something that smoldered down deep in his blue eyes and made itself felt in that trademark slouch of his, the one that said "Leave me out of this" but drew attention to his long, rangy legs and hard muscular torso just the same.

He hadn't been happy about this boat trip. But his displeasure hadn't been enough to kill that old watchful gleam in his eyes. Kelley had noticed him taking whatever opportunities came his way to chat with the other passengers.

Except Kelley, of course.

And Susan Gustaffson hadn't missed it. Kelley resisted a sigh.

"We've both been working too hard lately," she said, falling back on the excuse Sam had used with the intrusive handyman yesterday. "It may take us a few days to unwind."

Susan nodded sympathetically. "Boy, I know how *that* feels," she said. "My firm was having a tough time a couple of years ago, and I was working one seventy-hour week right after another. That's why Jon and I decided to buy the cottage, so we could at least get away on the weekends."

Kelley made another mental note next to Susan's name. *Firm in trouble recently,* it said. *Check it out.* Was it possible that Susan and Jon might have turned to counterfeiting to make up for a dip in Susan's income?

"You should consider buying a vacation place, too," Susan suggested. "I heard the prices on the Windspray properties are probably dropping again soon. You should make an offer." She glanced over her shoulder at Sam. "Judging by how uptight that man of yours looks, you two need some kind of getaway."

"He's just not crazy about boats," Kelley said, recalling Sam's words on the subject when she'd told him about the planned excursion. "He says he'd rather be on a bucking bronco any day—at least that way you know you're going to land on solid ground if you get tossed off."

Susan's eyes widened. "Has he really ridden broncos?" she asked.

"Sure." Kelley had to smile at the other woman's obvious awe. "According to Sam, riding wild horses and Brahma bulls is the simplest thing in the world," she went on. "He says you always know where you stand with them. They want you off their backs, and that's that."

People, he'd always added, were a hell of a lot harder to figure out. But she didn't share that part of Sam's philosophy with Susan Gustaffson.

She didn't get a chance to share anything else, either, because Wayland Price was approaching them, insinuating himself into the small space between them at the railing. "And why are you two lovely ladies hiding over here away from your husbands?" he asked.

Susan rolled her eyes behind Wayland's back. "We're just talking girl talk, Wayland," she said. "Nothing you'd be interested in."

Wayland leaned his arms on the railing. "It's got to be more interesting than listening to my mother go on about how hard it is to get good help these days," he said. "If I hear one more harangue about that new handyman—"

"Which handyman?" Kelley asked.

"The redheaded one, whatever his name is."

"Helen doesn't like him?"

Wayland shook his head. Kelley couldn't read the expression behind his shiny sunglasses. "She says he's shifty, whatever the heck that means," he said. "Dad hired him because the guy was willing to work cheap in exchange for a place to live. But my mother's convinced he's got an unreliable look, and she wants to let him go. Can you imagine a personnel director at your company hiring and firing on that basis, Susan? Or at—what was the bank you said you work for, Kelley?"

"First Austin Savings and Loan," Kelley said, naming her old employer and hoping Wayland wasn't curious enough about her to check it out. "And I forget what it is that you do, Wayland," she added.

Wayland's conversation yesterday had mostly been about Cairo and his family's long-standing connection with the little town, and about his own marital woes with a lengthening list of ex-wives. He didn't seem any more eager now to talk about his work.

"Oh, I'm a consultant," he said. "I do some of this and some of that."

A lot of the people Cotter Investigations had helped to put behind bars had done "some of this and some of that." And "consultant" could be the vaguest job description in the world, when you wanted it to be, Kelley thought.

"I've often thought about going into consulting," she said. "Does it pay well?"

"Depends on the field." Wayland had suddenly become taciturn.

"And what field do you specialize in?"

"Oil." He didn't elaborate.

"Anywhere in particular that you—"

He didn't let her finish the question. "It's far too nice a day to be talking about work," he said, suddenly flourishing that brilliant smile of his.

"I'm really interested," Kelley insisted. "Who have you worked for?"

"If you're really interested, I'll print up a copy of my résumé when we get back to shore." Wayland seemed increasingly eager to change the subject. "And I insist that we stop discussing business. We should be enjoying this gorgeous day. And my mother, while she may be a trifle conservative when it comes to hiring maintenance men, does lay in provisions for a boat trip better than anyone else I know. Can I get either of you a glass of wine? Or rub some suntan lotion on for you? I wouldn't want to see either of you lovely blondes go home with a sunburn."

"I heard that, Wayland." Jon Gustaffson appeared behind his wife, sliding his arms around her. Jon was tall and boyish, with a ready grin and an ingenuous manner. "I'll have you know I personally slathered this woman from head to foot with sunscreen before we came aboard, and I'm standing by to do touch-up work whenever she needs it.''

Susan giggled and relaxed into her husband's embrace. "It's true, Wayland," she said. "And pregnant ladies aren't supposed to drink wine, so you're out of luck on both offers. But I would take you up on a soda, if you've got one.''

As the Gustaffsons and Wayland moved toward the galley, Kelley considered staying with them, then decided it was more important to talk to Sam while he was by himself. She headed for the cockpit and slipped off her sunglasses as she took a seat across from him.

The prow of the boat was lined with white molded-fiberglass benches, from which an adventurous passenger could look directly down at the hull slicing through the blue water, churning up white crests every time it met an oncoming wave. Above them, the tall sails were filled taut, and the little pennant at the tip of the mast rippled in the breeze, bright red against the blue and white patchwork of sky and clouds.

It should have made Kelley feel free and euphoric. But the memory of last night's adventure, and the terror she'd wakened into, kept seeping into the sunlit present, darkening her own mood as it had so plainly darkened Sam's.

At least she was doing her best to cover it up. But she frowned as her eyes met his, and said, "You know, there's a rumor going around that you and I aren't getting along very well.''

"Who says so?"

"Susan Gustaffson, for one. She just had a little heart-to-heart with me about it.''

"Hell.''

She waited, but that was apparently all Sam had to say. "Thanks,'' she said finally. "That's very helpful.''

"Why don't you just tell them I'm an antisocial bastard and there's very little you or anyone can do about it?" He leaned his head back against the railing as he spoke, closing his eyes.

Kelley reached down into her beach bag and pulled out a tube of sunscreen. She prodded Sam in the ribs with the end of the tube, startling his eyes open again. The surprise in them gave her more satisfaction than she'd expected.

"That doesn't reflect very well on my taste in men, does it?" she said. "It would be better if you just went along with the program."

"*Your* program, you mean."

"At least I've got one."

She felt her temper flash and hung on hard to that spurt of irritation. Anger, frustration, even bitterness—all of that was safer than letting herself be drawn into the awareness of how close he was, how the clearly defined muscles shifted in his thighs when he sat up, how the heat in his dark blue eyes was affecting her heart rate.

"At least I'm not trying to stick my head in the sand and pretend you don't exist," she added, holding out the tube of sunscreen. "We need to get on with this, Sam. Harold's banker only gave him until the beginning of next week, in case you'd forgotten."

"I hadn't forgotten." He ground the words out as though they tasted bad.

"Good. Then let's do what we're here to do. And you can start by rubbing some of this on my back for me. It's the kind of thing husbands do for their wives."

"Rub some of—" He looked suspiciously at the tube she'd put in his palm. "Why does this have to be a husband's job?" he wanted to know.

Kelley turned her back to him, lifting her fine hair clear of her shoulders and tilting her head forward slightly. "Most new husbands are *looking* for excuses to touch their wives," she told him, thinking of Jon's fond expression when he'd looked at Susan a few minutes ago. "Just do it, all right, Sam? And try to look like you're enjoying yourself."

He seemed to take a long time getting the lid off the tube. Kelley felt the warm breeze buffeting her, swirling her hair around her face as though it shared her restless sense that they needed to do this and get it over with. She was about to suggest that Sam hurry it up when he finally moved.

And the moment he touched her, Kelley's impatience turned to something quite different.

He curled his fingers around her left shoulder, holding her upper body still. With his other hand he smoothed sunscreen all the way across her shoulders, then began a slow massaging motion that caught her completely off guard.

She hadn't expected him to touch her as though he meant it.

She hadn't anticipated how good it would feel to have his long fingers digging so gently, so knowingly, into her skin. She felt something inside herself unclenching at the rhythm of it. Sam's hands seemed to release tensions she hadn't even realized she was holding inside her.

"I—have a feeling Wayland's employment record is going to be worth checking out." It was hard to get the words out as Sam's thumb and index finger followed a long, slow line up her spine.

"You have a feeling." Was it contempt she was hearing under the bass rumble of his voice?

"Yes. He seems—evasive about it. And you always said—"

"Go with your gut feelings. I know." He paused to put more sunscreen on his palm, then resumed the slow movements that felt more and more like caresses. "Maybe I've changed my mind about that."

Kelley wanted to close her eyes and let Sam's touch lull her into a pleasantly sensual haze. But his words were puzzling. "Why have you changed your mind?" she demanded.

"I just have."

"Come on, Sam. That's not—"

"All right." His voice grated over the words. "Let's just say that I've come to respect the value of cold, hard facts over any number of gut feelings. That's all."

There were questions she should be asking him, Kelley thought. Was it that night at the warehouse that had changed his philosophy so radically? Was it Kelley's own mistakes—mistakes her gut feelings had prompted her to make—that made Sam so determined to stick to cold, hard facts now?

There was just one problem.

The only question she really cared about at the moment was the one about why he was leaning closer to her as he spoke.

She could feel the warmth of his breath mingling with the brisk sea breeze. He'd encountered the curve of her shoulder now, and he paused, as though he'd just discovered buried treasure and wasn't sure whether to share the news with anyone. His thumbs traced the angle of her shoulder blade in an appreciative, deliberate way, pulling Kelley back into her own forbidden memories of how thoroughly Sam Cotter could love a woman.

"I don't suppose you could have brought a less—revealing bathing suit with you." His words were even rougher than usual.

Kelley made herself sit up a little straighter, trying to counteract the liquid pleasure of Sam's palms against her skin. The sun had gone behind a cloud momentarily, and the sudden cooling of the air made it even more tempting to lean back into the warmth of his touch.

"Wiley didn't exactly give me a lot of notice about this job," she told him. "There wasn't time to go shopping."

And anyway, her one-piece aquamarine bathing suit had never struck her as particularly daring until just this moment. It was only when Sam started to move his hands again, gliding along the length of her spine and circling back up from the soft hollow at the small of her back, that she realized how much of her body was on view.

She shivered as she tilted her head forward again. She wished she could blame her trembling on the clouds that were covering the sun, but she knew better.

Sam's fingertips were pushing under the elasticized edges of her suit now. The sensation was intensely suggestive, wholly erotic. Kelley closed her eyes without meaning to, suddenly lost in images of the way Sam's long, masculine hands must look against the whiteness of her skin.

"Sam—"

"Yeah?"

Don't stop, she wanted to say. *Don't ever stop.* The familiar strength of his touch felt too good. And his voice at her ear was like another caress, one that raced right through Kelley's frame and ignited brush fires all along the way.

But she couldn't give in to this. She just couldn't. She'd gone through it in her mind before facing Sam over breakfast this morning, and there were too many good reasons why she needed to keep her distance.

"Apparently—" If her own voice would work properly, this would be easier, she thought. She tried again. "Apparently Helen Price thinks there's something shady about that handyman, Steve Cormier."

"Shady how?"

"Wayland didn't say. I thought I'd see if I can find out when we stop for lunch."

"Get facts, then. Not just Helen's notions."

Kelley frowned and waited for irritation to seep into the pleasantly relaxed mood Sam's hands had created.

It didn't happen.

In fact, it was beginning to occur to her that she was actually enjoying arguing with Sam Cotter. Just as she always had.

"Don't worry, Sam," she told him. "I know a fact when I see one." And she still listened to her gut feelings, too, she added silently. Just because Sam seemed to have retreated into some cut-and-dried world where hard facts were the only thing that mattered—

He was pausing now, one hand still holding her shoulder, the other resting at the base of her neck. "You're not letting this go, are you?" he said.

She turned to face him. "Why should I?" she asked.

His quick smile had no mirth in it. "Hell's bells, sweetheart, somebody nearly killed you last night."

"Whoever it was, they tried to kill you, too."

He waved that off as though it didn't matter. "We're not talking about me," he said.

They'd both shifted positions by now. Sam had one leg planted on either side of Kelley, virtually imprisoning her where she sat at the edge of the fiberglass bench. When she glanced down, the hard, sinewy length of his thighs seemed too long for the small space of the cockpit.

She was astonished at how she was aching for that sham back rub to go on and on. But although it was important to convince the other passengers that their husband-and-wife act was for real, it was just as important to clear up the questions they hadn't yet found good answers to.

The sun came back out, brilliant as before. Somehow the brightness of its glare on the water made it easier to summon up the determination Kelley needed.

"Do you really think I would just walk away from this case?" she asked him.

He gave a quick shrug. "If you had any sense you would."

"Then why are *you* staying?"

"To get the job done."

That laconic style of his had always gotten on her nerves, especially when the turbulent look in his eyes told her he was just blowing smoke, trying to cover up whatever was really going on inside him.

"You mean you're staying because of your professional pride," she said.

"If you want to put it that way."

"Does it ever occur to you that I might have my pride, too?" she demanded. "Or that ever since the last time we worked together, my professional pride might be more important to me than ever?"

"More important than your safety? More important than your *life?*"

She hadn't even noticed when he'd taken hold of her hands, wrapping them in the broad palms that had given her such illicit pleasure just minutes earlier.

"There are days," she said slowly, picking her way across an emotional mine field that she'd hoped she wouldn't have to cross quite so soon, "when my job is the only thing that gets me out of bed in the morning."

Something in Sam's eyes flared at that, like a wild horse shying away from fire. But he didn't speak, not yet.

"This job is what keeps me going," she went on, glancing away from his face for a moment. "I care a lot about it." She paused. "I care too much to leave it half-done."

His words, when he finally grated them out, were the last thing she expected. They sounded hoarse, almost hostile. But there was no hostility in his eyes when she looked up at him again.

"You deserve better."

Suddenly she recognized the sound she was hearing in his voice. It was anger—the same anger she'd been feeling for the past three years—anger at her own stupidity, at fate, at the whole unhappy chain of events that had led her here.

And she didn't want it.

She didn't want to let Sam's anger open up all the things she'd worked so hard to keep under control. Most of all, she didn't want his pity.

Damn it, they *both* deserved better. But thanks to her inexperience, her overconfident belief in her own abilities, they'd been cheated out of the happiness they'd hoped for.

And the buried outrage in Sam's voice was reminding her of all of that. His touch had aroused her in some very dangerous ways, and his strength, in the dark reaches of last night's confusion, had been more welcome than she could have imagined possible.

But his sympathy made her mad.

"Let's not get into that, Sam, all right?" she said, starting to slide farther back onto the bench as she pulled her hands away from his.

Or at least she tried to slide away, tried to pull her hands free. Sam wasn't letting her move, wasn't breaking the intensely blue glare he had caught her in.

"Damn it, Kelley—"

She gave a more strenuous tug, noticing that the boat underneath them seemed to have stopped pitching some time ago without her noticing it. They were gliding into calmer waters, heading for the cove for lunch.

It was only inside Kelley that everything was still roiled up and unsteady. And she was more determined than ever not to let it show. If she accomplished nothing else on this assignment, she thought, she could at least show Sam Cotter that she was no longer the idealistic greenhorn who'd made such a tragic misjudgment three years earlier.

This time she managed to reclaim her hand, and got past Sam's barricading knee on her way out of the cockpit. "Unless you want people to catch us in the midst of yet another argument, I suggest we wrap this up," she said. "I'm going to go see what Harold and Helen know about Steve Cormier. Did you pick up anything useful from anybody earlier?"

"I learned that Jon Gustaffson knows every statistic for every player the Houston Oilers ever signed."

He didn't look pleased about it, or maybe there was some other reason for the black look that had settled on his features. The intensity of his gaze was hooded now, like a sheathed sword. Sam's personality was always a powerful force, Kelley thought, and somehow it only seemed more powerful when he withdrew into himself like this.

"But now that we've gotten past sports trivia, I'm hoping to get some more relevant information out of him this afternoon," he was adding.

"Good." Kelley moved away, toward the others on the deck.

"This really is just all business with you, isn't it?" Sam's voice followed her, faintly astounded under its gravelly rasp.

"What else *could* it be?" she asked. Although she didn't turn back to look at him, she felt his heavy-lidded gaze following her as she crossed the deck in search of their hosts.

Lunch was blessedly informal. It was easy to avoid Sam as everyone wandered around the big boat with plates of barbecued chicken and potato salad. Kelley saw him talking with Jon Gustaffson and Wayland Price, and hoped they'd gotten beyond sports scores. By then she was engaged in conversation with Helen Price.

The unseasonably hot day had cooled a little by now, as the clouds above them started to thicken and block out the sun. Helen had finished her lunch and announced that the light was perfect for sketching now. Kelley followed as the older woman took out a big sketchbook and settled herself in a deck chair facing several other big boats anchored in the same quiet cove.

"It's a pretty scene," Kelley said.

Helen nodded. "I love this part of the world. When I was young I studied art in Europe for several years, learning all the right ways to do things, but you know, the landscapes there never felt quite right to me. I got the best all-around art training that my father's money could provide, but I was never so happy as when I came back to Texas and could go back to painting the places I knew.''

She painted with skill, Kelley knew. She had admired Helen's big watercolors in the Windspray restaurant, and it was obvious now from the practiced movements of the older woman's hands setting out her materials that this was something Helen was very, very good at. Kelley almost hated to interrupt Helen's concentration with a question about Steve Cormier.

''I don't really know, dear,'' Helen replied, in answer to Kelley's query. ''There's just something about the man that makes me think he's not giving us the whole story. He turned up so conveniently when we had an unexpected gap in the staff.''

''Has he ever given you any trouble?'' Kelley asked.

Helen examined several soft lead pencils before choosing one. ''No,'' she said. ''And you'll think I'm odd for saying this—Harold certainly thinks it's odd—but that's one of the things that bothers me most about him. All of the other staff had questions and problems, especially at the beginning. But this Cormier man just does his job and goes back to his cottage. That's *all* he does. That's all he seems to want to do.''

''So he has a cottage to himself?''

''Yes. That was one of the reasons he wanted the job, he said. He was looking for a place to live, and Harold figured he might as well have one of the cottages that hadn't sold yet.''

''That makes sense,'' Kelley said.

Helen's gentle brown eyes were scanning the bay now, finally settling on one of the other sailboats, whose young occupants were having a diving contest.

''Oh, it makes *sense*.'' She began to rough in the scene with quick, confident strokes of her pencil. ''But he brought cases and cases of what he said was photographic equipment with him when he first arrived. But I've never seen him use any of it, not so much as to take a single snapshot. Doesn't that seem a little strange to you?''

It was certainly worth checking, Kelley realized. Counterfeiting had traditionally been a job that required big, unwieldy equipment, far bigger than anyone could move single-handedly. But with the technology changing so rapidly—

She was about to ask Helen whether there was any chance of getting into Steve Cormier's cottage when she became aware of a change in the happy yelling from the sailboat Helen was sketching. For some time now there had been high-pitched squeals of excitement as the young sailors propelled themselves off the stern of the boat, but now something seemed to be wrong.

Helen hadn't noticed it yet. To her eyes, the scene was still just an appealing jumble of shapes and angles. But one quick glance told Kelley what was happening, and it was enough to get her out of her chair and over to the railing in a hurry.

All the occupants of the other boat seemed to be children, unless there were adults with them who had gone below. One child, younger than the rest, had swum quite a distance away from the craft, in pursuit of a drifting beach ball.

But the swimmer was in trouble now, waving frantically, then sinking just below the surface of the water.

Cramps, Kelley thought. Or just plain panic. She didn't wait to think about it, or to answer Helen's startled question when she noticed Kelley tossing aside the pale blue cover-up she'd put on when the air had turned cooler.

''My dear, what on earth—''

The child's head bobbed up again. Kelley heard a frightened wail, answered by the occupants of the other boat, who'd finally figured out that something was wrong.

They were even farther away than Kelley, though. And there clearly wasn't any time to waste. Thanking her lucky stars that she'd learned lifesaving techniques a few years ago, Kelley swung both legs over the railing of the Prices' boat and let herself go.

It wasn't until she'd hit the water and come cleanly to the surface again that she registered a second splash off to her left. That was where Sam had been, she thought. And as she kicked herself into her fastest racing crawl, heading toward the floundering child, she caught a glimpse of a dark, drenched head and a pair of powerful arms speeding in the same direction.

Chapter 5

From the deck of the Prices' big boat, the scene had looked so clear. Now, though, the waves and spray were confusing the scene, disorienting her.

The chilly water temperature didn't help, although Kelley was swimming as fast as she could. By the time she reached the spot where she thought she'd last seen the youngster's head dip below the surface, Kelley could feel her teeth beginning to chatter.

She told herself to ignore it and tried to block out the increasingly urgent shouting from the other boat, as well. The only thing that mattered at the moment was finding the child who'd been flailing helplessly in the deep water.

To her left she could still hear the heavier rhythm of Sam's strokes, propelling him toward the same spot. Kelley paused, wishing desperately that her vision wasn't blurred by streaming water from her hair, when she heard Sam's voice.

"There!"

She got her eyes cleared in time to look over at him, but he wasn't pointing, just glaring with fixed intensity at a place halfway between them. Kelley scanned the area and saw what Sam had noticed—a slight roiling just below the surface, followed by a couple of big air bubbles.

She gulped a big mouthful of air and dove, not stopping to wonder why Sam had stopped moving or what the furious look in his eyes had meant. She forced her own eyes to stay open and focused on the place where the air bubbles had come from.

She saw the child right away, thanks to the neon-green bathing suit he wore. He was young—not more than eight—and almost swallowed up in the murky, tide-churned water.

Kelley gave a powerful kick and reached him just as he made a feeble effort to reach the surface again. It was hard to hold on to him, between the motion of the water and his own struggles, but she managed to get her arms around his waist and kick toward safety just as her own lungs started to protest the lack of air.

Sam was there when she came up, helping her hold the boy, rasping out the phrase "Good work" in a voice so hoarse that it startled Kelley out of her single-minded focus on the child.

Was something wrong with Sam? She thought she'd heard pain in his voice, but maybe it was just intense relief that she'd been successful. There was a sudden swarm of activity all around now, as a small motor-powered lifeboat—from the other boat, Kelley thought—zoomed toward them and a couple of other swimmers belatedly splashed their way to her side.

Kelley helped ease the coughing boy over the side of the boat, relieved beyond words to see that his eyes were open and he seemed to be all right. His friends—that had to be who the other swimmers were—were swarming around him, and the boat's driver, a shaken-looking youth of about twenty, was alternately patting the child on the back and trying to thank Kelley.

"God—we were only below for a few minutes—they said they'd stay close to the boat—if you hadn't been watching—"

The phrases tumbled out on top of each other. Kelley just nodded in reply. She was suddenly shivering uncontrollably, and the water around her felt icy.

She knew it was just a reaction to the adrenaline rush that had spurred her rescue effort. Now that it was over, she felt drained. As she turned to swim slowly away from the lifeboat, even her concern about Sam had faded from her mind.

Until she saw him.

A second motorboat, piloted by Wayland Price, had arrived without Kelley noticing it. Sam was still in the water, grasping the gunwale of the boat with one hand. And he seemed to be in worse shape than the boy who'd nearly drowned.

"Sam?" She breaststroked toward him, wishing she could control the shuddering in her own muscles. He looked drawn, gray and savagely angry.

And suddenly Kelley knew what it must be.

Sam Cotter had saved her life three years ago by putting himself directly in the path of a speeding truck. He'd been trying to swing aboard to wrestle the steering wheel out of the driver's control and run the vehicle into a dead end.

She'd seen his whole plan in her own mind the moment he'd jumped for the driver's door handle. *Turn the wheel— aim for that big stack of boxes—take advantage of the moment to get the gun out of the driver's hand.* It had been one of those moments they'd sometimes shared, when they'd seemed able to read each other's minds.

Things hadn't worked out quite the way Sam had intended. The driver cranked the wheel hard to one side, jolting Sam loose, slamming him against the loading dock with a bone-cracking force Kelley still couldn't bear to think about.

But by then she'd taken his cue and thrown her whole weight against the driver, wrenching the wheel around. By the time the truck came to a halt, cushioned by the stack of boxes, it was Kelley who'd been holding the gun.

Without Sam, she would probably have been dead, shot at the first opportunity the driver had been able to find.

And the white, clenched look of pain on Sam's face as he gripped the side of the dinghy told her the price he'd paid to save her.

Wayland was urging them both into the boat, commending them on their quick thinking, responding over his shoulder to his parents' shouted demands that he bring Sam and Kelley back to warm up and dry out.

Kelley barely heard him. She watched Sam haul himself painfully over the side of the small boat and winced at his angry refusal when Wayland offered to lend a hand. Wayland seemed pumped up about all this, Kelley thought, as though he'd played a much bigger part in the rescue than just jumping into the small craft fastened to the stern of his parents' sailboat.

And Sam, who'd put himself on the line again, was sitting silently, grim-faced, holding his torso in a way that told Kelley exactly how much it had hurt him to make that speedy dash through the water toward the drowning child.

Both of them stayed silent as they headed back to the big boat. Kelley submitted to the praise and concern that everyone was lavishing on them, but her thoughts were far away, drawn involuntarily back to that gloomy warehouse. The scene replayed itself over and over again in her mind as she let herself be shepherded below the deck into the main bedroom below.

"Here," Helen said, opening drawers in the built-in wardrobe against the inner wall. "Get dried off, and borrow whatever fits. You look chilled to death, and no wonder.''

She bustled away, saying something about hot coffee in the galley. Sam and Kelley were left standing next to the big bed, looking at each other.

Kelley couldn't imagine what to say. She'd worked so hard to make sure she had all the training and experience she needed to do her job efficiently and well. And none of it seemed to cover this.

It was Sam who finally spoke, and then it was only to point out that her teeth would probably come loose if she didn't dry herself off. ''Personally, I can't wait to see what Harold's got in his wardrobe that fits me,'' he said, tossing Kelley one of the thick white towels Helen had laid out and taking one for himself. ''Can't you just see me in sailing whites, with a captain's hat on my head?''

Kelley couldn't join in his grim attempt at a smile. She quickly toweled herself off and slipped into a pair of pale yellow sweatpants and matching top. But as soon as she was dressed, her heart was wrung all over again by Sam's slow, painful movements as he dried his upper body.

''It still hurts, doesn't it?'' She made her words blunt on purpose. She was aching with sympathy for the stilted way he was moving, and for the damage her own stupidity had caused to that magnificent body of his.

But sympathy was a dangerous thing to indulge when she was standing next to a half-undressed Sam Cotter. And so she fell back on the kind of toughness Sam had always told her was the first requirement for anyone doing their kind of work.

He started to shrug, then stopped abruptly. ''It's fine as long as I take it easy,'' he said.

Taking it easy didn't include no-holds-barred racing sprints across open water, Kelley knew. She frowned and stepped closer to where he sat at the edge of the bed.

''Can I see?''

She hadn't planned to ask the question. Suddenly, though, it seemed important to face the results of her mistakes of three years ago.

She'd faced her own physical trauma—the loss of the child she was carrying, in a miscarriage the doctors had said was probably prompted by the terror of her brush with death. But Sam had shut himself off from her after that horrible night. There had been no chance for her to see how badly he had been injured trying to save her.

Until now.

He seemed to be on the verge of saying no, but as her eyes met his—searching those steely blue depths for something, anything that would hint he'd forgiven her for her mistakes that night—he gave another half shrug and dropped the towel that had been covering his shoulder.

"Ain't much to look at," he told her. "They patched it up pretty well."

It was disconcerting to be looking down at him this way. His rangy body had been a kind of battlefield long before she'd come on the scene, and she remembered with sudden, aching clarity the way he'd pointed out all his old scars early on in their relationship.

She still remembered every one of them. The faint mark of an old rope burn on his palms. A horseshoe-shaped indentation courtesy of a crazy wild bronco at the state championship one year. The long white line of an old knife wound he'd gotten in a bar fight in the days when he'd been too hotheaded to know better.

And now, the scars from that night in the warehouse. He was right: there wasn't much to look at. The real pain, she realized, must be on the inside, where it didn't show.

Like her own.

Kelley reached out almost blindly for his injured shoulder, resting her fingertips on it as though she could absorb some of Sam's pain. She closed her eyes without meaning to and felt her own pulse throbbing at the ends of her fingers, where they touched Sam's hard, uncompromising muscles.

"I'm sorry." She half whispered the words.

"It doesn't matter." He was holding himself stiffly again, as though her touch was as excruciating as the way he'd torn up his shoulder plowing through the water a little while ago.

"It doesn't *matter?* How can you say that? After everything that went wrong that night—"

"I don't want to talk about this, Kelley. All right?"

Maybe it was the way she was standing next to him, looking down into his eyes. Or maybe there really was something new in that steel blue gaze of his, something very different from his usual take-charge attitude. He seemed to be pleading with her, or at least as close as Sam Cotter could come to pleading. Kelley withdrew her hand, startled by the change in his face.

"All right," she said, because her own memories suddenly seemed so raw and fresh that she was glad to escape them. "But there is something we need to talk about."

Sam got to his feet, drying off the rest of his body while glancing through the drawers Helen Price had opened. "What's that?" he asked.

"If we're going to stay here and finish this job, we're going to *have* to agree to work together. Can't you see that?"

He pulled a navy blue sweatshirt out of the drawer and lifted it—slowly, cautiously—over his head. He seemed to have lapsed back into silence, so Kelley went on. "We need each other, Sam. We needed each other just now, out there in the water."

His damp hair had fallen forward into his face again. He pushed it back impatiently, and said, "You saved that kid, Kelley, not me. I was too busy just trying to stay afloat."

He looked frustrated at having to admit it, and once again Kelley couldn't blame him. It was unsettling to feel such empathy for Sam, when she'd spent so much time trying to distance herself from him.

"I saved him after you'd pointed out where he'd gone under," she told him. "And you saved me last night, in case it slipped your mind already."

"If you hadn't called my name—"

She didn't let him finish. "You see?" she said. "It took both of us to get out of last night alive, and both of us to help that boy this afternoon. We're going to have to be partners in this, Sam, if we're going to do it at all."

Something flared in his face at that, something that made Kelley take a step back into the relative safety of the open doorway. Sam reminded her of a penned-up stallion at times, so angry and wild and unpredictable that he was a danger to everyone, including himself.

She knew why he was feeling that way now. The idea of being partners again was a terrifying one, given all they'd lost the last time they'd tried.

But it was tantalizing, too, to think of matching her wits and her strength with his again. She held her breath, waiting for his answer, refusing to let him hide behind that stubborn silence this time.

When he finally spoke, he didn't sound pleased. He sounded resigned, and cornered, and frustrated.

But he wasn't saying no. "I suppose it makes sense," he said, slowly. "Unless one or both of us decides to leave."

"Are you thinking of leaving?"

"Hell no." There was a slight gleam in his eye as he met her glance, catching the challenge in her words.

"Well, neither am I. So we might as well put our heads together on this thing."

It was a poor second best to what they'd once shared, Kelley knew. There wasn't a chance on earth of recapturing the kind of starry-eyed, anything-is-possible partnership they'd had when they'd first known each other. They both knew too well now that anything *was* possible, including the kind of loss that Kelley wasn't certain she could survive a second time.

But what Sam was telling her, as he gave her a slow nod and ushered her out of the bedroom toward the welcome smell of coffee in the main cabin, was that at least he wasn't going to shut her out anymore. He was giving her a chance to redeem herself, a chance to use the hard lessons she'd learned from everything that had gone wrong three years earlier.

And at the moment, that was all Kelley could imagine asking him for.

You can do this, Sam told himself.

It didn't matter that his whole arm was shaking or that his shoulder felt as though someone had kindled a bonfire inside it. It was possible to push through physical pain. He'd done it before.

And he could do it again now.

He squinted into the afternoon light and raised Kelley's pistol to shoulder height one more time.

She'd kept the same gun, he noticed. He'd helped her buy it—"So romantic, Sam, helping your girlfriend choose her first weapon," she'd teased him—when she'd first come to work for Cotter Investigations. It was a Smith & Wesson .38, a Model 52 that they'd been lucky enough to find in a pawn shop in Houston. The thing was accurate and reliable, a real peach, in Sam's expert opinion.

It was also heavy.

He hadn't actually fired a gun in a long time, and the three-plus pounds of metal at the end of his arm now felt like a ton. His muscles were quivering badly enough that the sights were a blur and there was no chance of him hitting the paper bulls-eye on the other side of the sunlit field.

"Hell," he said, and lowered his arm again.

He'd slept like a baby last night. So had Kelley, apparently. They'd both been tired after their interrupted sleep of the night before and the adventures of the afternoon—and maybe, too, from the emotional highs and lows of being together again.

At any rate, there had been no replay of the danger of their first night at Windspray, for which Sam was profoundly grateful. But that didn't mean he'd forgotten that someone had nearly managed to kill Kelley right under his nose.

He had phone calls to make and information to run down today. But he'd decided first to head over to the local gun club for some target practice. If their unknown assailant had plans for another attack, Sam wanted to be ready.

There was only one problem.

He couldn't do it.

He switched the weapon to his left hand and took a few long strides out onto the field, then back to the distance marker he'd been standing behind. With the toe of one sneaker, he scuffed the grass next to the white line painted on the ground. The fresh morning breeze kept blowing his hair all over the place, and he pushed it back, suddenly annoyed with the weather and everything else.

He felt inadequate as hell, and he didn't like it.

He tried to remind himself of how good he'd gotten at the new specialty he'd made his own at Cotter Investigations. He'd mastered all the tricks of the financial-investigation trade, and both his brothers agreed that there was nobody quite like Sam when it came to sniffing out bad money.

He even found himself thinking about his dad, that charming con man, J. D. Cotter. J.D. had had a fine collection of inspirational sayings, left over from his days on the lecture circuit. The lectures had been genuine enough, although the hundreds of prepaid book orders J.D. had taken after his speeches had always gone mysteriously unfilled.

The line that seemed to cover Sam's current difficulty went something like, *Son, ain't nobody can tell you no if you don't already have no in your heart.*

It was horse manure, of course, and J.D. had known it. But Sam found himself grinning, remembering how sincere his dad's handsome face had always looked when he'd come up with one of those little platitudes.

Wiley and Jack still couldn't get past the memory of J.D.'s fast-and-loose conscience and even looser morals. But Sam had loved the old scoundrel. He still missed J.D. Nobody—until Kelley Landis had come into his life—had ever made Sam feel so alive, so special, so all-around *good.*

His grin faded. He didn't want to think about Kelley right now. He wanted to fire this gun and hit the damn target so he could go back to the cottage and do the work he was being paid to do.

"All right, old man," he muttered, shifting the pistol back into his right hand. "I've got yes in my heart at this very moment—let's see what it does for me."

He didn't give himself the opportunity to choke this time. He frowned hard at the target and raised his hand to shoulder height in one smooth motion. The breeze was blowing his hair into his eyes again, but he ignored it, keeping his gaze on the target across the field.

As he squeezed the trigger, his whole arm started to shake as if Sam was nothing but a sideshow marionette and the devil himself was pulling the strings.

And the bullet missed by at least a country mile.

"Thanks for your note." Kelley looked up from the laptop computer on the table as Sam came in the kitchen door.

"Yeah, well, I thought it was the kind of thing a husband would do."

It hadn't been flowery—Sam didn't do flowery—but it *had* occurred to him, as he'd been going out the cottage door two hours ago, that Kelley might wonder where he was. He could see his own scribbled note on the round dining room table next to her elbow now: *Gone out for a while, back by noon.*

Kelley had been out with Susan Gustaffson when he'd gone. Susan had invited her to work out at the health club again. If nothing else, this assignment was going to leave her in peak physical condition.

Sam took a seat across from her now and reflected that there was nothing wrong with Kelley's physical condition to begin with. She was wearing casual white trousers and a dark pink flowered sweater today, and the ensemble perfectly suited her long-legged elegance and fair coloring. She'd pulled her honey blond hair back in a loose braid, but a few wispy strands, as usual, had pulled free. They were framing her high, gently curved cheekbones, making Sam's fingertips ache with the urge to stroke the fine softness of her hair, her skin. She looked as calm, as composed as ever.

You're perfect, Sam wanted to say to her. *You're perfect, and I'm a wreck.*

Instead, he watched as she finished keying something into the computer, then asked, "Any luck with Susan?"

"Lots." Kelley pointed one slender index finger at the small screen in front of her. "Susan *loves* to talk about real estate. So it was easy to find out how much they paid for this place, and how much of a down payment they made, and how much their condo in Houston cost them."

"So you've been doing a statement of application of funds." That was the quickest way to size up a suspect's financial situation and spot any large, unaccounted-for amounts of money.

"Right." Kelley nodded and picked up a pencil, tapping the eraser end of it lightly on the tabletop. "It's still fairly rough, but it seems to me that the year they bought this vacation property, there was a big bump in their income. I'm working on getting more accurate figures for their salaries right now."

"If you can't get exact numbers, sometimes a professional organization—"

"Will be able to provide ballpark figures. I know that."

Sam felt his stomach clench a little. She'd always been this way, he recalled—a quick learner, and just as quick to put her knowledge to work. She'd soaked up everything he'd been able to teach her, just as fast as he could come up with it.

It was the ultimate irony that by letting her go too far, too fast, he'd scotched whatever chance at happiness they might both have had.

"What about the bank in Cairo?" Kelley asked him. "Any luck there?"

Sam had visited Cairo's one and only bank yesterday morning and had spoken with the manager. The man was a nobody, in Sam's estimation—a nervous, disorganized little character who already seemed to be regretting the week's grace he had let Harold talk him into.

"It's just that we have so few business concerns here in Cairo," he'd told Sam yesterday. "And really, the fortunes of the town could turn completely around if Mr. Price makes a go of this resort development. On the other hand, banking regulations are very specific, and—"

Sam didn't have a lot of patience for people who made up their minds and then changed them. He'd contented himself with asking to see the records for the Windspray Community's accounts, which the manager had turned over to him willingly enough.

Today, though, he had more specific questions in mind. He'd visited the bank again after his abortive trip to the firing range this morning, and this time he *had* found out something concrete from the anxious manager.

"Well, many of the Windspray staff do have accounts with us, of course," he'd said, in answer to Sam's question. "Most of them are local people. Steve Cormier? Let me check. Yes, here he is. He opened the account at the beginning of the summer. And—well, look here. There's one quite sizable deposit and then just a few withdrawals. No other activity.''

"Cormier deposited ten grand when he first arrived, and nothing since then,'' Sam reported to Kelley now.

"Is that so unusual? He's not being paid much to work here since he gets a free place to live,'' she countered.

"Then why does he need the ten grand? And where did it come from in the first place?''

"Good question.'' She wrinkled her brow as she thought about it. Sam wished he could smooth his thumb over that fair skin of hers, the way he'd done so many times before.

One of the times he'd done it—their first night here, after they'd been shot at—he'd been courting death for both of them. *Shape up, Sam,* he told himself, and forced his mind back to the question of Steve Cormier.

"That one-time lump deposit seems strange to me,'' he said. "It makes me wonder if it's a payment for something.''

"Have you got any ideas how to find out?''

"Well, for starters, I intend to talk to Steve Cormier again, on his turf this time.''

"His cottage, you mean?''

"Right.'' He would ask to borrow a tool of some sort, Sam thought. And then he would see if he could lead the conversation toward photography, and the boxes Helen Price had said Steve Cormier had arrived with. Sam had spent enough hours in the Cotter Investigations darkroom back in Austin that he was sure he could tell a real photographer from a fake one after just a few minutes' talk.

"Any sign of Cormier's job application form from Harold and Helen?'' he asked.

Kelley shook her head. "Helen was getting pretty irritated about it when I was over there. She says it's absolutely the last time she's letting Harold hire anybody.''

"Well, I think it's worth pestering them about. Cormier looks to me like he might be our man."

"I agree," Kelley said, "with a side bet on Wayland Price."

"Anything new on him?"

"Yes, as a matter of fact. He showed up as Susan and I were finishing up at the health club—he seems to have this sixth sense that tells him whenever there are women using the place. Fortunately for Susan, Jon came looking for her, so she had an excuse to leave and I got stuck with Wayland."

"I don't like the way that guy looks at you." Sam tried to stop the words, but they got past him.

Kelley smiled at him, with the serenity that always seemed to find its way deep inside him. "There's something poignant about Wayland," she said. "He's not very happy, underneath that slick act of his. And once you get past the flirtation, he seems genuinely eager to have somebody to talk to."

"Kelley." Sam made his words as blunt as he could, to counteract the beguiling softness he could see in her eyes. "Attila the Hun would probably have softened up and started confiding in you about his problems, if he'd known you. You're an easy person to talk to."

Hell, Sam knew that better than anybody. Within days of meeting him, Kelley had seemed able to look into his heart and see things buried there that no one else had ever noticed. He'd never forgotten the way it felt to have Kelley's searching blue gaze turned on him with love and concern.

But—

"But try to remember the guy's a suspect, all right?" he added. "You're investigating him, not—"

"I haven't forgotten."

Sam hated the way the warmth in her eyes cooled at his words, but he wasn't sorry he'd said them. It made him crazy just thinking about that night three years ago when she'd trusted her diplomatic skills too far.

"And I did get some hard information out of Wayland, since hard information is what we're after," she added. "I asked him on the boat yesterday about the consulting work he'd done, remember? And this morning he brought me a list of companies he says he's worked for. He kind of flourished it at me, like I'd issued him a challenge and he was taking me up on it."

Her brows drew together in a frown. "But here's the really odd thing—when I called the companies to check up on Wayland, they all praised him to the sky. Said he was a great guy and knew the business inside out. It's just about the last thing I expected."

"Hmm." Sam drummed his fingertips on the table, then moved to stand behind Kelley's chair. Quickly, trying not to let himself be distracted by the sweet scent of her recently shampooed hair, he keyed in a few strokes and pulled up one of the lists he'd copied onto the hard drive yesterday: a list of oil companies he'd pulled off a financial statement.

"Look familiar?" he asked Kelley.

She half turned to face him, ocean blue eyes wide with interest. "All the companies I contacted are there," she said. "But how—"

Sam flicked a finger at the screen. "Harold Price is on the board of directors for all these companies," he told her. "Looks to me like the only work Wayland gets is through his daddy."

Kelley turned back to the list. "And that's why he was getting such rave reviews," she said.

"Right. Nobody wants to offend the powerful Harold Price."

Kelley was frowning again as she pushed her chair back and stood up. "I can understand that," she said. "I never met anybody as overbearing as Harold. And Helen, in that gentle way of hers, is just as forceful. When I tried to suggest—as tactfully as I knew how—that I thought we should check out Wayland's finances, both of them hopped all over me.''

Sam could imagine it. ''Better you than me, sweetheart,'' he said. ''That's the kind of scene where my inclination is to tell the client to get the hell off my back until I'm finished doing the job I was hired to do.''

''It's not as easy as that, Sam. You can't just avoid your clients. They're the ones who're paying you.''

He started to shrug, before his shoulder reminded him of several good reasons not to. ''Half the time, the client is as much trouble as the criminal, and I'm getting too old to go looking for extra trouble,'' he told her. ''As my dad used to say, if you can see the steam rising off of it, you're better to take the long way around.''

For a moment he thought she was puzzling over what he meant, but then he realized it was something else that had caught her attention.

''I've never heard you mention your dad before,'' she said slowly.

''I don't talk about him much.''

''Wiley says he was a real son of a bitch. Is that true?''

Somehow it bothered Sam that his big brother had been talking to Kelley about their father. It wasn't just what Wiley had said—J.D. *had* been a real son of a bitch, among other things. Then why was he feeling this sense of betrayal, as though something very private in his life had been invaded?

Damn it, why were they talking about J.D. at all? It must be because Sam had just been thinking about the old buzzard, out there on the firing range.

He didn't want to get into this with Kelley. Nobody, not even Wiley and Jack, had ever really understood how Sam felt about his father. It wasn't likely that Kelley Landis would get it, even if Sam chose to try to explain it to her.

And it wasn't something he was comfortable putting into words, anyway. Without answering her question, he stepped into the living room and picked up a small ceramic table lamp from one of the end tables. He removed the shade and held the lamp over the kitchen garbage can, aiming carefully.

One quick downward motion shattered the glass bulb, leaving the base still screwed firmly into the socket. That ought to be a good enough excuse to ask Steve Cormier for a pair of pliers, Sam thought. He told Kelley what he was doing and made his escape into the noonday sun without pausing to look too deeply into the bottomless blue of her questioning gaze.

Chapter 6

Stick with the facts, he told himself as he walked into Steve Cormier's kitchen. *Going with your gut will screw you up every single time.*

The problem was that his gut was telling him very strongly that there was something wrong with Cormier's setup.

It wasn't just the fact that the red-haired handyman seemed to have virtually no belongings of his own in his cottage. It was something about Cormier's demeanor, something so watchful that Sam felt almost certain the guy was hiding something.

The question was, what was it?

He managed to take a quick look into the single bedroom while Cormier was searching for a pair of pliers in a kitchen drawer. There was no sign of the big carrying cases Helen Price had mentioned. But then, if the cases *did* contain counterfeiting equipment, it was hardly likely that Cormier would leave them in plain view.

"Helen tells me you're a photographer," he said, as the other man carefully began to extricate the base of the lamp bulb. Sam had purposely broken it off as close to the socket as possible, so the process was a tricky one.

"An amateur," Cormier said, without looking up. "I haven't had time to do much since I've been down here. The Prices keep me busy." He headed off Sam's next question with one of his own. "You and your wife getting any chance to relax?" he asked. "Seems like I hear the phone ringing every time I'm near your place."

And how many times had that been? Sam wondered. It was true that the phone was ringing a lot—that was what happened when you started putting out inquiries in a case and information started coming back in. But he hadn't figured on anyone overhearing the process. He made a mental note to turn the ringer down when he got back to the cottage.

"Just some loose business ends that we couldn't tie up before we left the city," he said. "Listen, you mind if I use your bathroom?"

"Help yourself. Just step around my stuff."

In addition to the master bathroom off the bedroom, each of the Windspray cottages had a half bath accessible from the living room. Sam had glanced into the bigger room when he'd ducked into the bedroom, but the door to the smaller bathroom was closed tight, something that had struck him as odd.

The "stuff" Cormier had referred to was photographic equipment, a small portable darkroom setup that occupied most of the short counter space. As he ran water and flushed the toilet to cover his real purpose there, Sam took a good look around, trying to figure out what Cormier had been developing.

There was no way to be sure. But he'd been working in here recently, judging by the fresh chemical smells. And photography was still an integral part of most of the counterfeiting methods Sam knew about.

Cormier had the bulb base free of the socket when Sam came out again. And he seemed eager to wrap up their conversation, in spite of Sam's attempts to draw him out on the subject of darkroom techniques.

That was odd in itself, Sam thought. Most amateur photographers were happy to discuss their hobby. But Cormier was putting the pliers away and reaching for a plumber's snake as Sam joined him again.

"Gotta go clear a drain at the Gustaffsons' place," he said. "The whole development is built so close to the water that things are always backing up. Time I leave this job, I'll be a plumber in all but pay scale."

"You planning on leaving?" Sam kept the words as light as he could, but something in the quick flash of Cormier's eyes made him think the other man was on his guard against any and all personal questions.

"Not for a while," he hedged, and gave Sam a grin that Sam recognized for what it was—a diversionary tactic, designed to show that Cormier had nothing to hide. "Although too many more blocked drains could do it to me. How Harold got a permit to build so close to the water table is beyond me, but then, I guess you can do anything you want if you've got money."

Sam went out onto the deck, but as he left he couldn't help turning and taking one more look around the nearly bare kitchen. There might be *something* there, he thought, some clue, some sign of who Steve Cormier really was and why he'd come to this out-of-the-way resort.

If Sam hadn't been raking the room with his practiced gaze, he would have missed it. It wasn't in the kitchen itself, it was in the way the redheaded handyman was adjusting the fit of his worn denim overalls as he stepped out of the cottage.

It lasted only a fraction of a second—a quick motion of Cormier's right hand toward a spot on his hip under the baggy covering of the overalls. But Sam recognized it immediately as the kind of last-minute check he'd performed countless times himself, in the years before he'd stopped carrying a gun.

Steve Cormier was armed.

And dangerous, Sam's gut insisted on adding as he stepped out onto the lawn.

Sam and Kelley's cottage faced south, toward the ocean. The sky, shadowed now with clouds that seemed to hint at a shift in the weather pattern, was beginning to do some spectacular things as the sun set.

Kelley watched the colors in the west change from yellow to deep, saturated orange, wondering what it would be like to stay at a place like this just for a holiday, with time to drink in the beauty and the quiet of the place.

As it was, the darkening sky made her feel apprehensive, not calm. And the isolation of the Windspray Community—all by itself at the end of this sandy point—was anything but restful. Somewhere in this attractive cluster of cottages, after all, there was a person who had tried to kill her and Sam.

The constant tapping of the computer keys at the table behind her only added to her sense of unease. Sam had been working like a demon all day, and he showed no signs of slowing down now that night was falling.

They'd shared a hasty lunch of leftovers from the night before and hadn't discussed dinner yet. Something about the dimming light outside, about Sam's silence for the past hour and her own empty stomach, was beginning to leave Kelley feeling depressed. If this *had* been a vacation, instead of a working trip, or if she and Sam hadn't split apart three years ago—

Those thoughts were useless. But they were creeping into her mind, anyway, dampening her mood.

"There."

Sam spoke without warning, startling her. He sounded tired but satisfied as he leaned back in his chair, still looking at the screen of the laptop computer.

She knew the tone in his voice. It was the one that said, *Well, if nothing else, at least I'm working hard and getting results.* She must have told herself the same thing on a thousand different occasions during the past three years. The sound of it in Sam's voice didn't do anything to lift her spirits.

"I finally got something on the second of those references Steve Cormier gave when he came to work here," Sam said. "The office management company he said he worked for last year went out of business three years ago. That makes two phony references out of the three, and I'm willing to bet the third one is just as bogus."

Steve Cormier's job application form had finally turned up on Harold Price's desk—"Right under his nose the whole time," Helen had said, looking disgusted at what she clearly considered a long-standing flaw in her husband's filing system. And once Sam and Kelley had begun to check it out, the application had given new weight to the idea that the Windspray Community's handyman was not who he had made himself out to be.

Not only did Cormier's references not check out, but no one had heard of him at his previous address. "And he doesn't show up on any of the credit listings I've tried," Sam said.

From his trip to Cormier's cottage, Sam had brought back the news that one piece of photographic equipment in the handyman's cottage had a label from a mail-order firm. Yet when they'd called, the firm had no Steve Cormier on its mailing list. *Nothing* about the man seemed genuine.

Kelley herself had continued working on constructing a financial picture of the Gustaffsons, and she hadn't given up on her hunch that there was something shady about Wayland Price. But there were simply too many gaps in Steve Cormier's story to ignore.

"I'm beginning to agree with you that he's our first choice," Kelley said, watching Sam lift his arms above his head to stretch out the kinks in his neck and shoulders. "And we've got plenty to back us up. Now, the question is—"

She'd been about to say that what they needed now was some physical proof that Cormier was involved in counterfeiting money. But before she could say so, the look on Sam's face stopped her.

He'd paused with one long arm curved over his head. The other one had reached up to clasp the first at the elbow. It had been a casual movement, she thought, prompted by muscle stiffness after too many hours hunched over the computer keyboard. But it had turned into something else.

Everything about him had gone still, including his face. His eyes were closed, and Kelley could see him fighting for the careless expression he always wore when he didn't want to show what was going on inside him.

But it wasn't working this time. He didn't look careless. He looked like he was in pain.

For three years Kelley had held herself aloof from Sam's pain, because it seemed like the best defense against the way he was holding himself aloof from *her*. But now—maybe because of that unexpected moment yesterday in the cabin of Harold and Helen's boat—she couldn't keep her distance from it any longer. The distress on his shuttered face was something she was a part of, whether she liked it nor not.

And suddenly she needed to know whether she could have a hand in fixing it.

She didn't give herself time to change her mind. She moved quickly, quietly, around the circular table until she stood behind Sam's broad back.

The fiery sunset outside was dying into mere embers now. Kelley felt as though her thoughts were doing the same thing, plunging back into the darkness that was always there waiting for her whenever she thought about Sam Cotter.

But ignoring the darkness hadn't made it go away. Kelley took in a slow, deep breath and put her hands on Sam's right shoulder.

She felt him tense under her fingertips, tightening the hard knot that had stopped his stretch in the first place. At first she thought he was going to shrug her off, and she paused, waiting for his deep, gravelly voice to tell her she should mind her own business and let him mind his.

But he didn't speak. He just lowered both arms, slowly, in a gesture that looked almost like a silent surrender. After another long pause, Kelley began to probe, as gently as she knew how, into the tight mass of muscle that had been damaged and then slowly restored.

It was easy to feel the places where that slow therapy process hadn't really worked. She was reluctant to push too hard, afraid of hurting him even more, but as she pressed one palm firmly over the spot that had tightened so cruelly, she heard him exhale on what sounded like a note of relief. And that gave her enough confidence to go on.

She leaned into his tense muscles with the heel of her hand, rubbing in slow circles that seemed to loosen the rock-hard spot. She saw Sam tilt his head forward slightly, and wondered why it was that the exposed back of his neck, with the dark hair curling untidily over his collar, should make her feel so strong, so protective.

Was it because he was opening himself to her in a way he hadn't done for what seemed like forever? She didn't let herself linger over the question, but kept her thoughts focused on what she was doing, exploring his old injury with unhurried thoroughness.

She curled her fingers around his shoulder and flexed it, still massaging it with her other hand. She had no technical idea what she was doing. She only knew that Sam's body seemed to be telling her what felt right, and she was following his instincts, and her own.

She heard him exhale in another deep sigh as she lifted his shoulder a little higher and pressed a little more insistently into the damaged muscle. The sound was almost a groan this time, but the edge of pleasure in it was very clear. Heartened, Kelley became bolder, flattening both palms against his skin and moving in wider circles that rocked Sam's whole body and left her amazed at how relaxed, how trusting he was becoming under her touch.

"You have no idea," he said at last, "how good that feels."

She had some idea. The change in him was remarkable, and the sound of relief and pleasure in his voice made her feel suddenly lighthearted.

Her gloomy mood of a few minutes ago had vanished, and even the dark night outside had disappeared from her awareness. The only thing that mattered was the warm circle of light around the table, and the ragged honesty in Sam's voice, and the silent, certain way their bodies were communicating with each other, after all this time apart.

That silent language of theirs had been so perfect once. They'd each seemed to know exactly what pleased the other. Their lovemaking had always opened new worlds to Kelley. It had been as though Sam had seen directly into her thoughts, into her fantasies.

She felt her own body stirring in response to those half-forgotten fantasies now, and realized she was in danger of letting her old feelings for Sam completely overwhelm her.

"You must have had physical therapists who could do this as well as I can," she said, trying to keep her thoughts practical.

But he was shaking his head, flexing his neck like a big cat stretching in the hot sun. "Not like this," he murmured. For a moment Kelley had the hazy impression that he was actually purring. "Nobody ever made me feel like this except—"

Except you. Had that been what he'd been about to say? Kelley stopped moving, startled by the idea that both of them had been drifting back into deep waters without really meaning to.

Sam didn't finish the sentence, but he wasn't making any move to swim to a safer harbor, either. For a long moment Kelley just stood there, feeling the rhythm of her own escalating heartbeat where her palms rested against Sam's shoulder.

She knew she should step away, but somehow she didn't want to break this unexpectedly comforting contact until she'd told him she knew how he felt—knew, perhaps, better than anyone else could know.

"It's not enough, is it?" She said the words quietly, flicking one hand toward the green light of the computer screen. "You work and work, and there's still something—hollow about it."

She felt him grow tense under her fingers again and wondered if her words had just erased whatever benefit he'd gotten from the massage. And his voice sounded harsh again when he answered her.

But he didn't move. And he didn't argue.

"No, damn it, it isn't enough," he said. "But I don't know what else to do."

Kelley gave a startled half laugh. The anger and bewilderment in his voice was exactly what she had been feeling for so long.

"Me, too," she told him. Impulsively she ran both hands over the broad surface of his back again, warmed into the gesture by an unexpected sense of solidarity.

He captured one of her wrists suddenly, startling her even more, pulling her around to face him. She was drawn down onto his lap without realizing it, surrounded by his strength before she'd had a chance even to think of resisting.

And the moment she looked into his eyes, she didn't want to resist, anyway.

Sam Cotter kept the world at arm's length most of the time by making it clear—with his trademark slouch, his blunt speech, his flint-hard glare—that he didn't give a damn what anybody might think or say about him. Even when he smiled, his expression hovered halfway between warning and mockery. His eyes never changed when he smiled like that.

But Sam had another smile, one he rarely used. It was slow, and surprised looking. And tender. And infinitely sexy, because it was a window into the real Sam Cotter, with none of the usual barriers and barbed wire in the way.

It was one of the most beautiful things Kelley had ever seen.

And against all her expectations, she was seeing it now.

His eyes caught her, held her. She felt wrapped in his slow smile, drawn into the genuine warmth she could see in his face. She lifted one hand to smooth back his dark, tousled hair and felt herself smiling in answer.

Neither one of them tried to put their thoughts into words. Words were inadequate, anyway, Kelley knew, for the kind of empathy they were sharing right now—the empathy that had drawn them together when they'd first met.

And she wasn't sure her voice would work even if she wanted to talk. The way she was nestled into the hard angle of Sam's lap was overpoweringly erotic. When she shifted her weight slightly she could feel the masculine line of his thighs and another telltale ridge—just as masculine, even more arousing—under her body.

His smile faded, leaving only the naked hunger in his blue eyes. Kelley ran her fingers through his hair again, wondering how she'd managed to live through these past three years without the searching adoration of Sam's gaze. And then—she wasn't sure which one of them moved first— their mouths met, and the same long-denied, all-consuming hunger overran both of them.

She felt his fingers threading into her hair, holding her face against his as he kissed her. There were so many things she wanted him to do, so many feelings she knew he could arouse in her. She wanted to feel his mouth caressing every inch of her, his hands exploring parts of her that were suddenly crying out for his touch. She wanted to be joined to him forever, holding him safe in the cradle of her body, keeping the darkness around them at bay.

Sam drew her deeper and deeper into the moment, into the kiss, murmuring her name against her lips, groaning deeply as the satin softness of her tongue met his, inviting her into the warm recesses of his mouth and the untapped strength of his desire.

One of her hands was resting at the open collar of his worn white shirt, and she could feel his pulse hammering under her fingertips. That pounding beat echoed in her own body, calling up an answering moan of undisguised need, making her almost painfully aware of how her body was responding to Sam's kiss.

If they went on from here . . .

If they somehow crossed the distance from the table to the bedroom door, where the big queen-size bed was waiting . . .

Her own wanton thoughts didn't surprise her. This undercurrent of passion had been there all along. It needed only the merest touch to flare into high-voltage life.

And this was much more than a mere touch. . . .

She felt him slide one possessive hand along the line of her throat, as though he was searching for something. He followed it a moment later with a trail of slow kisses that left Kelley gasping.

His hand was sliding lower, over the collar of her loose white shirt. He met the first button and flicked it open with casual skill. Kelley moaned again, letting her head fall even farther back as Sam reached the second button.

''Sam—maybe—we should move—''

She wasn't sure how she managed to get the words out. Everything inside her seemed to be vibrating, humming, as though Sam Cotter had been heaven-sent to make glorious and erotic music with her body.

Or maybe it was the devil who'd sent him. There was something diabolically brazen about the way he was now kissing the inward curve of her breast. It felt unbearably right, as though she belonged to him and he knew it, and he was only claiming what had been his all along.

And Kelley wanted him to do it. She twined her fingers through his hair and let him rock her in an embrace that was becoming more and more provocative with every slight shift in the way they were holding each other. Her heart was beating so hard now that it seemed to be knocking at her eardrums, urging her in very primitive language to touch Sam, to hold him, to feel him in the core of her, where it was so clear he belonged.

The knocking of her heartbeat had gotten harsher, somehow, and Kelley frowned without opening her eyes. What on earth—

Sam had noticed it now, too. He lifted his head from the soft valley between her breasts and looked around the room. The darkness in his eyes told Kelley he'd been as caught up, as far away, as she'd been herself.

But something had dragged them back to earth. And after a few confused seconds, they both realized it was Helen

Price, tapping insistently at the screen door just a few feet away from them.

Sam's low expletive barely made it through the hoarseness in his throat. He seemed, if anything, even more startled than Kelley was. He stayed motionless for several heart-stoppingly long seconds, until Kelley finally shifted her weight and eased herself off his lap, away from his embrace.

Even then, as she quickly buttoned her shirt and tried to rally her wits, she seemed to be recovering more quickly than Sam from the shock of Helen's arrival. Kelley slid the kitchen door open, wondering what on earth she could say to their half-puzzled, half-embarrassed client.

They'd slipped up. They'd let themselves be distracted—devastatingly, powerfully distracted—from the job they'd been hired to do. And Helen had caught them at it.

There was no point making excuses. Kelley felt her face flushing an uncomfortable red and wondered what she must look like, with her hair disheveled from Sam's caresses and her eyes no doubt darkened by the desire that was still pounding through her veins.

Fortunately Helen jumped straight into the reason for her surprise visit. "Something very strange has happened," she said, her astute brown eyes glancing at Sam and then away again. "Harold noticed Steve Cormier packing some things into his car earlier this afternoon and asked him where he was going. Cormier said he was just going into town on an errand, but he hasn't been back yet. And when I went over to his cottage just now to ask him about something, it looked very much to me as though he had taken his few things out of it."

Kelley heard Sam swear softly again. She didn't blame him for not standing up—she'd felt the evidence of his runaway desire when her hips had pressed against his body, and she was sure he was staying put because he didn't want

Helen Price's inquisitive eyes taking note of how thoroughly aroused he was.

But he seemed to be trying to gather his wits, in spite of his shock. "Do you have a key to Cormier's cottage?" he asked.

"Of course. We have keys to all the—"

He didn't let her finish, and Kelley winced inside at his brusqueness. But at least Sam was working again, shifting back into the professional frame of mind they'd both slipped so far out of.

She'd wanted it to happen, Kelley realized. She'd wanted their embrace to go as far as it could possibly go. She'd been so completely caught up in her feelings that she hadn't even stopped to consider anyone might be watching them through the windows of the kitchen, or that it might be dangerous to let her thoughts drift so far away from her real reason for being here.

She'd done the one thing she'd sworn she would never do again: she'd let Sam Cotter make her forget everything in the world but him.

Suddenly she was furious with herself, with both of them. She reached for the dark green sweatshirt she'd hung on a peg by the kitchen door and tossed Sam his rust-colored windbreaker while she was at it.

"Has Cormier ever done this before?" he asked, as he pulled the garment over his head.

"No, not for this long. And the Gustaffsons' drain is *still* not working, and—"

Once again Sam cut her off, and this time Kelley couldn't blame him. She was sharing the urgency she could see in Sam's long-legged strides, feeling the same need to find out what was happening around them.

When she thought of what had nearly happened, she felt herself blush all over. But she resolutely shoved the thought of it to the back of her mind and preceded Sam—now safely cloaked by his windbreaker—out onto the deck where Helen stood.

"We'll turn the place over," Sam was saying, sounding angrier all the time. "If he's given us the slip—"

"Then it proves he must be the counterfeiter, right?" Helen sounded tremulous but determined.

"Looks like it. And unless he's more obliging than I think, he's not likely to have left us any clues, any proof, any—"

Helen interrupted him a second time, and Kelley had to wonder, as the three of them started across the grassy hill toward the handyman's cottage, whether their client was trying to make a point about the way Sam had cut her off a few moments ago.

"I'm assuming," she said, lightly but meaningfully, "that what I just saw through your kitchen door was all just a part of your act. Because otherwise, when I think about the possibility that our forger may have managed to get away without anyone noticing—"

Sam growled as his strong, rangy legs propelled him to the top of the knoll ahead of the two women. "Don't worry," he said, and even in the darkness Kelley could see the savage look of guilt and anger and sexual frustration on his face. It almost seemed that the man who'd held her so intimately just moments ago, the man who'd smiled into her eyes with such slow pleasure, had disappeared into the night.

"If Steve Cormier is our forger, we'll find some way to prove it," he said. "And as for what you saw through the door—"

He paused, glaring at Kelley briefly as though daring her to contradict him. "I can guarantee you that it won't happen again," he said finally, and stalked down the other side of the little hill at a pace that left Kelley breathless as she tried to keep up.

Chapter 7

The cottage had been cleaned out, all right. Sam hadn't expected anything less. But the sight of it—the closet doors standing open, the bare countertop where he'd seen Cormier's developing equipment only this morning—made him burn inside. If he'd had his whole mind on this job—

"He left his tools." Kelley was checking the kitchen drawers while Sam inspected the bedroom.

"Actually, most of the tools belong to us," Helen Price said. "I suppose we should be grateful that he wasn't a petty thief as well as a counterfeiter."

As far as Sam could see, there wasn't a whole lot else to be grateful for. Cormier seemed to have packed his few belongings in a hurry, judging by the half-closed drawers in the dresser. But he'd had enough time to be thorough about it.

"I don't suppose there's any chance of tracing him now." Helen sounded disheartened as Sam joined the two women in the little hallway.

"Chances are he's long gone, maybe over the border by now," Sam confirmed. He was feeling too angry at himself even to think about sugarcoating the news for their client. "I'll make some calls, just in case. Wiley has contacts in most of the law-enforcement agencies in the state, and maybe they can help us turn up something."

"It might be worth checking in Cairo, too," Kelley put in. "He was pretty noticeable, with that bright red hair. If anybody happened to spot him, we might get some idea which way he was headed."

Sam had been about to suggest the same thing. "I'll do that next," he said. "But beyond that—"

A floorboard under Kelley's feet creaked loudly as she shifted her weight, and all three of them jumped.

"That was one of the many things Steve Cormier said he was going to fix around this cottage," Helen said, frowning down at the hardwood flooring at her feet. "I suppose he was too busy making phony bills to do what he was hired for."

"He always seemed to be busy when we saw him," Kelley said thoughtfully.

"Oh, he worked hard enough during the day. But if there was any kind of emergency after hours, it was like pulling teeth to get him to see to it. There was one evening I was *sure* he was in here, but he wouldn't answer the door when I knocked."

She sighed and patted at her soft brown hair, as though she wanted to make sure at least one thing in her life was where it was supposed to be. "That's the last time I'm letting Harold's practical considerations triumph over my instincts," she said firmly. "Although I've never been fond of saying 'I told you so'—and frankly, I'd rather have our criminal than the satisfaction of knowing I was right."

Sam cursed silently as he took the cottage keys from Helen and stalked back outside to where his pickup truck was parked. Kelley followed him into the vehicle, refusing to let herself be left out. But Sam had no intention of letting his attention be waylaid by her beautiful, insistent presence a second time this evening. If only the honeyed scent of her hair wasn't swirling around the truck cab—

"Sam—"

He started the engine with a roar, not caring whether he disturbed the peace of any of the Windspray residents who might be enjoying a leisurely dinner. Still seething, he jammed the truck into gear and pulled out onto the gravel driveway. Kelley had to grab the dashboard to keep from sliding into him.

"Sam, we made a mistake. Is that any reason to—"

"We made more than one mistake, sweetheart." He got the words out through tight lips, and wished like hell he'd left a pack of cigarettes in the truck. "First of all, we let Steve Cormier slip through our fingers. He must have figured out this morning that I was after more than just a pair of pliers. *Damn.*"

His frustration boiled over, and he slammed the steering wheel hard with the flat of his palm. The muscles in his shoulder tensed in protest, but he told himself grimly that he didn't mind. Pain could be a useful wake-up call, if you paid attention to it.

It was only when you started letting yourself go soft, thinking about comfort and sensuality and solace—

He growled deep in his throat and fought off the memory of the way Kelley had felt in his arms, how the touch of her soft skin had made him want to cry out for more of her. There had been the sweet promise of comfort in her kisses, her embrace, the eager response he'd always found so exciting.

But comfort had a high price. And Sam wasn't ready to risk paying it again. Aside from the danger to his heart, he had a job to do, and an investigation agency to take over as soon as this case was wrapped up. Losing his head over

Kelley Landis again was a complication he simply couldn't afford.

"Cormier must have been thinking of bolting before now," she was saying. "I'm sure it wasn't just you—"

He refused to let her finish. He knew she was trying to make him feel better, but sympathy was the very last thing he wanted right now.

"Even if I didn't scare Cormier away, we still screwed up big time by letting Helen walk in on us like that. We both ought to have our heads read for getting so carried away."

They'd reached the end of the Windspray lane now, and Sam had to wait as a passing car turned at the intersection of the beachfront road that led to Cairo. The brisk wind off the Gulf rocked the black pickup slightly, and Sam felt as though the weather outside had joined with his own conscience, buffeting him with strong, accusing gusts.

He'd spoken bitterly, abruptly, and Kelley didn't seem to have an answer for his words. Had he hurt her, or just stung her into the realization that he was right? At the moment he couldn't afford to care.

"Sam."

She finally spoke just as the light changed and Sam was shifting back into first gear. Kelley's quick touch on his wrist stopped him.

"That floorboard—"

At first he couldn't imagine what she was talking about. He was working hard to collect himself, to dispel all the longings and memories that surfaced when he'd taken Kelley in his arms. He didn't have a lot left over for original thinking.

And then it suddenly clicked. "The floorboard Helen stepped on," he said. "The one that creaked—"

"Cormier said he was going to fix it, but he didn't." She'd turned toward him now, her blue eyes shimmering with the quick intelligence Sam found so captivating. "Do you think—"

"I think it's worth checking on."

He'd been intending to turn Cormier's cottage inside out later, but Kelley's idea was too good not to act on right away. Stomping on the clutch pedal, he ground the gearshift into reverse and started back through the low stone gates into the Windspray Community.

It was a good thing Cormier had left the tools behind. Sam ransacked the kitchen drawers for a hammer and a small pry bar while Kelley located the spot they were after.

"If I'm wrong, Harold and Helen aren't going to be too pleased about what we're doing to this nice hardwood floor," she commented as Sam began tapping the blunt end of the pry bar into the line between one piece of flooring and the next.

"Yeah, but if you're right—"

It was beginning to look as though she was right. The floor in the hallway was smooth, polished maple, but the boards were cut wide for an intentionally rustic look, and there were slight spaces between them. Sam hadn't noticed it earlier, but now, on closer examination, it was clear that someone had pried up this particular board before, with a little more finesse than he was now using. He could feel his excitement mounting as he began to lift the floorboard, catching a glimpse of a dark space underneath, where there should have been only plywood subflooring.

Kelley was stooping next to his shoulder, her thigh grazing him. Even now, even after the silent lecture he'd just given himself, Sam couldn't ignore the subtle perfume of her skin or the way the warmth of her breath curled itself around the back of his neck.

He frowned with the double effort of lifting the floorboard and resisting Kelley's nearness. If he couldn't keep his mind on his job, after what had happened earlier this evening—

In a moment it became very easy to focus on the job. What they saw, when Sam had finally pulled the strip of hardwood loose, was a small stack of twenty-dollar bills, neatly bound with a rubber band. It was impossible to be sure at a glance, but this time Sam decided to listen to his instincts, which were telling him loudly and clearly that the money would probably turn out to be counterfeit.

"So that's it."

Kelley speared her last shrimp thoughtfully but didn't raise it from her plate. She and Sam were sharing a late dinner at the little restaurant in Cairo, sitting at a table for two near the back of the softly lit room. The place was quiet on this Thursday evening, and the staff were showing signs of cleaning up for the day.

Kelley had thought she was ravenous. The Gulf shrimp in tangy Cajun sauce, served over rice, was the kind of thing that usually tickled her taste buds. And the restaurant was a pleasant place to linger over a meal. The walls were painted in a pale peach-colored wash, in contrast to the rich green carpet underfoot. Local art—Kelley had recognized a couple of Helen Price's watercolors—graced the walls, highlighted here and there by the soft light of the candles on the tables.

She should have been enjoying the food, and the atmosphere.

She should have been happy that this assignment was over.

She should have been convinced that it *was* over.

But she wasn't.

And neither was Sam, judging by the black looks he'd been giving his marinated steak. Kelley watched him toss his napkin onto the table as she finished her meal, wondering if he was sharing her doubts, in that uncanny, intuitive way of his.

"So that's it." Sam echoed her words. "I can't say it's a resounding success, with the perpetrator on his way to God knows where by now, but at least the mystery's cleared up."

"And the clients are happy."

"That's an understatement." He gave her a grim smile. "I thought Harold was going to pump my hand right off the end of my arm when I told him we'd found solid evidence connecting Steve Cormier with the counterfeiting."

The twenty-dollar bills under Cormier's floor had indeed proved to be phony. A close examination at Kelley and Sam's cottage had verified it. And although there hadn't been many bills left in the stash, Harold's guess about it—"He must have put them there when he first arrived and forgot there were any left when he took off"—seemed to be a plausible explanation.

Except—

Except that neither Kelley nor Sam had been able to concentrate on dinner. Even their waiter had noticed and had asked them three times if everything was all right.

"Dessert and coffee?" he asked now, as he cleared their plates.

They both shook their heads. "Just the check," Sam said, leaning back in his chair. He'd changed into a clean white shirt before leaving the Windspray Community, and the crispness of it highlighted the worn creases of his blue jeans and the unruly tangle of his dark hair. Kelley watched the candlelight moving over his thoughtful features and felt her own thoughts flickering just the same way.

The case is over, she told herself. *Harold and Helen are satisfied. It's not your problem anymore.*

But she'd worked so hard, trained herself so exhaustively to be a thorough professional. And all her experience was telling her that this was wrong.

"All right, cowboy," she said to Sam at last. "What's on your mind?"

Her words seemed to startle him. He raised one dark eyebrow and tapped his long index finger rhythmically against the tabletop.

But he answered her readily enough. And his words were as blunt as ever. "I feel like we've been set up," he said.

She was more relieved than she'd expected. So she wasn't the only one feeling this way. "Me, too," she said. "I've been in this business long enough to know that the obvious answer is often the right one, but this is—"

"Too obvious." He finished the sentence for her, seeming unaware that he'd even taken over her thoughts. "You're right. I just can't believe that Cormier would go to all the trouble of making that hiding place under the floorboards and then leave his stash there when he took off."

"Or that he'd disappear without clearing that ten grand out of his bank account."

It had taken some doing to convince the local bank manager to check the bank's computer records when Sam had called him after hours. But after some persistent urging, the man had done it, and had confirmed that Cormier's account was untouched.

"So where does that leave us?" Kelley wondered out loud.

"Out of the loop." Sam crossed one long leg over the other, frowning down at his cowboy boots as though they'd said something to insult him. "The case is over. Harold and Helen aren't going to pay us to continue, now that they're satisfied Cormier is the culprit."

"They did offer to let us stay out the rest of the week as a bonus, if we wanted," Kelley reminded him.

He snorted. "Wonder what Wiley would say about that," he mused.

She knew what he meant. Given the way Sam had kicked about working with Kelley again in the first place, it would be an abrupt about-face to extend their stay instead of heading home at the first available opportunity.

But—

"Wiley would say that Cotter Investigations has a well-deserved reputation for getting things right," she murmured.

Sam was still tapping the tabletop. The sound was beginning to make Kelley feel edgy, or maybe it was just that the faint, insistent drumbeat echoed her own unsettled feelings.

"If we assume Steve Cormier isn't the bad guy, then the person who tried to kill us is still out there," Sam said slowly.

"That's not a pleasant thought."

Their words were only skimming the surface, Kelley thought. Their eyes were holding a separate conversation, digging deeper, raising more troublesome questions.

Can we turn our backs on this thing now?

Do we trust each other enough to go on?

It was an uncomfortable challenge to keep her eyes level with Sam's, reading his unspoken thoughts in those blue depths. Kelley cleared her throat and was glad when Sam finally spoke.

"Do you want to keep this investigation going, under the table?" he asked.

"Well, I don't want to walk away from here leaving some son of a gun thinking we've been fooled, if that's what you mean."

"Fooled, or scared off."

"That, too." She leaned back in her chair. "Which son of a gun are you thinking it might be, Sam?"

"Well, there's Wayland. Although if we stay, we're going to have to find a way to check him out without his parents knowing we're doing it."

Kelley agreed. Harold and Helen had reacted with scorn to any suggestion of treating Wayland as a suspect. If Sam and Kelley accepted the Prices' offer of hospitality, their investigation of Wayland was going to have to be extremely discreet.

"But you agree he's worth looking into," she said.

"Hell yes." Sam stopped drumming on the table and held up one strong hand, listing his points on the ends of his fingers. "He has access to keys to all the cottages, through his parents. His job is an obvious sham. He knew his mother already had her suspicions about Steve Cormier. And he showed up here exactly two days before the first phony bill surfaced. If Cormier *isn't* the real counterfeiter—and it sure as hell feels to me like he isn't—then Wayland Price is the obvious next choice."

Kelley nodded. "And somehow I can easily picture Wayland trying to shove the blame onto somebody else," she said. "He seems to think the world was made for his personal pleasure."

"Good point." The waiter had brought their bill, and Sam dropped a pile of cash on top of it. "Let's get out of here, all right, sweetheart? I think better when I can stretch my legs while I'm doing it."

The restaurant was only a couple of blocks from the beach. They left Sam's truck parked where it was and walked toward the water. Kelley was glad she'd put on her heavy yellow cotton sweater earlier. The wind off the Gulf was steadily rising, and the air seemed to be turning cooler.

There was something eerie about Cairo's streets at night. The little town had so clearly been a busy place once. But the wind whistling across vacant lots and down deserted side streets made it seem like the ghost town Harold Price had jokingly called it.

Sam seemed to be reading her thoughts again. "Finding buyers for the rest of those Windspray cottages sure would make a big difference to this little burg," he commented.

"I know. And it's such a beautiful spot."

Cairo's waterfront was the prettiest part of the town. Even at night the long sweep of sand beach, bolstered by the stone breakwaters, made a clean, pleasing line along the shore. And the big fishing pier seemed to beckon to them, drawing their steps toward the broad, brightly lit platform that ran several hundred feet out into the Gulf waters.

"If we're going to stay, we shouldn't confine ourselves just to looking into Wayland," Sam said. He shoved his hands into his jeans pockets as they started onto the pier. "Most of the other names on Harold's list have turned out to be dead ends, but—"

"There's still the Gustaffsons." Kelley hesitated, then added, "There's one thing I probably should have mentioned—"

A particularly strong gust of wind whipped the words away and made Kelley wrap her arms around her midriff for warmth. At least she told herself it was for warmth. Deep down, she knew it was the thought of Susan Gustaffson's unborn child that chilled her.

"The Gustaffsons knew how Helen felt about Steve Cormier, too," Sam said, loping comfortably toward the end of the pier. Kelley could hear the clunk of his boot heels echoing in the dark, empty space between the dock and the water. "And assuming that somebody did plant those bills in Cormier's cottage, it could very well have been Susan or Jon. They knew he wouldn't be around, because they'd arranged to have him come and fix their plumbing."

"How would they get into his cottage?"

"I don't know. We'll need to see how accessible the cottage keys are. I know there's a master set in the maintenance room at the main building, but I don't know how easy it would be to get at it."

His strides had lengthened, making it harder to keep up with him. He really did think better when he was in motion—always had, Kelley thought. He was as restless as any true cowboy, always keeping one eye on the horizon no matter where he happened to be.

"I think we'd have better luck with the Gustaffsons if we try to talk to them separately," Sam said. "Aside from that first morning, when you found Susan by herself in the exercise room, I've barely seen them apart. Hell, they're more like newlyweds than any real newlyweds I ever saw."

If the reference to newlyweds made him think about the honeymoon act he and Kelley were going to have to continue, his face showed no sign of it. She watched his brows lower and recognized that his mind was working hard.

"I wonder if Susan and Jon might be sticking so closely together so they can corroborate each other's stories," he said. "Or maybe—"

"Sam."

"Maybe neither of them wants to take a chance on slipping up, so they stay close for backup. Even the best liars miss a step now and again. Maybe Susan and Jon—"

"Sam, listen to me."

They'd reached the end of the fishing pier now. The waves churned against the big pilings under the wooden structure, and the big floodlight over their heads shone ominously down into the heaving depths of the the ocean. Somehow the sight made Kelley uneasy, as though the muddy water might hold secrets that could come bobbing to the surface without warning.

Sam was leaning on the railing at the edge of the pier, looking sideways at Kelley. The wind whipped his dark hair back from his forehead, and his features suddenly looked harsh and bleak.

"What is it?" he asked impatiently.

Kelley took in a deep breath. "Susan Gustaffson is pregnant," she told him. "They just found out about it last week. That's why they're sticking so close together. They're happy, that's all. Happy that they're going to have a baby. It's how expectant parents behave, Sam. It's how we behaved, in case you'd forgotten."

She hadn't realized her voice was going to falter until it happened. It was the word *baby* that tripped her up.

And the sweet, half-buried memory of those few days when she and Sam had looked forward to their future together with the same kind of joy and hope that had shone in Susan Gustaffson's eyes when she'd told Kelley about her pregnancy.

She wasn't prepared for the way her whole body started to shake as Sam turned to face her. He looked as though she'd hit him, hard, without warning, and his eyes were nearly as black and wild as the night sky overhead.

"Susan told me this morning she already feels sure she's carrying a boy." The words were out without Kelley planning to say them. "It's funny—I had the same feeling, early on. Remember I told you I was sure it was going to be a girl?"

"Don't do this, Kelley."

She barely heard his gravelly protest. Suddenly she couldn't hold this back, couldn't rein in the words she'd kept inside her for what felt like a lifetime.

And who else could she say this to, if not to Sam? They hadn't shared the news about the baby with anyone else. And so they were the only ones in the world who could share the grief of its death.

She could hear that grief in her own voice, and feel it in her belly as she said, "It's amazing, Sam, how close you can feel to a child who isn't even born yet. Do you remember that day in the hospital, when I seemed like such a zombie?"

"I remember." He'd closed his eyes, and there were deep furrows in his brow, making him look older, impenetrable.

"It was because I couldn't believe it," Kelley said. "I couldn't believe she was gone."

Suddenly everything around them—the wind, the water, the circle of light from the tall pole at the end of the pier— seemed to have turned to a gigantic swirl of pain, washing out of the past and over her without warning. Kelley caught her breath and heard a sob forming in it.

But she still couldn't stop. "It took the longest time for it to sink in," she said raggedly. "I would find myself walking around with one hand pressed over my stomach." She pressed a hand there now, unconsciously, and saw Sam's eyes open again, taking in the gesture, wincing at the sight of it. "And I'd look down and *tell* myself there was no baby there anymore, but some part of me just wouldn't accept it. I felt as if she was still there—that everything was going to be all right—that you—"

She had no words for the silent hope that had tormented her for so long. *I was so sure you would come back to me. I couldn't believe you would just leave me alone....* How could she say that out loud, when Sam's stormy gaze was warning her not to say anything at all?

She was suddenly appalled at what she'd done. She'd ripped the lid off her carefully concealed hurts, letting them spill out unprotected into the night air.

And the cold wind and the blue steel of Sam's eyes were withering those fragile feelings, leaving her more vulnerable than she'd felt since that awful day when he'd turned away from her in the hospital.

"You—you said you thought the baby was never meant to be." Could he hear the soft words over the gusting of the wind? Suddenly she didn't care. She just needed to say this out loud, once, in Sam's presence. She hadn't known how badly she needed it until she'd already spoken the words.

"But you were wrong, Sam." She wrapped her arms around her midriff again. "Babies are gifts, not mistakes. I just didn't realize then how precious a gift they are."

And because she hadn't realized it, she'd let her own overconfidence and inexperience get her into the situation that had led to a miscarriage. The image of that night still haunted her thoughts, waking and sleeping. Kelley felt the familiar clenched knot of loss low down in her body and wondered if it would ever go away.

And there was another image that haunted her, too.

"She would have been nearly three now." She closed her eyes, although her inner vision of a smiling three-year-old—with fair braids like her own, she always wondered, or dark, unruly hair like Sam's?—was almost as hard to face as the wounded look on Sam's face. "Do you ever think about that?"

"No."

The word was so blunt, so unequivocal, that it rocked her. *No?* Just like that? How could he—

"I can't think about those things, Kelley." He was speaking slowly, as though something inside him was trying to keep the words in. "I just—it doesn't do any good. It won't change anything that happened."

He was right.

Kelley had thought incessantly about everything that had happened, and yet nothing had really changed. She still felt the same pain, lived with the same guilt.

But still—

"Can you really do that?" she asked. "Just turn off all those feelings like you were turning a tap?"

He turned briefly to look out over the water, and Kelley shivered again as she followed his gaze. The ocean was so vast, so dark, utterly without comfort or mercy.

And Sam's eyes, when he swung them back to meet hers, were just as dark, just as bleak and comfortless.

"I don't know what else to do," he said.

Slowly, heavily, as though he'd aged in the past few minutes, he stepped away from the wooden railing and started to walk back toward the shore. The angle of his shoulders looked forlorn, almost defeated.

It took a little while before Kelley could make herself follow him. She was still in the grip of too many memories, too many unresolved feelings. And she'd never found a way to put all of these old hurts behind her.

Something in the past few days had fractured the careful control she'd prided herself on. The ragged sound of her own voice when she'd poured out her thoughts a few minutes ago only proved that.

And unlike Sam, she'd never learned how to turn around and just walk away.

Chapter 8

Son, you've got a pair of ears that could hear a flea crossing from one side of a cat's belly to the other.

At first Sam thought it was the memory of his father's voice that had wakened him. That in itself was surprising enough to make him roll over on the sofa and prop himself on one elbow, blinking in the near-darkness.

He didn't usually think about his dad any more than he could help. Yet in the past few days he'd been hearing J.D.'s deep, affectionate growl in his head, almost as though the two of them were together again. It was beginning to get on his nerves.

Then he heard something else, and realized what had alerted those sharp ears his father used to tease him about.

The wind was still blowing hard outside, and the high-pitched hiss of the waving beach grasses overlaid the occasional gusts. But there was another sound out there, too, one that had gotten through to Sam even in his sleep.

Someone was walking across the deck.

It was the faintest of steps, just a soft padding of feet on the wooden boards. But it was enough to make Sam roll over and settle Kelley's pistol into his palm. He'd been keeping it close to him these past couple of nights. If it turned out they were under attack again—

He rolled off the sofa and into a low crouch on the carpeted floor.

The light footsteps on the deck seemed to be moving away from the back door, not toward it. Puzzled, Sam followed the sound as it rounded the corner of the cottage, and realized when it stopped abruptly that whoever was out there must have stepped off the deck onto the lawn.

He was on his way cautiously through the kitchen when he saw her.

It was Kelley, her fair hair blown into disarray by the wind. And she was moving quietly but purposefully toward the Windspray road, or perhaps toward the dunes that lay beyond it.

Sam cursed silently and slid the kitchen door open. He put the safety on the gun and jammed it into the back pocket of his sweatpants as he went down the wooden steps.

Was she sleepwalking? Her pace was unhurried, her long limbs as graceful and poised as ever. He couldn't see her face, but something about the way she was moving made him think she was paying no attention to her surroundings. She seemed to be far away, maybe wandering in some dreamworld of her own.

She crossed the gravel road at the same deliberate gait and leaned forward into the wind a little as she reached the soft sand of the dunes. She was having a tougher time walking now, but she still seemed completely focused on whatever inward voices had prompted this midnight stroll.

If she was dreaming, what was it about?

Was she imagining their lost child, perhaps following the ghostly image of a three-year-old girl across the shifting, sandy dunes?

Sam shivered suddenly. He was beginning to feel surrounded by a past that he'd hoped was safely dead and gone. The look in Kelley's sea blue eyes this evening, when she'd talked about their baby, had forced him face-to-face with things he thought he'd managed to outdistance a long time ago. And now—

Kelley had reached the end of the ridge of dunes and stopped at the flat stretch of beach.

Behind her, Sam stopped, too.

And another wave of memory hit him so hard he could feel it rolling right through him.

It had been a night nothing like this one, a calm, starry night many miles north of here. Flat country, ranching country.

And it had been angry voices that had wakened him, not soft footfalls.

He'd heard his parents shouting at each other, heard his mother's shrill demands.

Get out. Get out and don't come back.

And the door slamming.

And the rising dismay in his mother's sobs.

At seven years old, Sam had been shaken by the sound of his mother crying. But the idea of his father leaving had alarmed him even more. He'd hurried down the stairs of their little house as quickly and silently as he knew how and wriggled out the loose pantry window the same way he'd wriggled in whenever he'd been out later than he was supposed to be.

Nobody had noticed him.

It had been nearly morning—when his father stopped the truck for gas—before Sam poked his head out from under the canvas tarp in the truck bed and announced his presence. There had been traces of tears on his father's face— had the whole order of things gotten turned upside down in one night? Sam remembered wondering—but J.D.'s broad grin at the sight of his youngest son had made up for everything.

At least for a while.

Sam realized he was clenching his hands tight at his sides. It took a surprising amount of effort to flex them again.

He'd overturned his whole life on that starry night, following one path, running like hell away from the other.

Was he doing the same thing now?

He frowned into the windy darkness ahead of him, to where Kelley stood wrapped in her own thoughts, and knew that even if he was, he didn't have a choice. He'd been drawn after her tonight by something he hadn't even tried to resist.

"Kelley."

She didn't seem to hear him. The wind was coming directly off the water, blowing Sam's words back toward the cottages.

"Kelley, what the hell are you doing out here all by yourself?"

He could tell by her expression that he'd startled her. But there was something else in her face, too, something that tugged Sam's memory back to the day she'd sat at the foot of his hospital bed, staring at him with that dazed, questioning look in her eyes.

She hadn't cried then. But she was crying now. He could see the tears glistening in the faint light from the Windspray entrance.

"Ah, hell." Sam took a step closer to her, then stopped. The fine sand shifted under his bare feet, slipping out from under him.

Did Kelley want him here? His mind flickered back to the memory of his father's face lighting up at the sight of Sam curled up in that canvas tarp. His whole life, Sam had never forgotten that feeling of having somebody really want him.

But Kelley—

"You shouldn't be out here." His doubts made his voice harsher than he'd intended. "You don't even have your gun."

"I don't care about the gun." Her voice, normally so honey smooth, was clogged with tears now. "I just wanted to be by myself."

Well, that was pretty blunt. But he still couldn't leave her. And it wasn't just because he was worried about her safety.

"You were by yourself in the bedroom," he reminded her.

A fresh gust of wind tore through what was left of her decorous braid, and for a moment she looked almost ghostly. Her hair, warmed by the sun over the past couple of days, had turned blonder on top. It caught the distant light now, glinting gold against the dark sky. Her face was pale, her eyes wide and haunted. For a confused moment Sam wondered if he was dreaming all this—the beach, the pounding waves on the sand, the impossibly fair-skinned loveliness of the woman ahead of him.

Then she raised her hands to her temples, holding back her swirling hair. The gesture was so familiar, and so unhappy, that it brought Sam back to the present moment with a jolt. This was no ghost—it was Kelley Landis, the only woman he'd ever really loved.

And she was as miserable as he'd ever seen her.

"I know I was alone." She sounded angry as she repeated his words. "I just had to get out, Sam. I just—I needed—" She stopped and looked over her shoulder to the waves that were hurling themselves on the hard sand of the beach. "I don't know what I needed," she finished finally.

He took another step closer to her. "That doesn't sound like you," he said. "You've always known exactly what you needed to do."

"And now I don't. You don't have to rub it in." The anger was still there, but Sam had a feeling she was only using it to mask the tears he could hear in her voice.

The sound of those tears affected him more than her cool elegance ever had. He'd always been in awe of her grace, her poise. But now—

His feet still shifting under him in the sand, he closed the distance between them.

"Kelley, I—"

Damn it, what was it he was trying to say to her? It had started to be a lecture about not going out alone at night, but somehow he couldn't get those words to come out.

Kelley waited out his silence, hands at her sides again, the wind whipping insistently through her hair and around her dark sweatpants and T-shirt. The longer he looked into those troubled blue eyes of hers, the closer Sam came to realizing what it was he wanted to say.

And he wasn't sure he could do it.

"Kelley—" He tried again, and couldn't quite manage it.

But then Kelley swallowed hard against something that looked like a sob, and Sam suddenly knew what had brought him to this point.

He'd seen bitterness and resolve and unhappiness in Kelley's eyes these past three years. But he'd never seen her beautiful face without some faint, persistent light of hope behind it.

Until tonight.

Tonight she looked beaten. Empty. Exhausted. And Sam couldn't stand the sight of it.

"Kelley, I just wanted to tell you—"

He couldn't do this just standing here, he thought. He needed to touch her, to hold her. He took a step closer and ran one palm slowly up the length of her arm.

She didn't respond, but he thought she was breathing faster. So was he.

"That day—in the hospital." The sentence ran into a dead end. Sam pursued it anyway. "There were things I tried to say to you then. But—I just couldn't."

He wasn't sure he could say them now. It seemed as though the three intervening years should have made this easier, but it hadn't.

"I just felt dead." His short laugh was harsh. "I know you needed me. And I had nothing to give you. Not a damn thing. But that doesn't mean I didn't want—that I wasn't thinking—"

It was hard to get his next words out at all. Maybe if he pulled her against him—like this—and felt the soft swirl of her hair against his face—

He finally managed it.

"Kelley, I'm sorry about the baby." It was like struggling through heavy seas to get the simple words out. "Sweetheart, I'm so sorry."

It felt as though everything that had stood between them came crashing down in that one instant. Kelley gave a low cry that seemed to have Sam's name buried somewhere in it. She clutched him around the waist as though she, too, had been drowning in deep waters. And Sam closed his own arms around her so hard that his shoulder ached with the effort of it.

Hell, all of him ached, from the strength of everything that was shuddering through him. Kelley was crying again. Maybe Sam was crying, too. He wasn't sure. And he didn't care. He felt as though the two of them had become part of the rising storm around them, buffeted by their own memories and holding fast to each other to keep from being swept away.

He shifted his grip slightly and heard Kelley's voice rise in protest.

"Sam, don't leave me."

"Don't worry, sweetheart. I'm not going anywhere."

He kissed her tangled hair, and the spot at her temple where her heartbeat pulsed, quick and urgent. She raised her arms to his neck and drew him even closer. Sam kissed her cheekbone and tasted tears there, salty as the sea but sweet, so unimaginably sweet to him.

"You're all right, Kelley." He didn't know where the words were coming from. They weren't phrases he'd ever thought he would use again. "You're going to be all right."

"I'm just so tired of hurting this much."

Sam's brief laugh was whirled away from him on the wind. She'd just voiced his own thoughts, the ones he'd never quite dared to put into words.

And it wasn't just surprise he was feeling.

It was relief.

And understanding.

And a sympathy so strong he thought it might tear him apart.

He had no idea how long they stood there, wrapped in each other's arms. He gave up trying to speak and just held Kelley close, waiting until her body was no longer wracked by those quiet sobs. When she'd gone still against him, he kissed her again, smoothing her hair with his hand and whispering her name against the soft skin of her forehead.

She made no move to step away, and Sam couldn't imagine ever wanting to let her go. But he was suddenly weary, as though he'd just run for miles to reach the safe haven of Kelley's embrace. And something in the way she was leaning against him made him think she was feeling the same way.

"It's late," he murmured against her ear.

She nodded. "I know."

"Do you want to go back in?"

"I suppose we should."

They still had a case to unravel and a criminal to catch, Sam remembered. The recollection of it astonished him.

"Going to be a big day tomorrow." He wasn't sure if he was reminding himself or Kelley.

But their assignment seemed to be the last thing on her mind as she lifted her head and looked into his eyes. She seemed to be searching for something, although Sam couldn't imagine what it might be.

"It's been a big day *today*," she said.

She was right. Sam snorted, hardly able to believe he'd started the morning at the target range, feeling like a complete failure.

And now he was walking back across the dunes with one arm clasped tightly around Kelley's shoulders, feeling the soft strength of her fingers at his waist. They walked in step so perfectly—always had, he recalled now.

He was remembering a lot of things that he hadn't let himself think about for a long time. And not all of them were painful.

He remembered, as they stepped back into the kitchen, how it had felt to come home together.

He remembered the naturalness of it, and his own sense of amazed gratitude that he *could* feel at home, after so many years of restless wandering.

The silence in the cottage seemed to wrap itself around them as Sam closed the sliding door. With the cool night wind locked outside, their cottage became a refuge, a resting place. Sam almost laughed to think how it had felt like a trap only a few days ago.

Kelley moved toward the bedroom door, but she paused, looking over her shoulder at him. Her hair was gloriously tangled, a soft mass of tendrils that softened her face and warmed the cool elegance of her features.

Sam wanted to move closer to her again, to step through the open bedroom door and lie down on the rumpled bed with Kelley in his arms. His hands ached with the need to hold the soft weight of her breasts, to set her whole body on fire with the intimacy of his touch. And his soul ached, too, with the loneliness of too many long nights without Kelley Landis.

But he knew he wouldn't do it.

She spoke as he was starting to move back toward the living room sofa.

"Sam, I—"

Sam shook his head. "Shh, sweetheart. You don't have to say anything."

She put a gentle hand on his arm as he passed her, and Sam stopped short. Even in that soft touch, Kelley had the power to calm some of the restless demons that were chasing around inside him.

And her touch awakened something, too—something Sam wasn't ready to deal with yet.

"You didn't have to say anything, either," she told him. "But you did. It means a lot to me, Sam."

He knew she was talking about the words that seemed to have been torn out of him after such a long silence—the ragged admission that he, too, had felt the loss of their child, had mourned the brief life that had been so cruelly cut off. He drew in a long, slow breath, amazed at the relief of finally sharing some of the blackness of that loss with Kelley.

But that didn't mean he'd forgotten all the hard lessons he'd learned on that night at the warehouse.

He was tempted to pull her close to him, to breathe in the sweet, salty perfume of her hair once more tonight. He could imagine how it would feel to kiss her good-night, to feel the gentle contours of her body fitting against him with tailor-made perfection.

But he couldn't let it happen.

He just couldn't.

"Good night, sweetheart." He ground the words out, and saw her eyes widen at his tone. If she only knew how much it was costing him to keep his distance from her....

He refused to think about it, or about the seductive possibility that she might actually *want* him to follow her into that dark bedroom. He strode past her into the living room and picked up the pillow that had fallen onto the floor when he'd awakened earlier. He beat it back into its original shape with fierce energy, not caring that the movements hurt his shoulder.

"Good night, Sam." From the bedroom doorway, Kelley's voice sounded almost wistful.

Sam grimaced and pulled the pistol out of his pocket. He didn't want to hear the soft regret in Kelley's words, any more than he wanted to be settling down on this too-short sofa by himself again.

He wanted Kelley Landis, more than he'd imagined it was possible to want a woman. He wanted to recapture what they'd once shared. The humming in his blood reminded him in some very specific ways of how it had felt to make love to her all night long, to give way to everything that she made him feel.

But those days were gone.

And in spite of what had just happened between them out on the beach, one of the things Kelley Landis made him feel now was remorse. Pure and simple.

He'd failed to keep her safe three years ago. He'd failed to protect their unborn child, failed to secure the future they'd both dreamed of. He'd been the experienced agent, the one in charge. But he'd ignored everything his own experience should have taught him.

And he'd be damned if he would let himself forget it again.

"I'm not wild about this."

"Of course you're not." Kelley poured milk into her coffee mug and stirred it with maddening calmness. "Admit it, Sam, you still think you have to oversee every piece of this investigation personally if it's going to work at all."

The annoying thing was that she was right.

The *other* annoying thing was that she seemed to have regained all her poise overnight. Sam, on the other hand, was a mess.

"We don't have the time to indulge that lone horseman complex of yours," Kelley continued. "You said yourself that we're running out of time. Besides, you're quicker with locks than I am."

"Wiley said you could pick a lock without even thinking about it."

She gave him that faint, catlike smile that always drove him crazy. "I'm good," she admitted, "but I'm still not as good as you."

It was a surprise to hear her say it. But then, maybe she'd been surprised to hear him speaking up for her professional skill, too. It was a far cry from their defensiveness when they'd started working on this case.

Her next words brought Sam back to earth. "And you're not as good as I am at making small talk with people, which is what I'll probably end up doing all morning with the Gustaffsons and Wayland," she said.

"You never know. You might pick up something useful. Keep your ears open."

"You don't have to tell me that, Sam."

"I probably don't have to tell you to be careful, but I'm going to do it anyway. These people are our three main suspects, after all. Any one of them could have been the person who fooled with that gas tank on Tuesday night."

"I know." The catlike satisfaction on her face went away, leaving a vestige of the haunted expression that had drawn him to her in the night. "Do you want more coffee?"

Sam felt as though he'd barely slept, between the throbbing in his shoulder and the thought of Kelley tossing and turning in the queen-size bed while he'd been doing the same thing on the sofa. He'd heard her, heard the faint rustling of the sheets as she'd tried to find her way toward sleep. It hadn't exactly been a restful night for either one of them.

And he needed to be sharp this morning, because he was probably going to have only one clear shot at searching those two cottages. "All right," he said, draining his cup and wincing as the hot coffee seared its way down his throat. "Let's go over the story one more time. I want to make sure we've both got it straight."

All the Windspray cottages shared the same layout. And that meant Sam didn't have to waste a lot of time getting his bearings once he'd picked the Gustaffsons' lock.

He'd gone in the sliding door off the living room as soon as he'd seen Susan and Jon pull out of the driveway with Kelley in the back of their car. While he'd worked on the lock, cautiously holding the wire picks in place, he'd imagined the conversation taking place in the car right now.

You and that husband of yours have just got to start doing more things together, Susan Gustaffson would probably be saying. *I'm sure he's a busy man—we're all busy—but he can't work all the time, not if you're going to have a good marriage.*

Susan and Jon evidently found the time for each other, not to mention for starting a family together. Had they found time to create a series of phony twenty-dollar bills, too? Sam frowned over the lock and told himself he couldn't afford to let his thoughts about Susan and Jon's unborn child get in the way of his view of them as possible counterfeiters.

The interior of the Gustaffsons' cottage was expensively and comfortably furnished. A big-screen television dominated the end wall of the living room, and in the kitchen a set of copper pots and pans hung from a rack in the ceiling, gleaming even in the dull light of this breezy, cloudy morning.

Sam hadn't done a physical search in a long time. Since his accident, he'd preferred hunting for clues in computers, not in people's homes. But the old pattern came back to him now as he moved quickly around the cottage.

He started in the kitchen, where the drawers and cupboards offered the most convenient hiding places. He took a hard look at the floorboards, just to make sure, but there was no sign of the kind of hiding place that had been created in Steve Cormier's kitchen.

The sofa and chairs—a favorite with many criminals bent on storing away incriminating evidence—turned up a few stale pieces of popcorn, some loose change and a hairbrush, but nothing else. The seams showed no signs of having been ripped open and sewn up again.

Sam figured he had about forty minutes to go through each cottage, less if the weather turned nasty. Kelley had suggested a drive to the wildlife sanctuary west of Cairo, and the Gustaffsons and Wayland had seemed eager to go, but Sam knew their enthusiasm could easily wane if the threatened rain started to fall.

He'd already used up twenty minutes in the Gustaffsons' kitchen and living room. He debated whether to launch a more thorough search in either room, then decided it was more important to have a look in the bedroom and master bath first.

Almost instantly he was glad he'd done it.

The gun in the bedside drawer was half-hidden under a paperback novel and a couple of sheets of loose paper. Sam examined the gun first, spinning the cylinder to determine that all the chambers were filled.

That told him nothing. The gun appeared to have been fired recently, judging by the powder residue left on the metal, although there was no way of telling exactly how long ago it had been used. *Tuesday night?* Sam wondered. *Had it been Susan or Jon Gustaffson firing those shots from the hill behind the cottages after the gas had failed to do its intended work?*

The gun itself couldn't answer those questions for him. But its presence in Jon Gustaffson's bedside table was certainly suggestive.

The lined pages on top of it seemed to have been used as scratch paper. There were several names and telephone numbers jotted down at random on the sheets, and Sam knew they were worth noting. People scribbled down the damnedest things sometimes. He'd once tracked down a fleeing embezzler because the guy had jotted down the time and number of his airline flight right next to his office telephone.

He was halfway through copying Jon Gustaffson's notes into his notebook when he heard Kelley's voice.

At first he thought he was just imagining it, the way he'd been imagining the serene grace of her smile and the newly washed softness of her honey blond hair. But then it came again, clearer this time, and Sam realized he was in trouble.

He couldn't hear her words, but her voice was distinct enough that he could pinpoint where it was coming from. She and her companions—he could hear their voices now, too—were heading for the east side of the cottage. Any moment now they would probably be coming through the side door.

And barely ten feet away, Sam was sitting on the edge of the Gustaffsons' bed.

Kelley's voice was usually as low and melodic as a sultry jazz solo, but now she sounded almost sharp. It didn't take a genius to figure out why. She was trying to send Sam a warning, letting him know the expedition had returned too soon.

"You'll feel better after you lie down for a while." He caught her words as he slipped the gun and the loose pages back into the drawer and cast a quick eye around the bedroom.

Part of his brain registered a guess that Susan Gustaffson wasn't feeling well. Another part—the cynical side of him, the part that couldn't help questioning everything and everyone—wondered whether Susan might be faking it.

But by far the largest part of his mind was simply occupied with trying to figure out where to hide.

He heard the sound of a key being turned in a lock, then the soft hiss of the glass door sliding open. By then he'd rejected the master bathroom—it was a dead end, aside from the possibility that someone might want to use it— and the window, which wasn't big enough for him to get out of easily.

That left one option, and almost no time to make use of it.

He had to press his face right into the carpet to get flat enough to fit under the bed. And he'd only just managed it when the room was suddenly filled with people.

Chapter 9

"Here. Let me get you a damp washcloth for your forehead."

Kelley ducked into the Gustaffsons' master bathroom, her heart pounding. If Sam was here—

She flicked the shower curtain open and felt herself relax a little when she saw the empty bathtub. Had he managed to get out, then? There'd been no immediate trace of him in the living room or kitchen, although she knew he could still be hiding in the half bath or in some more devious spot.

She hadn't seen him anywhere around the yard when the Gustaffsons' car had driven back along the Windspray road. He'd announced his intention of going through this cottage first. Had he changed his mind for some reason?

If he hadn't, and if he hadn't gotten out in time, that meant he was still somewhere in the building. Jon was sitting next to Susan on the bed now, holding her hand, asking if there was anything he could get for her. Wayland was hovering around somewhere, too. If Sam was out there, and Wayland stumbled on his hiding place—

She sat down on the edge of the bed and pressed the damp washcloth over Susan's forehead. Susan didn't look noticeably ill, although Kelley remembered from experience that the early phases of pregnancy could have their sudden ups and downs. If Susan really was feeling sick, the obvious thing to do was to offer sympathy and leave discreetly. But if Sam was stuck in the cottage somewhere, she couldn't just abandon him. Partners didn't do that do each other.

The feeling of a hand curling itself around her ankle nearly made her jump.

"Something wrong, Kelley?" Jon Gustaffson had noticed her quick intake of breath. He was looking anxiously at her, as though he didn't want to be stuck with *two* sick women.

Oh, God, Kelley thought. The bed. Sam was under the bed, and she and Susan and Jon were all parked right on top of him. She felt his lean fingers biting into her ankle now, telling her silently to get him out of this.

She managed to come up with a reassuring smile for Jon, and said brightly, "I'm fine, Jon. It's just that something came back to me, from a long time ago. My grandmother always used to make ginger tea whenever one of us kids had an upset stomach. Do you happen to have any ginger in the kitchen?"

"There's some in the refrigerator." Susan spoke faintly, without opening her eyes.

"Good." Kelley made no move to get up. "Why don't you chop some up, Jon, and let it steep in boiling water for about ten minutes? I'm sure it'll help."

Jon took the hint. And the moment he was out of the bedroom, Kelley got to her feet, too. "And I think maybe some fresh air would be a good idea for you," she said to Susan. "It's a little stuffy in here."

"It's kind of cool outside."

"I know." Susan's answer suited Kelley just fine. "If we leave the sliding door open for a few minutes, that should do it."

It was a risk, she knew. But she couldn't imagine how else they were going to manage it. She slid the glass door open and went back to Susan, rearranging the damp washcloth and effectively blocking Susan's view of the doorway at the same time.

Getting past Wayland and Jon was going to be Sam's problem, not hers. She didn't dare look over her shoulder in case she alerted Susan that something was going on back there. But she had a vague impression of stealthy movement behind her.

He must have seen his opportunity and taken it. Kelley let out a breath she hadn't realized she was holding and started to take her own departure.

She went out the front door, hoping to draw attention away from the side deck in case Sam was still skulking around out there. But on the steps just outside the living room, Wayland Price caught up with her.

"Wait a minute," he said, stepping outside the cottage after her. "I've been wanting to talk to you alone."

Great, Kelley thought. Wayland's unwelcome attentions were about the last thing she needed at the moment.

But it wasn't flirtation that was on Wayland's mind. He was wearing a dark blue jogging suit today, and as he caught up with Kelley he slid his mirrored sunglasses into his hip pocket, frowning at her with blue eyes that seemed to be honestly concerned about something.

"It's about Steve Cormier," he said, and instantly Kelley came to a halt on the wooden steps.

"What about Steve Cormier?" she asked slowly.

Wayland was picking his words carefully, she thought. It wasn't like him, and that made her pay even closer attention to what he was saying. "Do you happen to know anything about where he went, or why?" he asked.

"Why do you ask?"

He looked away from her for a moment. She had a sense that he was girding himself to ask a direct question he would have been just as happy to avoid.

"Well, he disappeared just about the same time you and Sam showed up," he said. "I wondered if—you know—either of you might have met him before somewhere."

"Why would that make him leave?"

Wayland shrugged. It was painfully clear how hard he was working to seem casual. "The man obviously wasn't who he said he was," he answered. "I know I've made fun of my mother for getting nervous about things, but I think she had a point about there being something shady in Cormier's past. And then the coincidence of him taking off just as you and Sam arrived—"

"It *was* just a coincidence. It must have been." Deep down, Kelley wasn't so certain about that. But she wasn't certain she could trust Wayland's sudden candor, either. He was worried about something, that was clear. But she doubted she was getting the whole story on what it was.

"What is it about Cormier's disappearance that worries you?" she asked, watching him carefully.

His eyes slid to one side and then the other, confirming her suspicion that he didn't want to tell her. "My mother is upset about it," he said, "and when my mother's upset, the whole family is upset. That's all."

There was more, Kelley was certain of it. For one thing, Wayland hadn't shown any particular concern for his mother's state of mind before this. And for another, he seemed just as anxious to wrap up the conversation now as he'd been to start it a couple of minutes ago.

"I'll see you later," he said as he stepped past her onto the lawn. "Maybe we can try that trip to the wildlife sanctuary another time."

She was still puzzling over the brief exchange when Sam joined her on the gravel road back to their own cottage. He must have doubled around toward the entrance to the community, she realized, then waited for her to appear.

He was walking with a spring in his step that she hadn't seen for a very long time. "Damn, you are *good,* lady," he told her, as he put one long arm around her shoulders and fell into step next to her. "You never so much as quivered when I grabbed your ankle from under the bed."

She knew this mood—knew the euphoria that could take over when you'd gotten boxed into a corner and found a way out of it again. But it was a surprise to see Sam's dark blue eyes glittering this way, and to feel herself responding to the maverick charm of his grin.

"I grew up with four brothers who took every possible opportunity to scare the daylights out of me," she reminded him. "It takes a whole lot more than grabbing my ankle from under a bed to make me flinch."

"So I noticed. And I remember the four brothers, now that you mention them. But the old grandmother with the herbal remedies?"

In spite of everything, Kelley felt herself being drawn into Sam's lighthearted mood. How long had it been since the two of them had joked together like this? How long since they'd instinctively relied on each other's wits the way they'd just done inside the Gustaffsons' cottage?

Too long, something inside Kelley was telling her now.

She shook her head and refused to follow that train of thought.

"The folksy old grandmother was an inspiration of the moment," she confessed. "My real grandmother was one of the first women ever admitted to the state bar in Oklahoma, and as I recall her, she was far too busy writing briefs to have time for brewing any kind of tea at all."

"Well, I salute your powers of invention, sweetheart. And I salute your real grandmother, too." He shot her a sideways grin that made Kelley feel short of breath. "The Landis women are a quick-witted bunch."

She didn't know which was more disconcerting, the compliment or the way her left hip was rocking against Sam's as they walked. They'd always eased naturally into step together, exactly the way they were doing now.

And walking wasn't the only time when their bodies had seemed to find an instinctive, pleasurable pace.

Kelley felt her cheeks redden slightly as Sam tightened his grip around her shoulders. Making love with Sam Cotter had been like nothing else she'd ever experienced—a primitive, joyful free-for-all where the only thing that had ever mattered was the pounding rhythm urging them both on.

And she could feel a faint echo of that erotic pulse now as she and Sam turned onto the lawn in front of their own cottage.

This is crazy, she told herself. *What Sam is feeling is professional satisfaction, nothing more.*

But the sight of his lanky legs in those worn blue jeans kept getting in the way of the sensible thoughts she was trying to focus on. And the sensation of his lean hip riding against hers with every step kept reminding her of the way their bodies had felt against each other without any clothing in the way, without anything at all between them.

Including any kind of protection, she tried to tell herself. They'd always been so hot for each other that it wasn't surprising that they'd slipped up once or twice. The thought of what had resulted from those lapses should have been enough to quell the treacherous feelings that were rising in her now.

But it wasn't.

Was it because of last night's nearly silent moment of comfort out on the sand dunes that the past seemed to weigh less heavily on her today? *Something* had changed, and Sam seemed to be aware of it, too. The atmosphere between them as they reached their cottage was charged in a way that Kelley hadn't felt for a very long time.

She could sense the silent challenge in the way Sam turned toward her, resting his strong forearms on top of her shoulders.

And she could sense his interest, too.

And the same kind of purely physical longing that had taken over her bloodstream while they'd been walking along the gravel road from the Gustaffsons' cottage.

This *was* crazy, she knew. Walking had surely never been on anybody's top ten list for foreplay. Yet her heart was beating unsteadily and insistently at her ribs, and she could see a telltale brightness in Sam's eyes that told her she wasn't the only one responding to this sudden, unexpected closeness.

The question was, what were they going to do about it?

"I don't—"

"This isn't—"

They both started to speak at once, then laughed with the same note of embarrassed rapport.

"You first," Sam said, giving her that slow smile that always turned her knees to water.

There was no way on earth for Kelley to resist the tenderness of that smile. She smiled back at him and raised her hands, clasping them around his waist.

"I'm not sure what I was going to say," she admitted.

His arms circled her now, pulling her closer. Kelley leaned back in his grip, aroused and suddenly feeling carefree. When he lowered his head for a quick kiss, it was the casualness of it more than anything else—the familiarity, the sense of belonging together—that made her heart race a little faster.

She kissed him back, loving the feeling of his mouth against hers. His hair had fallen forward again, but his face didn't have its usual suspicious shadow. The unruly coil of hair across his forehead made him look almost playful, as though he, like Kelley, had momentarily managed to escape the dark burdens he usually carried around with him.

Where do we go from here? She was sure he was wondering the same thing as he gazed down into her eyes. She couldn't imagine ending this moment, breaking the happy spell that suddenly enclosed both of them. She couldn't bring herself to insist that they get back to work on the case, not just yet.

But were they ready to do anything else?

Sam was tracing one thumb thoughtfully around the curve of her cheekbone when the matter was decided for them.

She didn't hear the car engine at first, because she was too caught up in the soft pressure of Sam's skin against hers, and the searching, hungry expression in his eyes.

But then there were voices.

Loud voices. Familiar voices.

"Hey, lovebirds." Kelley jumped as Wiley's words cut through the erotic reverie that Sam's touch had created. "Sorry to drop in on you without warning, but we were in the neighborhood and figured we'd say hi."

There were a lot of things Kelley didn't understand.

This surprise visit was confusing enough. She'd checked in by phone with Wiley early this morning, as she'd been in the habit of doing since she'd arrived at the Windspray Community. But for him to come pelting down here, bringing his fiancée, Rae-Anne, and his brother Jack, a federal agent—

Kelley shook her head as she pulled coffee mugs down from the cupboard and carried them to the living room table. Besides the perplexing visit itself, Wiley's manner, and Jack's, had been odd. They'd both been hearty, congratulatory, playing along with the honeymooner pose to the hilt.

"You can knock it off now," she'd said to Wiley when the five of them had entered the cottage.

But he'd shaken his dark head at her. And he'd kept the conversation on purely trivial matters while Kelley had made coffee for all of them and Sam had started pulling pertinent files up on the computer.

And then there was the fact that Jack was searching the cottage, in spite of Sam's objections that there was nothing to find.

It was all very strange. And Kelley hated to admit it, even to herself, but she wasn't feeling up to fielding all the curveballs that were suddenly coming at her.

Her body was still humming from Sam's gentle embrace. Every time her gaze met his, she could see such a welter of uncertainty and desire in the blue depths of his eyes that all she could think of was being closer to him again, trying to recapture the sweet moment of solidarity they'd just shared.

But there was no chance to do it.

And she couldn't think what else to do, either, until Jack found whatever it was he was looking for. So she'd made a pot of coffee, because it gave her hands something to do while her mind was busy running in useless circles.

"Got it," Jack said at last.

"Great." Sam's voice held all the pent-up frustration Kelley had been feeling herself. "What the hell is it?"

Jack was holding up a tiny metal dot, no bigger than Kelley's little fingernail. The wires trailing from it were mere filaments, almost invisible in the overcast midday light.

"This," he said, "is a state-of-the-art listening device, courtesy of our very own government. The only other one I've seen was an FBI lab prototype."

As if he didn't believe his eyes, Sam switched on the two lamps in the living room, frowning at the object his brother had pried out of one of the electrical outlets next to the bedroom door.

"I checked this place," he said slowly, as if challenging Jack to disagree with him.

"Not your fault, little brother. These little critters are changing the whole ball game as far as bugging is concerned. Hell, I only found it because I knew what to look for, and where to look. As far as we know, nobody outside the bureau has access to this technology yet." He handed the tiny device to Sam, who held it up to the light and glared at it.

"Think there's more?" he asked.

"I doubt it. These things are unbelievably sensitive. One would have been all he needed."

Kelley didn't like the idea that they'd been overheard. It was bad enough to know that someone had listened in on their discussions about the case, but when she thought about the more private exchanges she and Sam had shared—

"When you say 'he,' are you by any chance talking about Steve Cormier?" she asked Jack.

"You got it."

She took in a deep breath. She'd been starting to feel that she had her bearings in this case, but suddenly everything had changed.

"Well, if you're sure there aren't any more little ears listening in the walls, may I suggest we all sit down and have coffee and share some information with each other?" she said. "Because I, for one, would really like to know just what is going on here."

Sam's grim nod confirmed her words. He took a seat beside her on the sofa, with Jack next to them in a chair. Rae-Anne was sitting across the room, watching the whole scene with bright, interested blue eyes. Wiley had taken up his usual relaxed stance next to his fiancée, one broad shoulder leaning against the wall, his ankles crossed so that the embroidered patterns on his expensive cowboy boots showed under the hem of his jeans.

Wiley had one hand extended so that his fingertips rested on Rae-Anne's shoulder, and the sight of it—of any of the Cotter men reaching out so naturally toward a woman— startled Kelley. It was still hard to understand how tough-talking, lone-wolf Wiley Cotter had changed and softened in the past short while.

She shook her head and reminded herself that it was law enforcement, not love, that they were here to discuss.

"Maybe you'd like to start by explaining how Steve Cormier happened to have one of the FBI's brand-new bugs at his disposal," Sam was saying.

"He had one," Jack said, "for the simple reason that he was working for the FBI."

"He was *what?*"

Kelley could feel Sam wanting to shoot to his feet again, wanting to pace the length of the small room and back. She put a hand on his forearm without planning to, sending him the silent message that they needed to stay focused, because time was short and there were obviously surprises in this case that they hadn't foreseen.

"It would have been helpful if we'd known this sooner," she said to Jack.

The middle Cotter brother gave her a rueful smile. "It would have been helpful for all of us," he said. "Unfortunately the bureau didn't know you two were investigating this place until I happened to hear about it through Wiley."

"And I didn't know the FBI had Windspray under surveillance until Jack put two and two together this morning," Wiley said. "Once we connected the two cases, we figured we'd better hustle on down here and set you and Sam straight, because it looks as though things are a whole lot more serious than we originally thought."

Between Wiley and Jack, the story fell into place. The FBI had been trying to track a West Coast counterfeiting operation back to its roots, and had gotten as far as determining that there was some connection with the Windspray resort on the Gulf coast of Texas. A special agent—Steve Cormier—had been assigned to infiltrate the place.

"When you two showed up, Cormier thought there was something fishy about you," Jack said. "Apparently he felt you were worth keeping an eye on." He nodded toward the little bug that lay on the coffee table.

"So that explains why he kept turning up around our cottage," Sam said.

"And why he seemed to have something to hide," Kelley added. "It explains his photography setup, too." Photography was one of the investigator's most valuable tools. "But it doesn't explain where he's gone," she finished.

Jack's handsome face grew more serious at that. "No, it doesn't," he said. "And our people are pretty worried about it. It's never good news when an agent goes missing."

"Will they send somebody new?" Kelley asked.

"You're looking at him." Jack leaned forward, elbows on his knees. His shirt cuffs were neatly rolled to the elbows, and his dark hair was impeccably cut, as always, but under his handsome exterior Kelley could see how seriously he took this.

"Obviously there's a lot at stake here, if somebody's willing to shanghai a federal agent to keep it secret," he added. "The bureau wants this wrapped up, and Cormier found, as quickly as possible. But we don't want to shake things up to the extent that the perpetrator gets spooked and does something reckless."

"Like bolting," Sam suggested.

"Right. Or killing Cormier, assuming he's still alive."

Kelley felt a cold shiver run through her. She'd managed to accustom herself to the violence that occasionally went with this job, but she'd never learned to like it. Whenever she could, she still preferred to talk rather than fight.

But this case seemed to be turning into one where the option for negotiating didn't exist. "So what do we do now?" she asked Jack.

His level hazel eyes met hers. "You find the bad guys," he said plainly. "My bosses figure it's more practical to work with you rather than duplicate what you're doing. You've got a cover story already in place, after all."

Sam and Kelley exchanged a glance. "It seems that whoever the counterfeiter is, he or she has already figured out that we're not just honeymooners," Sam said. "Somebody tried to take us out of the picture the first night we were here."

Jack considered it. "Has anything happened since then?" he asked.

"No." Kelley almost laughed as she answered the question. So much had changed between her and Sam that it was getting harder, instead of easier, to keep her mind focused on her job.

But Jack's words were clear enough. "Maybe the perpetrator decided the warning had been enough to scare you off," he said. "I'd say it's worth keeping up the newlywed pose."

The flicker of interest in his hazel eyes made Kelley realize that her hand was still resting lightly on Sam's arm, and that Sam had reacted to it as though it was something that happened all the time. What did Jack think about that, and about the embrace he'd overseen when he'd arrived at the cottage?

Whatever he thought, he was keeping it to himself. "The difference now is that you'll have the backing of the FBI, if you need it," he told them. "I'll be your go-between. I'll need access to whatever you've dug up, and you'll be able to look at the reports Cormier sent in before he disappeared."

Kelley glanced at Sam again. She could see him thinking hard, tossing all the alternatives around in that quick mind of his. But her own thoughts were running on a different track.

The potential danger in this case had just skyrocketed, and the grim look on Sam's face told her that he realized it, too. At the beginning of the week he'd done his best to lock her out of the case. Would this new development erase all the progress they'd made, all the tentative steps toward the partnership they'd been rediscovering?

There were a lot of questions demanding her attention right now, but somehow that felt like the most important one. Kelley found herself holding her breath, waiting to see whether Jack's news would drive all of Sam's reawakening trust back underground.

She didn't get a chance to find out until Sam suggested they all have a look at the financial records he and Kelley had been compiling on their computer. As their three guests moved toward the kitchen, Sam took Kelley's arm, holding her back.

"I didn't know you called Wiley this morning," he said, his voice low.

"I've been calling him every morning." She said the words matter-of-factly.

"Why?"

"We've been through this, Sam. I believe in keeping the channels of communication open when I'm working on a case. You don't. That's all." But it wasn't all, and she couldn't resist adding, "If you ask me, it's a darn good thing I told Wiley about Steve Cormier when I checked in this morning."

Sam snorted. "Go ahead," he told her. "Say 'I told you so' if it'll make you feel better."

His snort was earthy, companionable, not angry, as she'd been half expecting. It was an unimaginable relief to realize that he wasn't cutting her off, after all.

"I don't need to say it," she replied.

The quick slant of his grin sliced through the serious look on his face. "Good," he said, "because I don't need to hear it. But it is a good thing we found out who Cormier really is. And Kelley—"

His fingers tightened around her arm. She could feel the heat of his skin stirring all those forbidden responses inside her.

"Let me know what you're up to from here on in, okay? Things just got a whole lot stickier, and we need to be together on this."

He didn't give her time for more than just a quick nod before sliding his grip down to capture her hand and walk with her into the kitchen.

Outside, the weather was still blustery and gray. It looked as though it might start raining at any moment. And inside the cottage, all five of the faces gathered around the table were serious and thoughtful as they contemplated the tangled mass of information they were trying to pull apart.

But none of it felt as turbulent or tangled to Kelley as her own thoughts.

Sam's words a moment ago had been so open, so spontaneous. *We need to be together on this . . .* That was what she'd wanted when she'd accepted this assignment: Sam's trust, his acceptance that they were equals and partners again.

Then why did she suddenly find herself wanting more?

And why, at the very back of her mind, was there a little voice telling her there was something she hadn't shared with Sam, something he might need to know?

She searched her memory for it, but her thoughts were too scattered and too confused. It would come back to her, she told herself. Once all these new facts settled down into some sort of pattern, she would remember what it was that was nagging at her.

For now, she had her work cut out for her. Anything else—any leftover bits of information, any buried longings, most of all any troublesome thoughts of the old passion and hope that had once gone along with the trust she and Sam had shared—all of that was simply going to have to wait.

Chapter 10

"Wiley tells me you and Sam used to be partners."

Rae-Anne dropped back to walk beside Kelley as the five of them headed for the Windspray restaurant. It was early afternoon, and Sam and Kelley had decided that lunch at the restaurant and a tour of the resort would be the best way to provide the orientation Jack was looking for.

Rae-Anne seemed to be looking for something different. The petite red-haired woman sounded casual enough, but Kelley had the feeling that Rae-Anne's intelligent blue eyes were taking in a lot more than she was letting on.

"Did Wiley tell you why we *stopped* being partners?" she asked.

"He said something about an accident. He didn't go into a lot of detail." Rae-Anne paused, glancing over at Kelley. "Looks like nobody wants to go into detail about it," she added.

Kelley gave her a faint smile. "It wasn't a very happy occasion," she said.

"So I gathered. The thing is—" Rae-Anne looked at the gravel road ahead of her, where the three Cotter brothers' long strides had already carried them out of earshot. "The thing is, Wiley gave me the definite impression you and Sam practically had to be roped and tied to get you into the same room together. But it looks to me like you get along pretty well. Is there a part of the story I'm missing somewhere?"

The weather was continuing to worsen, and Kelley pushed her hands deeper into the pockets of her tan canvas jacket as she tried to figure out how to answer Rae-Anne's question. Before she came up with the right words, Rae-Anne spoke again.

"If I'm being nosy, you can just tell me so," she said. "I've spent a long time as a bartender, so I kind of expect people to pour out their troubles to me. But if you'd rather not—"

"No, it's okay." It was a surprise to realize that she *wanted* to share this with someone, after keeping it to herself for so long. And Wiley's fiancée, with her perceptive eyes and her personal experience with one of the famously difficult Cotter men, suddenly seemed like the ideal confidante.

"Sam and I were a lot more than just working partners," she told Rae-Anne. "We were engaged to be married. And we—I was pregnant, when the accident happened."

The dismay in Rae-Anne's pretty face was more vivid than Kelley had been expecting. "You were pregnant," she echoed. "What happened?"

"I lost the baby. It was my own fault—I made a stupid error in judgment. If Sam hadn't stepped in, I probably wouldn't be alive to be telling you this."

She took in a deep breath and wondered when she had stopped walking. She and Rae-Anne were facing each other on the gravel road now, frowning as the faint wind-driven rain flicked against their faces.

"I'm sorry, Kelley." Rae-Anne sounded more than sorry. She sounded as though she understood. It was amazing how comforting that felt. "I really am."

"It's okay," Kelley said again. "When Wiley told me about this assignment, I figured it would be a chance to put some of what happened behind me finally. The only thing is—"

She paused, not sure how to end the sentence. It was both a surprise and a relief when Rae-Anne finished it for her.

"The thing is, it's hard to put things behind you when the old feelings refuse to go away," she said.

"How did you know that?"

In Rae-Anne's quick smile it was easy to see the spirit that had won over Wiley Cotter so completely. "I've been there," she said, and inclined her auburn head at the three lanky men on the road ahead. "It's not easy, especially with one of those three."

"Amen to that." Kelley's own smile felt a little shaky.

"You still love him, don't you?"

Rae-Anne's question hit her out of the blue. Kelley had barely used the word *love* even to herself, and to hear it put so bluntly—

"I don't know," she hedged. "I don't know what's happening."

Rae-Anne raised an eyebrow and began to walk again. "I haven't known Sam very long," she said, "but I saw the way he was looking at you when Wiley and Jack and I arrived. And if you want my opinion, he's having some trouble putting *his* old memories to rest, too."

Her words seemed deliberately challenging, and her pace deliberately quicker as she started to catch up with the three brothers. Kelley followed, but more slowly, trying to grasp all the loose ends that were swirling around in her mind as though they were being stirred up by the steady Gulf Coast wind.

You can handle this, Sam told himself. He cranked off the shower tap and reached for his towel. *You can keep things together.*

His brother Jack was ensconced in the nearest motel, a few miles down the road in Port Lavaca, available by phone or modem if Sam felt they needed backup.

Wiley and Rae-Anne had gone back to Austin, but not before Wiley had taken a lot of very detailed notes about Susan and Jon Gustaffson, and promised to do some digging that Sam and Kelley couldn't do on-site.

It wasn't getting any easier to be around Kelley, but Sam was finding ways to cope. Showering in the morning, for example, had come to seem too suggestive. He couldn't deal with the thought of stripping his clothes off and standing under the hot shower while Kelley was still in the bed just a few feet on the other side of the door. So he'd taken to cleaning himself up whenever she wasn't around—and this evening, that meant while she was over at the Gustaffsons' cottage checking on how Susan Gustaffson was feeling.

Things were progressing, he told himself. Things were under control.

Then why did he feel as restless as the wind howling outside the cottage? Why had his mind been filled with a steady parade of erotic imaginings even while he'd been trying his hardest to focus on this case? Kelley in that outrageously sexy blue bathing suit of hers...Kelley in the shower with him, slick and warm and willing...Kelley looking into his eyes with a sea blue gaze that was as close to paradise as anything Sam could imagine...

He growled at himself as he toweled most of the water out of his hair. This part of the job wasn't under control at all. He dried the rest of his body with fierce energy and stepped back into the bedroom, where he'd left his clothes at the bottom of the bed.

And almost ran right into Kelley.

Sam stopped as though he'd hit a brick wall. For a moment he wondered if he was still just fantasizing about her. Her shining eyes and the soft disarray of her fair hair made her look like something out of a dream.

But then she threw the canvas jacket she'd been holding onto the bed, and Sam heard the rustle of fabric as it fell. He groaned inwardly, still not daring to move.

She was real. She was here.

And he was stark naked and already half-aroused by the racy visions that had been keeping him company in the shower.

Shoot, he thought. He'd gotten himself out of a lot of sticky situations in his thirty-six years, but he'd be damned if he could see a graceful way out of this one.

Kelley cleared her throat.

"I—just came back to get my raincoat," she said. "And my gun."

That should have done it. If she wanted the gun, it was because she thought she might need it. And that should have been enough to get Sam's overheated mind back on track.

But it wasn't.

"What do you want the gun for?" He got the words out, but it was like speaking from underwater. His mouth felt slow and reluctant.

He knew why that was. He didn't want to talk business. He wanted to be kissing Kelley Landis, every inch of her. He wanted to feel his lips against her skin, to curl his tongue around the taut buds of her nipples, the seductive indent of her navel, the soft curve of her belly.

She was wearing her plain white shirt underneath the jacket she'd just taken off. And Sam could see those tightened buds under the smooth white surface. He felt himself growing a little harder at the sight of it, and cursed his body for its instinctive, undeniable response.

"I just ran into Wayland Price." Kelley was speaking slowly now, too, holding her eyes level with Sam's as though after her first long look at him she didn't dare let her gaze wander any lower.

"And?"

"He invited me to join him for a drink. He seems to have something on his mind."

This was all wrong, Sam told himself. He was having to struggle just to remember who the hell Wayland Price even was. On the other hand, the memories of how Kelley's mouth had felt under his, how her soft moans of need had filled his senses, were achingly clear.

"The gun . . ." He tried to make it into a sentence, and couldn't.

"I just thought—" Kelley seemed to be having the same trouble. The thought didn't do anything to steady Sam's nerves. "He was asking me some questions about Steve Cormier this morning. As if he knew something he wasn't saying. I don't know what it is, but it just seemed like a good idea not to meet him alone without a weapon. That's all."

The last two words sounded absentminded, as though she'd tacked them on without realizing it. She glanced over her shoulder, toward the open bedroom door, and said, "Wayland said he was just going to secure the boat. The weather's getting rougher. I told him I'd meet him at the bar—"

This time the sentence ended abruptly, and Sam knew why.

She'd looked back toward him, and this time her gaze was explicit and direct. Sam felt his skin start to heat up all over again as she took in the whole length of his body with her blue-eyed stare. He'd let the towel drop to the floor in the surprise of finding Kelley in the bedroom, and there wasn't a thing in the world he could do to disguise the state he was in.

And suddenly he didn't want to disguise it.

He'd done his best to avoid this moment. But it had snuck up on him anyway. He couldn't deny that he wanted Kelley Landis, and he couldn't for the life of him force his thoughts back to the case they were working on. Even the little warning bell that jangled in his consciousness at the mention of her meeting with Wayland was lost now in the clamor of remembered sensations and all-too-present longings.

He wasn't sure which of them moved first. One moment they were at arm's length from each other. And the next moment they were a whole lot closer than that.

"Sam—"

Her voice was rough with unexpressed feelings. Sam groaned again—out loud this time—and pulled her into his arms.

The metal button on her jeans was cold against his skin. And the feeling of denim and rayon was such an intrusion that he shook his head and drew back slightly. It was Kelley's satin skin he wanted, not the barrier of her clothing.

"Do you think we should—" She didn't finish the question.

Sam shook his head. "Sweetheart, I've spent too much damn time thinking. About all of this."

And now he didn't want to think about it anymore. He didn't want to talk about it, either.

"I know." Kelley seemed to hear his unspoken thoughts. "Sometimes I get tired of thinking, too."

She lifted a hand and smoothed it over his newly shaven jaw, and Sam gave up trying to force any of this to make sense. What did sense matter, when instinct was telling him so clearly what he should do?

"One of us seems to be overdressed," he murmured.

She smiled at him, and he could feel her yielding to the same overpowering pulse of longing that was throbbing through him now. "I can take care of that," she said.

How did she still manage to sound so elegant when her honey-rich voice was overlaid with such pure and earthy sensuality? Sam chuckled and gave in to the temptation to kiss her—once, briefly, almost teasingly.

He shook his head and felt his hair, still heavy and damp from the shower, settling itself over his forehead. "Allow me," he said, and reached for the top button of her shirt.

Her pleased gasp when she understood what he meant jolted through Sam like a shot of pure moonshine. He'd worked so hard at trying to forget the way Kelley's passion had always matched his own, the way they'd met each other in desire and delight, time and time again.

He'd tried to tell himself she didn't want him anymore.

But now he knew it wasn't true.

The pulse at the point of her collarbone was beating to the rhythm of a dance Sam had never been able to forget. And her eyes were shining with a sapphire glint that Sam had seen only when they'd been making love.

It suddenly seemed like forever since he'd caught that reflected gleam of passion in Kelley's blue eyes.

The sight of it now made him want to rip the obstructing clothes from her body, to tear them aside with all the force of his own long-forbidden hunger. But he made himself move slowly, circling her slender waist with his left arm as he skillfully flicked the button open and moved on.

"You haven't lost your touch."

"I guess it's just something you don't lose the knack of."

Sam lowered his head and kissed the maddeningly delicate tip of her chin. And then the classy slant of her jaw. And her earlobe, half-hidden in the flyaway tangle of her hair.

He'd thought it wasn't possible for him to grow any harder, but when he finished with her buttons and tugged the soft white shirt free of the waistband of her jeans, the snowy expanse of her skin—her shoulders, her breasts in that lacy white bra—made him ache even more potently to be inside her, moving with her.

And the way he was moving against her now already seemed to be reaching places deep inside her. Sam heard her moan and saw her gleaming eyes darken as she met his. Her breathing was quick and erratic, just like his own.

He dropped her shirt to the floor and reached behind her shoulders, searching for the clasp of her bra. It gave way under his fingers without a struggle, and suddenly Sam was drowning in the sweet sensation of Kelley's breasts against his torso, touching him so intimately, so familiarly, that he thought his head might spin loose with the sheer pleasure of it.

"Sam, please." It was halfway between a demand and a question. Her hands had been clasping his shoulders, gliding seductively over his skin, but now he realized that she was zeroing in on her own waistband, heading for the metal clasp that had now turned as warm as the blood in his own veins.

"I said no."

He caught her wrists as she lowered them against his chest. The thought of Kelley wrapping her soft palms around him was almost painfully sweet. But he knew that the moment she touched him, his resolve about taking things slowly would disappear. And he didn't want that to happen. Not yet.

So he unsnapped her jeans himself and slid his hands flat under her waistband, reveling in the impossible softness of her skin under his palms and the tantalizing, lacy edge of her underwear at the tips of his fingers.

Their bodies remembered this slow dance so well, Sam thought, as he pushed Kelley's jeans toward the carpeted floor and felt her hips align themselves against his. Her arms twined around his torso again, holding him close, wrapping him in a sea of heavenly possibilities.

She must have kicked her shoes off without him realizing it. Her jeans followed, until she stepped free of everything that had covered her and joined Sam in an embrace more gloriously intimate than anything he'd allowed himself to dream about for the past three long years.

It was getting more and more difficult to remember that he'd intended to take things slowly.

Kelley gave a delighted half laugh as Sam bent his head and kissed the inner curve of one of her breasts, then the other, recapturing the caress that had been interrupted by Helen's presence the day before. Her skin under his lips was like cool silk. He shifted his grip and captured one tight nipple between his teeth, astonished at the high-voltage jolt that shot through him as he swirled his tongue around the small bud.

His self-control was unraveling by the moment. Kelley's hands, tangling themselves in his still-damp hair, seemed to be setting off sparks inside his head. He could feel them shooting into every corner of his body.

He'd slid to his knees without realizing it, intent on the small, pinpoint pleasure of Kelley's nipple in his mouth even while his hands were rediscovering the other hidden pleasures of her body.

She cried out loud when he slid one probing finger between her legs and penetrated the moist core of her. And Sam heard himself gasp in answer, astonished as ever by the openness of her passion, by the way she seemed to meet his own hunger halfway and impel him to find even more tantalizing levels of intimacy.

Sam felt as though the whole universe had narrowed to this one supercharged place, this small circle of heat and light where he and Kelley rocked in each other's embrace.

He probed her more deeply and felt her knees buckle against his chest.

He smiled as he kissed her gently rounded belly, and the soft nest of curls between her legs, and then moved lower yet.

He groaned against her as he kissed her into mindless satisfaction, easing her back onto the bed, caressing her with intuitive expertise until he heard those soft moans of pleasure turn to something different, something urgent and primitive and electrifying.

Her voice seemed to be connected directly to Sam's spinal cord. He felt as though she was singing through him as she arched her back and cried into the night on a long note of surprise and ecstasy.

Sam laughed out loud with the delight of it. The sound was ragged with need and welcome and a hundred other long-suppressed emotions. He joined her on the bed, sliding over her still-quivering frame without breaking contact with her, gazing down at her half-closed eyes with a lover's satisfaction.

She felt warm and pliant under him, soft and strong at the same time. Sam gathered her into his arms and propelled both of them into the center of the big bed, pausing only briefly to reach into the back pocket of the jeans he'd tossed there—had it been just a half hour ago, or a lifetime already?—when he'd stepped into the shower.

Kelley's eyes flared open at the crinkling sound of the plastic wrapper as he discarded it, but he shook his head, not wanting to talk, to explain how spooked he'd been the first night they'd been here to find himself responding to Kelley just as wildly, as naturally as he ever had.

He'd visited the little drugstore in Cairo the next day, foreseeing this moment but still not willing to take a chance that their unhappy past might repeat itself. And now—

Now it didn't matter. He'd protected Kelley this time, and he didn't want to think about it anymore.

He wanted to concentrate on the way her face changed when he lifted himself up and slowly moved inside her. Sam could see the astonishment, the wonder in her eyes, mirroring the way he felt himself.

It had always been this way, he remembered with sudden, blinding clarity.

It had been as though both of them had witnessed a miracle, every time they'd ever come together.

"Sam—"

"I know, sweetheart. I know."

He bent his elbows again and buried his face in her neck, loving the way her baby-fine hair swirled itself around him. Her hands on his bare back were gentle but insistent, and the way her hips rose to meet his thrusts was making Sam's head reel.

He heard her cries spiraling upward again, a long series of amazed exclamations that ended in a drawn-out *Ohh* as Sam gave up trying to hold himself back and finally buried himself in her so deeply he felt as though they had just fused and become one body.

He was aware of the slender length of Kelley's legs sliding up over his hips, drawing them even more closely together. He closed his eyes and felt himself being borne away by the perfection of the way they were moving against each other, by the almost painful pleasure that was humming in every part of him.

He'd thought he was far beyond any kind of thought at all. But as all the desire in his body began to collect itself with unstoppable strength in the very center of his belly, he had a revelation so clear he could almost see the words written on the dark, dazzled sky behind his closed eyelids.

I want you back.

He hadn't even known the notion was there.

And suddenly it was consuming him, gathering all his hopes and fears and desires into one overwhelming torrent.

I want you back....

The phrase rolled through him as he moved faster and faster in unison with Kelley, reaching for so much more than just the physical satisfaction that was spurring them on. If he could somehow undo what he'd done wrong in the past, if he could just erase all the old hurt, all the old uncertainties . . .

He felt his whole body contract and explode into release without warning. And even in the midst of the shuddering pleasure of it, the ache in Kelley's cry, the sweet sense of deliverance, he clung to the words that had come to him out of the darkness.

I want you back. He was reaching far beyond pleasure, far beyond passion, as he held Kelley close and eased with her into the silent peace following the storm they'd just shared.

He was reaching for something he knew he didn't deserve, something he'd never been able to hang on to for more than a fleetingly short time.

But he was holding out his hand for it again anyway. And if it was to be found anywhere, he knew it would be here, inside the soft circle of Kelley Landis's arms.

What he was reaching for, awkwardly, tentatively, hardly daring to believe it might be his again, was pure and simple hope.

Chapter 11

"Sam, I've got to get up."

Her words reached him from a long way away. At first he couldn't make sense of them.

He didn't know how long they'd been in each other's arms, still wrapped in the aftermath of their loving. It had been long enough that Sam's skin was starting to feel slightly chilled. He couldn't bring himself to move, though, not when it meant loosening his hold on Kelley's slender body, separating himself from the silky sensation of her legs alongside his, or her soft, fine hair against his face.

But now she was talking about getting up.

"I've got to go meet Wayland," she said. "Remember?"

Remember? The only thing Sam could clearly remember was the realization that in spite of all his efforts to get over this woman, in spite of the harshness of the lessons he should have learned, he was just as smitten as ever, just as hungry for her love, just as tangled up and distracted by her as he'd been when they'd first met.

In the throes of passion, that had seemed like a gift, a blessing.

Now he wasn't so sure.

Kelley was struggling to sit up, and Sam reluctantly moved aside. But he wasn't quite ready to let her go. He kept one arm firmly clasped around her as he fought to get his wits back in order.

The problem was that he was badly knocked off course by what had just happened, badly shaken out of the pattern he'd worked so hard to make for himself.

And now Kelley was trying to step straight back into that pattern.

Sam felt an unexpected fear clutching at him, making his voice rough as he said, "You have to leave *right now?*"

The look in her eyes shook him even further. She looked startled, uneasy, as though the whirlwind of passion they'd just come through together had landed her in a very different place from the one where Sam had ended up.

He was grasping at hope, trying to reclaim lost dreams.

And Kelley seemed to be looking for a way out.

"I have to." She turned her face away from him as she spoke. He could hear the urgency in her voice. "Damn it, Sam, this is still a case, isn't it?"

"Is it?" He grated the two words out.

And sensed her impatience growing as he said them.

"You know it is."

She pushed past his restraining arm, and this time Sam didn't try to stop her. If she really wanted to leave—

He tried not to let himself pursue it, but he couldn't stop the thoughts that were crowding into his mind now. *She doesn't want you anymore,* a faint, mocking voice was telling him. *This was just a quick roll in the hay, nothing more. And now she's on her way back to work.*

He stared up at Kelley as she got to her feet and started retrieving her scattered clothes. Was it possible? Had this been nothing but a momentary diversion for her? Had he completely misread the signals between them?

He couldn't believe it.

But he couldn't get around the fact that she was walking out on him, either.

If it hadn't hurt so damn much, Sam might have laughed.

"I can't afford to pass up a chance to talk to Wayland," she said as she stepped back into her jeans. "He seemed very insistent about meeting me alone. He's definitely got something on his mind."

"As long as it's safe."

He said the words because he couldn't think what else to say. His concern for Kelley's safety had been a touchstone in the beginning of this case, something he could fasten his thoughts to when he needed to fend off the treacherous longings he still felt around her.

"It'll be safe." She was zipping her jeans and hooking her bra with quick efficiency, as though being naked with Sam made her uncomfortable. The thought of it added to the pain that was stabbing him from the inside. "I'll be armed. And we're meeting in the bar. There'll be other people around."

Sam suddenly couldn't stand it anymore. Kelley was almost fully dressed, reaching for her shoes, and he was still sprawled across the bed buck naked like a trick rider who'd been tossed off the back of a particularly lively bronc.

It wasn't a bad image, he thought. He felt as stunned, as disoriented, as he ever had after a bad fall in his riding days.

He tried to pick himself up now, but even though he managed to get to the edge of the bed, and then onto his feet, he was still off-balance inside, as bruised and exposed as he'd ever been.

"How can you do this?" The words came out raw with the hurt he was feeling. "How can you just—walk away after something like this?"

He was startled to find his fingers shaking as he pointed toward the rumpled bed.

Kelley shook her head and ran her fingers through her hair. Apparently she felt she hadn't sufficiently repaired the damage, because she walked with quick steps into the bathroom and picked up a comb from the counter.

"I'm going back to work," she told him. "It's what we're being paid to do, remember?"

She sounded brisk, almost annoyed. She was lecturing him, Sam realized with a jolt. Reminding him what the limits to their partnership really were.

Reminding him that their loving—the pure starburst of experience that still had all of Sam's nerve endings singing—had been out of bounds.

Sam sat down again. He couldn't think what else to do.

And Kelley wasn't giving him time to come up with anything. She breezed out of the bathroom with her honey blond hair neatly back in order and pulled a teal raincoat out of the closet. The crinkling of its folds sounded loud in the room.

And suddenly Sam was aware of other sounds, sounds he'd managed to block out since he'd taken Kelley in his arms. The weather, as she'd said, was still getting worse. The wind was howling around the edges of the roof, and he could hear rain coming in gusts now, pelting against the windowpanes.

He shook his head. The sweet storm of their lovemaking had been enough to shut out the rest of the world for the past short while. But the world hadn't gone away.

That was what Kelley was trying to tell him now.

And it was his own damn fault that he was still too stunned to get the message.

He watched her check the ammunition in her pistol, then tuck it into her raincoat pocket. He heard the determined zip as she ran the zipper up to her chin, and he listened to her parting words without really hearing them.

"I won't do anything stupid, Sam. You don't have to worry about me this time."

And then she was gone, sliding the glass door tightly closed behind her as she stepped out into the rain.

You don't have to worry about me this time . . .

The words cut into him like needles, like cold rain slicing down out of an angry sky.

She didn't want his concern. She didn't want anything from him, beyond the momentary pleasure they'd just shared.

She didn't want him. Period.

"Oh, God . . ."

Sam was shocked by the anguish in his own voice. There were other words pushing at him now, words he hadn't thought of for years and years, words so unexpectedly potent and primal that they frightened the hell out of him.

Please don't go away. Don't leave me alone.

"Please . . ." He hadn't meant to say it out loud. But it came out anyway, tossed uselessly into the space that Kelley had just left. "Please don't go."

Where were these words coming from? Sam never pleaded, never complained when things hurt. Life kicked you sometimes—that was the long and the short of it. You dusted yourself off and got back on your feet, if you wanted to survive.

But this was a hurt that went too far back to ignore.

Please, don't leave . . .

It had been a long time since he'd said those words out loud. But he still remembered the way they felt in his mouth: hollow, and flat. And useless.

Don't leave me! He remembered shouting the words at his father's retreating form, struggling against the adult hands that were holding him into a house where he didn't want to be, where he already knew he didn't belong.

Partners did that to you. They walked away, just when you grew to trust them.

The lesson had been perfectly clear, and Sam had learned it well. It was better to stay on your own, trusting nobody but yourself.

And the only time he'd broken that rule—

He leaned forward now, rocked by the hurt inside him. His eyes stung, and he covered them with the heels of his hands, pressing hard against the ache of memory and desire.

He and Kelley had been partners once. He'd broken his own rules, and they'd both paid a high price for it.

And now—

He couldn't stand the thought of it. He'd let himself want her again. Let himself *love* her again.

And she'd walked away.

The way partners always did.

Sam tried to clamp down on the wave of self-pity that rolled through him. But it was too strong—everything was too strong. The euphoria of loving Kelley again, the vivid memories of his father's desertion, the thought of everything he'd lost that night at the warehouse three years ago.

He felt as though he was losing it—everything, all of it—again right now.

His eyes still burned behind his flattened palms. It took a moment to recognize the sensation as tears.

"Damn it..." He fought against it, but the misery in his own voice told him he was losing.

He hadn't cried since he was a small boy, and he sure as hell didn't want to catch himself doing it now.

But the more he struggled against the pain racking him from the inside, the closer he came to the shameful admission that this time he'd somehow managed to get himself into a fight he might not be strong enough to win.

"Quieter than usual around here for a Friday night." The bartender refilled Kelley's glass with soda and moved back to the tray of glasses he was polishing. "Must be the storm that's keeping people in the city."

It felt like weeks since Kelley had listened to a weather forecast, read a newspaper, done any of the things that were part of her usual routine. She looked around the restaurant now, taking note of the few couples who'd come down to their vacation homes in spite of the storm warning, and then turned back to the bartender.

"I was supposed to meet Wayland Price here," she said. "You haven't seen him around, have you?"

The man shook his head. "Not this evening."

Kelley went back to watching the rain lashing against the windows. Anything—even letting her mind wander, distracted by the patterns of water against glass—was better than letting herself think about Sam.

The bartender's friendliness reminded her of Rae-Anne Blackburn. And that made her think about Rae-Anne's comment.

You're still in love with him, aren't you?

Wayland's absence—he'd told her he would meet her nearly forty minutes ago—made her wonder whether she should have stuck with him earlier, when he'd seemed in the mood to talk. Had she lost an important lead by going back to the cottage, taking the time to grab her gun and her raincoat and to fill Sam in?

Had she lost more than that by making love with him?

Stick to business, Kelley, she told herself. She'd been telling herself the same thing ever since she'd come back to her senses in Sam's arms an hour ago.

She wished she was having more success at following her own good advice.

"Thanks," she said to the bartender, suddenly fed up with waiting for Wayland and with the way her own thoughts kept circling back to Sam despite her best efforts. Surely there had to be a way to stop picturing the lost look on his face when she'd pulled away from him on the bed.

It's for the best, she'd told herself then. She repeated it now, and knew, deep down, that her own insistence on getting back to work was nothing more than a mask for her fears—fears about loving Sam again, about losing him again, about losing more than her heart could stand to lose.

She put a couple of bills down on the bar and left a message with the bartender in case Wayland finally came in. She had a feeling he'd stood her up, though. And that meant something was happening, something that Kelley wanted to get to the bottom of if she could. If nothing else, it was a welcome way to keep busy while she tried to get her thoughts about Sam back under some kind of control.

She zipped her raincoat as she headed back into the night. The wind was driving the rain harder now. There was a salt taste to it, as though the rising storm was picking up the big waves from the Gulf and hurling them onto the shore.

Wayland's cottage was at the far end of the curve, facing the new boat slip Harold Price had had built. Even behind the shelter of the hill at the center of the Windspray Community, the wind was strong enough that Kelley found herself hunching over as she walked, working hard to stay upright.

She'd pulled the hood of her jacket up, but her hair had already been tugged loose by the wind, and she could feel damp tendrils sticking to her cheeks and forehead. There was something ominous about the strength and anger of the storm coming in off the open sea, and she couldn't help connecting it in her mind with the way everything about this case seemed to have darkened in the past twenty-four hours.

There were no lights on in Wayland's cottage. But Kelley could see the beacon of the pier light shining in the distance. Against its beam, she thought she saw a figure moving, crouched over against the wind as she was.

She shoved her hands deeper into her pockets, feeling the reassuring weight of her gun there. She picked up her pace. Was it Wayland? There was something familiar about that outline.

She lost track of the figure as one of the cottages came between her and the light. But then she saw another light, a smaller one, and realized that it was Wayland, and that he'd just opened the driver's door of his car, which was parked next to his building.

Where was he going? Kelley called his name, but the wind hurled it in the wrong direction, and he didn't hear her.

He looked upset, she thought. It was more than just the way the wind had torn apart his sleek hairstyle. Wayland usually moved as though he was fully aware at all times of his muscled physique and well-groomed exterior. But now his motions were jerky, distracted, and Kelley thought she saw him nearly lose his balance as he got into the car.

He seemed to be in a big hurry to get to wherever he was going.

"Wayland!" She shouted his name again, hating to let him get away on her. But she was still out of range, and she saw the car's headlights flare on as she started to run. By the time she'd gotten close enough to be heard over the wind, Wayland had put the car in gear and it was heading away from her, gravel spurting from under its tires.

"*Damn.*" She shook her head in frustration.

And nearly jumped right out of her skin when a powerful set of fingers closed around her arm.

At first the driving rain kept her from seeing who it was. She felt herself being spun around and pulled away from Wayland's cottage.

Kelley had practiced self-defense techniques until she'd been able to trounce the people who'd taught her. But her shoes slipped on the wet grass as she struggled to get her balance now, and it was all she could do to stay upright as she was propelled back in the direction she'd come from.

By the time she got her feet under her again, she'd recognized her attacker.

"Come on." Sam's gravelly voice cut through the whine of the wind. "If we're fast, we can tail him."

Kelley didn't argue. She knew he was right. And after all, she'd been the one insisting that they keep their minds focused on the task at hand. Right now the task was figuring out where Wayland had taken off to in such a hurry, and why.

But there were a lot of other whys lashing at her now, too. Sam had shifted his grip to her hand, and his grasp was rough and hard, as though he was angry about something. *Why?*

He must have been following her, or else he'd been watching Wayland's cottage while she'd been waiting in the bar.

Why?

And why was she having such a hard time hanging on to her thoughts as she climbed quickly into the cab of Sam's truck and watched him jam the key into the ignition?

Why did the look in his eyes—that wild, rogue-stallion gleam—tear her up inside? Was it because she'd caught a glimpse of some other expression behind it? There was something more than just anger making his eyes so savage and his voice so harsh as he spoke over the growl of the truck engine and the spatter of the rain against the windshield.

"Did you talk to him?"

"No. He didn't show up at the bar. I was on my way to his cottage when I saw him getting into the car."

Kelley was used to strong language. But the string of profanities Sam let loose now startled her.

"Tell me what he said earlier that made you think he wanted to unload something," he said at last as he veered onto the road toward Cairo without even pausing at the flashing light.

It was hard to rally her thoughts, hard to draw her eyes from the way Sam was favoring his injured shoulder as he muscled the steering wheel into a turn, or the way his long legs seemed too big for the dark truck cab.

He reached his right hand toward her suddenly, wincing as he moved, and Kelley felt her breath quicken. But it was the crumpled cigarette package on the seat between them that he was after. He tossed it back after discovering it was empty and glared at Kelley as though it was her fault. His eyes were dark and unreadable in the slight glow from the dashboard.

Wayland. He'd asked about Wayland. Kelley tried to push past her own awareness of Sam's big body and forced herself to recall her conversation with Wayland earlier this evening.

"He said he was afraid I'd gotten the wrong impression when he asked me about Steve Cormier this morning," she said. "He seemed to have been thinking it over, and worrying—"

"Hold on." Sam's voice grated across her words. "When exactly did Wayland ask you about Steve Cormier?"

Oh, hell, Kelley thought. That was it—the loose fact she hadn't been able to come up with this afternoon. There'd been so much else going on—

"It was this morning, after we'd gotten you out of the Gustaffsons' place," she said. "Wayland seemed to think we knew Steve Cormier somehow. He seemed concerned about where Cormier had gone, and why."

"And were you planning to tell me about this eventually, or was it your own private clue?"

His voice was caustic now, and Kelley didn't blame him. She'd had plenty of reasons to forget, but excuses didn't count in this business, not when you had a partner who was counting on you. Sam's tone was making that abundantly clear.

"How the hell are we supposed to work together if you aren't putting everything on the table?" he asked.

"I know." Her own words were soft. "I slipped up. I'm sorry."

That simple admission could have encapsulated their whole relationship, Kelley thought miserably.

I slipped up. I'm sorry...

And all the apologies in the world couldn't bring back the trust they'd lost. They'd been starting to recover it as they'd worked together this past week, but she could see in Sam's expression now that this most recent slip had cost her a lot of the ground she'd gained back.

He shook his wet, dark head as he stared out into the pelting rain. If the steering wheel had been a living thing, it would have been gasping for breath under his grip by now.

"I don't see how in hell we're supposed to make this work." He muttered the words, speaking to himself, it seemed. She could hear the frustration in them.

They were on the road that skirted Cairo's small downtown section, heading north toward the highway. Sam had the wipers on as fast as they would go, and in the distance, whenever the blades momentarily cleared a patch of windshield, Kelley could just make out the hazy red glow of a set of taillights.

"Think that's Wayland?" Sam asked.

"I'd say there's a good chance of it. There don't seem to be very many other people out tonight."

"No big surprise there." Sam, like Kelley, was wearing a raincoat, but both of them were still soaked by the driving rain they'd run through. "The question is, where is Wayland off to in such a hurry in weather like this?"

"I don't know." Kelley pushed her hands into the pockets of her coat, trying to stave off the chill inside her.

"When I ran into him at the health club, he seemed so eager to talk to me. And eager to dispel any impression I'd gotten that he might be worried about who Steve Cormier really was."

"Tell me what else he said."

Kelley frowned, concentrating as hard as she could. "He said he wanted to get the sailboat under wraps before he got together with me, because the weather's supposed to turn really nasty overnight. His parents weren't around to do it because they'd gone up to Houston this afternoon for some big charity art show that Helen contributed to."

"Hmm." Sam drummed both thumbs against the wheel. Kelley recognized the gesture. It meant he was thinking hard. "I wonder if Wayland had gotten some inkling about Steve Cormier's real identity."

"That Cormier wasn't who he appeared to be?"

"Right. And it could have seemed suspicious to him that Cormier disappeared at just about the time you and I showed up."

"So he had some idea that we might be connected to Cormier somehow."

"Or even just that we recognized Cormier, which scared him off."

"The big question is—"

He finished the sentence for her. "Why would Wayland be worried about it in the first place?"

Kelley nodded, barely noticing the interruption. "Wayland must have something to hide, or he wouldn't have seemed so worried when he talked to me this morning," she said.

Sam briefly raised his hands from the wheel, turning his palms flat to the roof of the cab. "This case beats anything I ever worked on," he said. "We no sooner get one thing nailed down than something else pops up. I was sure, when I found that gun in Jon Gustaffson's drawer, that we'd pinned the blame on the Gustaffsons. And now..."

Kelley knew exactly how he felt. And it wasn't just clues that were hard to pin down in this assignment.

Her feelings were on a roller coaster, too, down one moment, up the next.

Five minutes ago it had seemed impossible that she would be able to keep any kind of partnership together with Sam. And yet here they were playing off each other's thoughts again, bouncing ideas around in the same old instinctive rhythm.

Making love with Sam this evening had been more exhilarating and frightening than anything she'd experienced in a long time. It had sent Kelley scrambling for safety, trying to distance herself from emotions and desires she didn't feel ready to handle again.

And yet they kept finding their way in. In spite of her efforts to keep her thoughts fixed on the case, she was still half-seduced by the deep growl of Sam's voice, still all too aware of his big shoulders and lean waist as he turned toward her again.

"Check the glove compartment, would you, sweetheart?" His brows were lowered into a long, belligerent line. "There's got to be a cigarette *somewhere* in this damn truck."

There wasn't. Kelley checked. It didn't seem to do anything to improve Sam's temper.

And neither did the roadblock they hit a few minutes later.

Sam had been pushing the truck to go as fast as it could on the slick pavement, and they'd been managing to keep pace with the car ahead of them. But Kelley could see more lights in the distance now, flashing blue and white, swallowing up the faint red taillights as Wayland's car neared the scene.

"Damn." Sam pressed the gas pedal a little harder. "Something's up."

It quickly became clear that most of the flashing lights belonged to a police cruiser parked in front of a trailer truck that had skidded sideways across the road. A police officer in a glistening slicker was directing Wayland's car—it was Wayland, Kelley could see now—around the truck as Sam and Kelley neared the scene.

But when Sam tried to follow, the officer barred the way. The truck driver was evidently attempting to get his vehicle back on the road, and now that Wayland had passed by—

Sam rolled down his window, ignoring the rain that lashed his face when he leaned out. "We've got to get through," he called to the policeman.

"Sorry, sir. It'll just be a minute."

It was two minutes, according to Kelley's wristwatch. The second hand seemed to have slowed to a crawl as she watched the time tick away, and she could feel her impatience building to match Sam's as the truck driver jockeyed cautiously back and forth.

By the time he'd finally finished, it was too late.

There was no sign of Wayland's taillights on the road ahead of them. Sam kept his foot mercilessly on the accelerator, but they knew when they reached the main road that they were out of luck. The night was black and empty in both directions.

"No way to tell which way he went," Sam said gloomily.

"I know." Kelley shook her head. "This night is just going from bad to worse."

She couldn't decipher Sam's inarticulate snort, and he didn't add anything to it as he turned the truck around and headed back toward the Windspray Community.

Chapter 12

There'd been a large puddle at the Windspray entrance when they'd pulled out a half hour earlier.

Now it was a small lake.

And there was no way around it.

"It's a good thing the Prices have that boat," Sam muttered. "We may need it yet. Hold your breath, sweetheart—this truck's not overfond of deep water."

Kelley held her breath, but it didn't help. Sam's pickup charged vigorously into the axle-high puddle, but halfway through it started to sputter. In spite of everything Sam could do—and every profanity he could come up with in the process—the truck succumbed to a violent attack of coughing and stopped dead.

"Damn." Sam's face looked grim as he zipped up his raincoat. "I'm going to have to get out and push. The longer we sit here, the longer it'll take to get it going again."

He was out of the cab before Kelley could volunteer her help. She looked out her window at the water surrounding the truck and shivered at the thought of how cold it would be. The wind was howling around them, and the rain was making angry pockmarks on the surface of the huge puddle.

But she couldn't just sit here while Sam struggled to move the truck all by himself. Cinching her hood down as tightly as she could, Kelley got out of the cab and joined him.

He was already straining against the rear fender, his face twisted with the effort of it. "Are you out of your mind?" he demanded when Kelley appeared at his side.

"No, but you may be." She sloshed through the frigid knee-high water and leaned her right shoulder against the truck. "Don't waste time yelling at me, Sam. Let's just do this and get back inside, all right?"

It wasn't as simple as that. They were both drenched already, and it was hard to keep their underwater footing long enough to get a steady rocking motion going. By the time they managed it and the truck rolled up over the hump at the edge of the puddle, Kelley felt as though she'd been standing under Niagara Falls.

The wind seemed to cut right through her soaked clothing as she and Sam ran for their cottage door after parking the truck. Her fingers were chilled and clumsy as she fit the key into the lock, and she had to work hard to keep her teeth from chattering.

Sam seemed to be having the same problem. "There's been too damn much water in this case so far to suit me," he muttered as he stripped off his sodden raincoat and dropped it by the door.

Kelley did the same, pulling her pistol out first and placing it in the nearest drawer. She laughed as she looked down at her dripping-wet jeans and shirt. "Not much point trying to avoid leaving puddles, is there?" she said.

"No." Something flared in Sam's dark blue eyes as he looked at her, something that made Kelley think he was trying to salvage his usual steely glare and having a hard time doing it. "Look, a hot shower is the best answer to this, if we're going to avoid catching pneumonia. And I'm willing to wait my turn, but I'd just as soon not wait forever, and—"

Suddenly Kelley knew what was behind the struggle in his eyes. She was feeling the same uneasiness herself, the same awareness that what they were really approaching, out of pure necessity, was a situation where they both needed to get out of all their clothes.

Kelley tried for the lighthearted tone she'd used as a cover-up a moment ago, but she couldn't quite manage it. "Go ahead," she told him. "Just let me get some towels first."

In the bedroom they kept running into each other.

Kelley ducked into the big bathroom and came out with an armful of clean white towels, but Sam was blocking her way. They both stepped aside at the same moment, self-consciously. Kelley managed to put a few steps between her and Sam's big body, but she realized she'd only done it by backing herself against the bedroom wall in a posture that was far more defensive than she'd intended it to be.

And one good look at Sam told her exactly what she was trying to defend herself against.

With his hair plastered to his head like that, and his blue eyes haunted by heartaches he was refusing to put into words, he looked startlingly young, unexpectedly vulnerable.

His long frame looked anything but young. His plaid shirt, turned nearly black by the rain that had soaked it, draped his broad upper body in a way that outlined every hard muscle, every masculine angle.

And the way his wet jeans clung to his hips was heating Kelley from the inside out.

She closed her eyes and felt desire beginning to build at the center of her own body as she remembered how Sam had looked stepping out of the shower earlier tonight.

The dark hair on his torso had been softened and disheveled by the rough toweling he'd been giving himself. Those dark curls had still thickened low down on his belly, drawing Kelley's gaze seductively lower.

The long, hard sweep of his thighs had always driven her half-crazy. At his most maddening, Sam could be an arrogant son of a gun. But his arrogance had another side, and Kelley had seen it tonight in the confident swagger of his step as he'd come into the bedroom. He had a kind of rough-and-ready integrity, and an outlaw appeal that she'd never been able to resist.

She couldn't resist it now.

And she couldn't be certain, not under the damp folds of his jeans, but she thought she was seeing the same telltale bulge at his loins that meant he couldn't resist her, either.

Oh, God, she thought desperately. *Just go. Step into the shower and let me get out of here. Don't tempt me like this again, not twice in one night.*

But he wasn't moving.

"You didn't have to help me with the truck." His words were slow, his gaze heavy as he looked at her.

"I wanted to—" She stopped the sentence midway, not sure what she really wanted to say. *Are you looking at me that way because you're undressing me in your imagination exactly the same way I'm undressing you?* It was a disturbing thought.

"It didn't seem right to let you wrestle with it all by yourself," she said finally.

"It seemed right to leave me earlier, though, didn't it?" He was still holding her gaze, and Kelley could feel the connection between them growing stronger, finding its way into her bloodstream.

She tried again for a light tone, but it didn't work. "I— I was scared, Sam." Her own honesty startled her. "I *am* scared," she amended. She lifted both hands in the air, aware of the dampness at her shoulders where her back was pressing against the wall.

"Can't you see what we're doing?" she asked him. "It's just like it was before. What if—" She paused. "I couldn't stand it if something like that happened again."

He growled, but it was a sound of agreement, not argument. "I know," he said. "Damn it, do you think I don't see—"

He broke their gaze finally and looked toward the curtained window, where the wind was whipping rain against the panes.

When he looked back, he seemed to have decided that searching for any more words was a waste of time.

He was only a couple of paces away from her. He moved without warning and reached her before Kelley could even think of sidestepping him. His palm landed hollowly against the wall next to her ear, cutting off her only escape route.

And suddenly his other hand was cupping her face, so gently that Kelley heard herself moan in response, drawn toward him, as always, by the buried need in his eyes and the hidden tenderness of his spirit.

She knew he was trying to crowd her, trying to push past all the unresolved questions that stood between them.

She let him do it.

It was impossible, when she was looking into his eyes like this, feeling the heat of his body pressing into hers through their damp clothes, to resist the longing that surged between them like the swell of a high tide.

She'd been fighting this for so long. She'd been fighting it when she'd left him after they'd made love earlier. But suddenly she just didn't have the strength to fight anymore.

She lifted her arms to circle his neck and felt him let go of the breath he was holding. He'd just given in, too, she

thought. The realization was like a warm wave, pooling ir-
resistibly at the pulsing juncture of her thighs.

When he kissed her, the last of her doubts dissolved.

His kiss was a slow exploration, a question, not a demand. Kelley could feel him trembling against her, as
though for all his strength he was still overawed by the
power that drew the two of them together.

His breath drew in quickly when she opened her mouth
under his and met the sensuous swirl of his tongue with a
silent caress of her own. She felt his fingers pushing
through her damp hair, pressing into her flesh, warming
her, cradling her.

Is this safe? The question skittered through her mind,
prompted by the threatening howl of the wind and the uneasiness of the situation around them.

Was it safe to let their guard down, to let themselves be
swept back into passion when there might still be danger
outside in the night?

The answer was perfectly clear.

It wasn't safe.

And there wasn't a thing Kelley could do about it.

Her body's responses were too ravenous, her imagination too fired by the sweetness of their lovemaking only
hours before. If an armed commando squadron were to
burst through the cottage door, she thought hazily, it might
only barely be enough to draw her away from the pleasure
she felt as Sam kissed her more deeply.

He was easing himself against her so she could feel every
inch of his body from the broad strength of his chest to the
hard ridge pressed so erotically across the bones of her hips.

"I'm afraid these clothes might stick to us if we don't get
out of them soon." The lightness she'd tried for earlier
came more easily now as she pushed Sam's wet hair back
from his forehead and tilted his face so he was looking at
her again.

The barest beginnings of a smile appeared in his dark blue eyes. "Might have stuck already," he said. "Let me see."

That gravelly drawl went straight to the core of her, as it always had. She'd been half in love with Sam Cotter the very first time she'd ever heard him speak.

He didn't linger over her shirt buttons this time. Seizing both sides of her sopping-wet collar, he tore the garment open, scattering small pearl buttons all around them.

Kelley gasped. And laughed. And gasped again when she felt Sam's tongue, warm and slick and explicit, gliding over her neck, her collarbone, her breasts.

He dispatched her bra with even less ceremony than he'd used on her shirt. By then Kelley felt as though she was floating under his touch, aching at the smooth, sweet sensation of his tongue over her skin. He was erasing all the cold of the storm outside, all the doubts she'd lived with for so long, sweeping them away in one long caress after another.

This was heaven. It was *better* than heaven. It was—

"Sam..."

She cried his name as he gathered her against him, and fought past his gentle grip until she reached his own shirt buttons. Her fingers stumbled over them—she didn't know if she was still cold or simply too aroused to be dexterous—and he ended up undoing the shirt himself, baring his lean, magnificent chest and reaching for the waistband of his jeans with a motion that Kelley found overpoweringly seductive.

Naked together at last, they were both shivering from the aftereffects of the dousing they'd gotten. Sam lifted the covers and they fell into bed together, burrowing back into each other's arms in a combined quest for heat and pleasure.

Kelley had imagined doing exactly this, every time she'd wakened in this bed by herself.

She'd wrestled with her own need to feel Sam's rangy body surrounding her this way, to have his hands touching and arousing her in a way that no other man had ever done.

She'd dreamed—how many times had she had this dream?—of the inexpressible freedom she and Sam had always found when they'd made love. There was no barrier between fantasy and reality when they were together. Sam's loving had always found and answered her most secret desires.

Those same tantalizing horizons were opening in front of her now. And she rushed toward them, eager, light-headed.

He wrapped his big hands around her waist and lifted her on top of him. Kelley shook her damp hair out of the way and looked down into his face, loving the taut, handsome lines of his features and the velvet black of his eyes in the dim light. When she shifted her bare legs against his, both of them cried out at the same moment, hungry for the same closer union.

"You're still so beautiful." Sam's voice was low and shaken with desire. "So beautiful . . ."

She felt his gaze covering her like a silken veil. He smoothed his palms over her shoulders, lower, across her breasts, then clasped her waist again and settled her more tantalizingly against the hard evidence of his need for her.

Passion took over what was left of Kelley's mind as she moved against Sam. She leaned her palms into his muscled chest and felt the dark, springy curls send racy messages to nerve centers all over her body. It was impossible to stay still, impossible to resist the urge to slide her hips from side to side, imitating the timeless rhythms of lovemaking so perfectly that it made both of them groan in unison again.

She lowered herself over him, meeting his kiss with a hunger that was quickly speeding out of control. She felt him growl against her mouth and felt herself spinning off into a swirl of physical sensation as Sam closed his arms powerfully around her and reversed their positions, pressing her down into the bed that was already warmed by the heat of their bodies.

She took advantage of the shift to wrap one hand around the length of his arousal, stroking him until he moaned her name in a voice raw with need.

"Kelley... if you don't stop that..."

She didn't plan to stop. But Sam's questing hands had found the liquid well of pleasure inside her now, and suddenly he wasn't the only one hovering on the edge of something he couldn't control.

His fingers were more knowing than they had any right to be. Kelley arched her spine as he slid in and out of her, and felt his long, strong legs wrapping themselves around her in an all-encompassing embrace.

"Sam, please..."

Through the haze of barely curbed desire that masked his features Kelley could see the faint gleam of a smile.

He'd been waiting for this, she thought.

He'd wanted to hear her calling his name with that note of longing in it, wanted to know that she was being torn apart by the same overpowering need she could see in his face.

She wanted to tell him not to look so satisfied, but the words wouldn't come out.

Her own impatience made her even bolder as Sam reached over the edge of the bed to the back pocket of the jeans he'd stepped out of. Kelley slid her whole body along the length of his and heard him groan again.

The low sound of his voice seemed to be caught in the noise of the howling gale outside the cottage. And their joined cries of satisfaction, as Sam finally slid inside her, felt like part of the tempest, too,

It was as though the turmoil of the sky and sea had somehow found its way inside them, lifting them higher and higher on waves they couldn't possibly hold back. Kelley was being swept into the darkness of the roiling storm around them, oblivious to anything but the way they were moving together, rising and falling with every renewed roar as it slammed into them.

Passion carried them on, far into the night.

And when it finally crested, there were no words left over, no way to tell Sam what she was feeling, no way even to understand it herself.

When she drifted into sleep at last, held close in Sam's arms, she had only enough awareness left to wonder where all the tumult and rage had disappeared to.

It must be the eye of the storm, her sated, sleepy mind told her. They must have stumbled into the center of the hurricane, where, for this merciful interval of quiet, no winds blew.

Still wrapped in this sudden sense of peace, Kelley let herself fall asleep.

"No..."

It was Sam's voice. But she hadn't been dreaming about him. She hadn't been dreaming about anything at all, as far as she could tell.

"No, don't..."

The sharp edge of protest in his words hauled Kelley back to consciousness. She blinked and heard the wind still buffeting the cottage in the gray predawn light.

"Don't leave me..."

Sam was mumbling, his face half-turned toward his pillow, but the words were clear enough.

And so was the panic in them.

Kelley pushed her tangled hair out of her eyes and rolled over. Sam had moved away from her in the bed. She could see his broad shoulders now, and his profile pressing into the pillow, facing the faint light that was reaching in around the edges of the curtains.

"Don't leave me..."

Panic had turned to pleading, and by now Kelley was fully awake and sliding her arms around him.

"Sam, it's okay." She held him close, trying to ease the anguish she could see etched in the lines cut across his brow. "You're all right. You're just dreaming."

He surfaced from sleep all at once, like a drowning man coming back to fresh air.

"Kelley?" There was amazement in his voice.

And the fear was still there, too.

"Shh, Sam." She wrapped her arms more tightly around him. "You were dreaming. You're okay."

"It wasn't a dream." He sounded angry and disoriented. "I was—" He shook his dark head and looked at her with eyes still clouded by sleep. "I was all alone."

The phrase was childishly simple, and at first Kelley wasn't sure why it affected her so strongly. She smoothed a hand over his forehead, unraveling the dark brown hair that had dried itself into unruly patterns overnight. Why were Sam's words tugging at her heart this way?

And then, suddenly, she understood.

I was all alone...

She'd seen that silent message in his eyes ever since she'd met him. It was one of the things that had kept drawing her quietly toward him even during the years when the pain of their breakup had forced them apart.

She'd never heard him put that buried anguish into words until this moment.

"Who left you alone?" She asked the question gently, trying to hold her own curiosity in check. He was so uncharacteristically vulnerable at this moment, so fragile in spite of the hard strength of his body.

His brief, harsh laugh made her think she'd pushed too hard and driven him back inside the armor he usually wore to defend himself against the rest of the world. But then he shook his head.

"Everybody," he said. His second short laugh, echoing the first, wasn't enough to disguise the desolation in his tone. "Anybody I ever really cared about walked out on me sooner or later."

Kelley fought down the little spurt of remorse inside her at the thought that she had walked out on him, too, after the first time they'd made love last night. "I've never heard you talk about this before," she said slowly.

She shifted onto one elbow as Sam rolled over onto his back. He was staring up at the ceiling now, eyes focused on some distant memory. But he kept one hand clasped over Kelley's where it rested on the warm expanse of his chest.

"It's not something I talk about." He tightened his fingers around hers for a moment, and then she felt his chest rise and fall in a slow sigh.

"I guess when I dream about it like that, it's my father I'm dreaming about," he said finally. "He walked out on the family when I was a kid."

"How old were you?"

"Seven."

"That must have been hard."

A slight, mocking grin tilted the corner of his mouth, and Kelley had to work hard to restrain the memory of the way he had kissed her last night. Her whole body was still pulsing with the pleasure of it.

"Oh, it wasn't so difficult." His grin quirked a little higher, then faded. "I just followed the old son of a gun."

"You followed him? Away from your mother?"

He nodded. "I adored my dad. Thought the world revolved around him. That was probably why we got along so well—he thought the world revolved around him, too."

His flippant tone didn't fool Kelley. There was real love—and real loss—in his eyes as he spoke.

"What happened, Sam?"

He shrugged, then winced, as though he'd let himself get so far lost in the past that he'd forgotten the more recent injury to his shoulder. "He dumped me," he said baldly.

"Dumped you? Just abandoned you, you mean?"

"We hoboed around together for a few years—great years, probably the best time I ever had—and then I guess he decided it would be better for me if I was in school, with somebody to teach me manners and stuff."

It was Kelley's turn to smile. Sam caught her eye and snorted. "Yeah," he said. "The aunt and uncle he turned me over to did their best, but I never cottoned on to etiquette much."

"How long were you with them?"

"Five years."

He didn't have to stop and count, Kelley noticed. These memories went deep with him.

And so did the hurt they'd left behind. For the first time, she felt she was getting a glimpse of the reasons for Sam Cotter's solitude, for the distance he put between himself and the rest of humanity. His father had been Sam's first partner—his only partner, until Kelley had come along years later.

And both partnerships had ended in unhappiness.

She didn't prompt him this time, and after a long pause he took up the story again. "Soon as I turned sixteen, I took off on my own," he told her. "I've told you some about those days—mostly I was just moving around, trying to find something I really wanted to do. Until Wiley managed to track me down a few years ago and offered me a job as an investigator, I just did whatever came handy, for however long it lasted."

"Following your father's footsteps?" she asked gently.

Sam snorted again. "My father was a con artist with a capital C," he told her. "And I loved the old bastard, but frankly, his business dealings always made me nervous as hell. He was like a magician—I remember the way he used to pull out his business card and flourish it at some unsuspecting dupe, like it was a rabbit he'd just yanked out of a hat. But at the same time, I knew the company name on the card was bogus. It used to amaze me, the way people would fall for any old line if it was presented with enough pizzazz.''

He shook his head, his eyes still focused on some distant place that Kelley couldn't see. "I was looking for some niche of my own, something where I could rely on more than just pizzazz," he said. "It just took me a long time to find one, that's all.''

Kelley sat up, pulling the warm sheet over her shoulder. Her mind was putting a lot of things together now, things that had always puzzled her about Sam Cotter.

Sam had a natural genius for sniffing out financial scams. And the news about his father explained how he'd gotten so good at it. Sam must have grown up watching financial crime from the criminal's point of view.

At the same time, he'd loved his dad.

And his dad had walked off and left him.

Was that why Sam was so quick to back off whenever a relationship threatened to go sour? Was he just trying to stay one step ahead of the risk and pain of love, refusing to take a chance on being left behind again?

There were a lot of things she wanted to ask him, but she wasn't sure how. He seemed to be fully awake now, and the unaccustomed openness in his face had hardened into the sharp, watchful expression she was used to seeing in his features.

What happened to your mother? she wanted to ask. *What about Wiley and Jack? What about us?* She hadn't been able to decide which question to start with by the time Sam raised himself to lean on both elbows, shrugging off her hand.

"Damn," he said, suddenly sounding frustrated. "Something's nagging at me, and I can't quite get hold of it.''

"Something about your family?"

"No." He shook his head and raked a hand through his hair. "Something about the Windspray case. Talking about my father just triggered it."

Kelley felt the cold touch of disappointment in her chest. *The Windspray case.* From the moment she'd eased herself into Sam's arms last night until just now, the thought of the case hadn't even crossed her mind.

And she resented it for intruding now. She'd tried to hide behind the case herself not long ago, but she didn't want to hide anymore. And she didn't want Sam to hide, either. They'd come too far for that now. Surely he could see—

"Sam, listen to me," she said. "You said yourself that there's something funny about this case. We seem to keep coming up with dead ends no matter which way we turn."

He wasn't listening to her. She could tell by the way his brows had lowered over his dark blue eyes, and by the taut outline of his mouth.

"Let's let Jack and his people clean this one up," she said, more urgently now. Suddenly it was impossible to imagine plunging back into the business-first attitude she'd been clinging to for so long. Now that she and Sam were finally opening up to each other again, finally beginning to grapple with some of the uneasy ghosts that had kept them apart—

"I've got it."

He threw the covers aside as he said the words, and Kelley's heart tightened as she heard his decisive tone.

Sam Cotter was back at work.

And the man she'd been holding so tenderly in her arms, the man who'd let her into his secret dreams, his secret fears, had suddenly disappeared.

"What exactly is it that you've got?"

He looked over his shoulder at her from the edge of the bed. "Do you remember how you described Wayland Price when he gave you that list of the companies he'd worked for?'' he asked.

She had to work hard to come up with it. "I said he waved it at me like it was the answer to a challenge," she said at last. "But I don't see—"

"I don't, either. Not yet. But I've got a hunch. And this time I don't intend to ignore it."

"Sam, wait."

She spoke to his retreating back, watching as he strode out into the living room in search of dry clothes. She reached over the side of the bed and discovered that her own jeans were still damp from last night's adventure. And her white shirt was buttonless, torn apart by Sam's eager hands.

The little white buttons were strewn around the carpet, winking in the early morning light like crystallized tears. Kelley fought back the tears that welled unexpectedly in her own eyes at the sight of them, and got quickly out of bed and into a pair of navy blue leggings and a loose blue sweater. She was sure her shoes would still be wet, so she pulled on a pair of low pumps and hoped she wouldn't have to do any cross-country running this morning.

"*Damn.*" Sam's frustration seemed to be building on itself. She could hear his long-legged steps as he moved around the living room.

"What's the matter?"

"Phone's out. Storm must have knocked down a line somewhere."

The news didn't do anything to calm Kelley's vague fears. She wasn't certain what was worrying her—maybe it was nothing more than regret at the lost tenderness of a few moments ago.

Whatever was causing her misgivings, it wasn't calmed any by the sight of Sam pulling her gun out of the drawer where she'd left it last night.

"What's going on, Sam?" she asked sharply. "What are you doing?"

"I'm heading into town to see if I can find a phone that's working." He picked up his own raincoat as he spoke, shaking the remnants of last night's rain out of its folds. "Grab your coat, sweetheart. If I'm right about this, it could change everything."

Chapter 13

She didn't want to do it.

She wanted to stay at the cottage and demand that Sam listen to her, that he ignore the Windspray case for just one more hour while they tackled the more important question of what was happening between them. At the moment the mystery of who had produced the counterfeit bills seemed remote, and not nearly as urgent as the questions her heart was demanding answers to.

But Sam's blue eyes were remote now, too, just as they'd been when he and Kelley had started to work on this case. And she knew from long experience that there was no getting through to him once he'd set his mind to something.

He'd found the list of companies that Wayland Price had done consulting work for, and he handed it to Kelley as they stepped outside. "You called all of these, right?" he said.

"Yes. And they all confirmed Wayland's story." She still couldn't see where he was headed with this.

"But they *didn't* tell you anything about the financial health of those companies, right?"

"Right, because I didn't ask them. Why would I?"

"Exactly."

"Sam, would you like to explain—"

"I will, sweetheart. I just have to check something out first, and I can't do that without a phone line. Once I reach Jack—" He paused before stepping into the truck and raised empty palms to the sky. "It's a hunch, Kelley. That's all."

The worst of the storm had blown itself out overnight, but the sky was still overcast, the clouds still racing in off the sea. Kelley could taste salt spray in the fine mist that touched her face.

"A few days ago you were telling me you'd given up playing your hunches in this business," she couldn't help saying as she slid into the truck next to Sam. "You said it was better to—"

"I know. To stick with 'just the facts, ma'am.'" He frowned and turned the key in the ignition. "I guess I was trying—" The engine sounded reluctant, and Sam seemed to be concentrating fiercely on it. "I've been trying to make everything go the way I wanted it to. But nothing in this damn case is going right. At this point, hunches are all I've got."

He didn't sound happy about it, either, but that seemed to be all he intended to say on the subject.

Kelley was silent as they drove into Cairo. She trusted Sam's instincts when it came to the detective business. Wiley had always said that aside from a few antisocial tendencies that occasionally got in his way, Sam was the best natural investigator Wiley had ever trained.

The problem was that Kelley had instincts of her own. And they were all telling her now that she and Sam had just passed up an opportunity that might not come their way again.

The local diner was already open for business at this early hour, but its phones, too, were out of commission.

"A big tree came down on the road up to the highway," the waitress told them. "Nobody in Cairo's got phones this morning. But we've got coffee and the morning papers, if that's any consolation." She poured them two cups without being asked, and Sam and Kelley slid into a booth while they considered what to do next.

"Tell me what you're thinking," Kelley demanded as she stirred cream into her coffee.

Sam's brows were drawn together in a scowl, a sure sign that he was concentrating on putting the pieces of a puzzle together in his mind. "What I'm thinking," he said, "is that your description of Wayland flourishing this list at you reminded me a lot of the way my dad used to flourish his credentials when he was trying to impress somebody with how legitimate he was."

Kelley finally saw the connection. "But your dad's credentials were mostly bogus ones," she said.

"Right. And it makes me wonder—" He waved a hand in front of his face in a frustrated motion. "Maybe it's nothing," he said. "But I still want to check out how those companies are doing. Something about it just doesn't feel right to me."

"But without a phone—"

"I know. Maybe we should head over to Port Lavaca and see what Jack can do for us. Let me think it over while I get some caffeine into my system."

He seemed to want to do his thinking silently, and Kelley didn't interrupt him. Her own thoughts kept drifting back to the warmth and intimacy they'd wakened into, and her sense that it had been a mistake to leave it.

Trying to chase those thoughts out of her mind, she turned her attention to the morning edition of the Houston paper. There was nothing in the world news that grabbed her eye. But when she came to the life-style section, Helen Price's name jumped out at her.

"Sam," she said, reaching a hand out to touch his forearm, "look at this."

The photograph that dominated the page showed three stylishly dressed older women in front of several framed pictures. Helen wasn't among the women, but the caption credited one of the artworks as hers.

And the story beneath the picture mentioned that Mr. and Mrs. Harold Price had been unable to attend the glittering charity art show at which Mrs. Price's watercolor *Gulf Dawn* had won a prize.

"'Unavoidable commitments elsewhere,'" Sam muttered, reading as Kelley's finger marked the spot.

"But they told Wayland they were going to be at that art show," Kelley said.

"Or at least that's what Wayland told you." Sam sat back, frowning at her.

Kelley pressed her fingertips to her temples. Now it was her turn to be nagged by some tiny detail out of the past, some fact she'd noted in passing but hadn't connected to anything at the time. What *was* it?

She closed her eyes and heard the soft slap of water and the jangle of metal fittings against a tall mast. And then she knew.

"Helen had a thorough art training in Europe," she said, looking at Sam again. "She learned all the standard techniques, she told me. That would include engraving, wouldn't it?"

"Engraving..." Sam echoed the word, frowning now. "But they hired us," he added. "They started this investigation. They—"

"No, they didn't." Suddenly it was all falling into place. "Their bank manager started it, when the counterfeit bills were discovered. He had to report it. But what if—"

"What if Harold and Helen are behind the bad bills?" Sam's eyes locked on to hers as they both chased down this new idea. "They'd have wanted to cover their tracks when the bills caught somebody's attention at the bank."

"So instead of letting the bank manager call in the feds, they called a private-investigation agency instead."

Sam shook his head, tangling the dark hair he'd just pushed back into place. "This can't be right," he said. "We can't actually be considering that our clients are guilty."

"But it makes sense, Sam. It explains why we've had this feeling of being manipulated. And why it's been so hard to get a handle on things. If Harold and Helen Price have been stage-managing this entire investigation—"

"And trying to get us to focus on Steve Cormier—"

Kelley put a hand down flat on the tabletop between them, startling the breakfasting couple in the next booth. "They could have rigged that leaking gas tank," she said, lowering her voice but unable to calm her excitement. "And they would have known it was fairly safe to do it, because—"

"They knew we weren't really honeymooners." Sam finished the sentence grimly. "They knew we wouldn't be sleeping in the same bed."

Last night they *had* been sleeping in the same bed. And they'd been swept away by the same passions, too, oblivious to everything in the world except their driving need for each other.

If something had threatened their lives last night—

Kelley couldn't stand to think about it. "What about Wayland?" she asked, aware that her voice was shaking slightly. "I wonder how he's involved."

"Maybe he's not. Wayland doesn't strike me as the kind of guy you'd want as an accomplice."

"Me, too. But—" Kelley snapped her fingers. "He does strike me as enough of a freeloader that he might have lifted a twenty-dollar bill or two from his parents if he needed some spare cash."

"And those bills did show up after Wayland came to live at Windspray," Sam commented.

"So maybe Wayland was an accessory without meaning to be." Kelley glanced down at the newspaper story again, and added, "None of this tells us where Harold and Helen *really* went last night. Or why Wayland took off in such a hurry."

"I know. But I'd be willing to bet my last nickel it has something to do with this case." Sam gulped down the rest of his coffee and slid out of the booth.

"Another hunch?" Kelley asked as she tossed a couple of bills onto the table and followed him.

Sam looked grim now, more than ever like the loner she'd first met three years earlier.

"Once in a very long while," he told her, "it turns out to be the smart thing to do."

When his eyes met hers, cold and steely and blue, it was as though they'd never loved, never trusted, never shared anything at all.

And Kelley had the powerful impression Sam was trying to convince her that he preferred it that way.

On the way to the truck, they took a quick, hard look at their options. It was tempting to head straight over to Jack's motel room in Port Lavaca and enlist the FBI's help in uncovering everything possible about Harold and Helen's personal finances, in the hope of turning up some hidden income or some hint of why the supposedly wealthy Prices had resorted to counterfeiting.

On the other hand . . .

"If they're not back yet, I sure would like to get a look inside their house," Kelley murmured.

"I know. And this may be the only chance we have."

The only chance we have.

The words echoed somberly in Kelley's mind. Were they passing up a chance at something more lasting, more important, in order to solve the case they'd been assigned to?

Or was their work, in the long run, the only lasting thing they had to share?

She swallowed hard and looked at the hard lines of Sam's profile. This wasn't the time to try to reach him, she knew. The only thing on his mind right now was the prospect of searching the Prices' vacation home, and her own professional experience was telling her that the idea was a smart one.

By the time they reached the big house, the cloud cover was starting to break up and there were patches of blue out over the cove that the Prices' home faced. The sun was still low on the horizon behind them, and the air around the coast was fresh with salt spray and all the ocean smells that the storm had churned up during the night.

This is it, Kelley thought, as Sam scouted all the doors of the Prices' house and finally chose the cellar bulkhead as the most likely way in. Things were finally coming to a head.

The last time they'd been in this situation together, she'd nearly gotten both of them killed.

And what really scared her now was that she was having such a hard time keeping her thoughts focused on her work.

For all the experience she'd accumulated since that night at the warehouse, for all her promises to herself never to take a chance on getting into the same kind of trouble, she found herself thinking about all the wrong things as she watched Sam picking the padlock on the bulkhead.

His long, agile fingers, probing at the inner workings of the lock with the metal picks he'd pulled out of his back pocket, made her think inescapably of the way he'd caressed her last night, the way he'd turned her nearly inside out with his knowing touch.

She could almost feel the heavy thickness of his hair as she watched the wind blowing it into his eyes.

And his long legs, taut and rangy as he half knelt on the slanted bulkhead door, were splayed at an angle that Kelley found too eye-catching and sexy to ignore.

This is all wrong, she told herself. But the intrusive thoughts kept coming.

"All right."

The lock slid open with a quiet click under Sam's expert hands. A moment later he and Kelley were standing in the basement of the old house, looking around them while they waited for their eyes to adjust to the low light.

Sam was muttering something about splitting up the search once they got upstairs into the main house. Half of Kelley was attending to him, while the other half worked at slowing her beating heart and fighting against Sam's nearness in the big, dim cellar.

In spite of her dangerously distracting thoughts, she was the first one to notice the locked room. "That's probably worth checking," she said, nodding toward the padlocked wooden door.

Sam made short work of the second lock. It was as though his mind was becoming more focused on the task at hand, while Kelley's was more and more tempted to wander into all the wrong places.

But she had no problems concentrating once Sam got the door open and they found themselves looking at a set of equipment that spoke volumes to their trained eyes. Presses, engraving tools, reams of paper—it was in various stages of being dismantled and packed into crates, but in the light from the small window high up on the wall, it was very clear what they'd found: a complete set of the tools needed to practice the counterfeiter's art.

She never saw the quick movement behind them until it was too late to do anything about it.

By the time she realized she and Sam weren't alone, she was feeling the hard edge of something cold and metallic between her shoulder blades. Harold Price's voice was calm

enough, but his words were laced through with a threat that
made Kelley's skin tingle.

"I'm sure you're armed," he was saying. "Unfortunately, as Ms. Landis can confirm, I am, too. I'd take it
very kindly if you'd hand over your weapons before we go
upstairs and continue this conversation."

Sam was only letting himself think about one thing:
finding a way out of this.

Thinking wasn't easy, not when his whole head still rung
from the impact of the butt of Harold Price's gun against
his skull. Sam had lunged at the older man just before
Wayland, at Harold's orders, had started to tie Sam's
hands and feet. But Harold had been on his guard.

Sam supposed he was lucky Harold had just hit him and
not shot him. Unfortunately that didn't do anything to ease
the throbbing in his head.

Ignore it, he told himself now, as the Prices' minivan
jounced underneath him. *Pain is the least of your problems.*

He couldn't stand to consider what the worst of his
problems was.

He couldn't—wouldn't—let himself think about what
might happen if he didn't come up with a way to get himself and Kelley out of the Prices' hands.

The minivan gave another jolt, and Sam deduced that
Wayland had turned off the paved road and onto a gravel
one. He scanned the map in his mind and realized that the
only gravel road this close to Cairo was the one leading toward the firing range.

It wasn't a comforting thought.

He could hear Helen and Wayland conversing quietly
now in the front seat. For such a gentle-looking lady, Hel-
en had turned remarkably fierce once she'd gotten a gun in
her hand. Sam was willing to bet she was still holding Kelley's pistol, and that even though her voice was low, she was

issuing definite orders to her son Wayland, who was driving.

Harold Price wasn't with them. He'd headed toward the boat slips once Sam and Kelley had been safely stashed in the back of the minivan.

And that meant that if the plan evolving in Sam's head had any chance of working, he had to set it in motion soon.

Kelley was sitting across from him. Her hands, like his, were tied tightly behind her back, and her ankles were knotted together with what seemed to be ropes from the Prices' sailboat. Her face was white and serious, her ash blond hair loose and disordered. Her eyes seemed focused on the distance, remote and endlessly blue, almost as though she was trying to withdraw herself from the mess they were in.

He didn't blame her. *If you'd just kept your mind on business,* he berated himself, silently, furiously. *If you'd gone straight to Jack, instead of playing that hunch of yours...*

It didn't help to know that Kelley had had the same gut instinct. Sam had *known* there was danger in this case. He'd felt it, sensed it—

He cut himself off. There wasn't time for this. And it was leading him too close to all the things he didn't want to think about, anyway.

He glanced at Helen and Wayland, who were still conversing in undertones, and managed to take advantage of another bump in the road to roll himself closer to Kelley.

She seemed to see immediately what he was up to. She tilted toward him, as though the two of them had just happened to lose their balance and had ended up with their faces close together on the floor of the minivan.

The feminine scent of Kelley's hair and skin seemed to reach out and envelop Sam—damn it, he thought he was even catching the earthy, seductive musk their two bodies had generated in the heat of their lovemaking last night.

He fought off the urge to drink in that heady perfume and concentrated on keeping his voice as low as possible.

"Listen to me," he murmured. His lips were close to Kelley's ear, and the memory of the way he'd cried out his need for her last night was driving him half-crazy. "I think Wayland is on the fence about this whole deal."

"I agree." The quiet strength in her voice surprised him. "If we get him talking, try to exploit whatever doubts he's having—"

So he'd been wrong. That distant look on her face had meant she was thinking hard, not simply wishing she was somewhere else.

The problem was that her thoughts were the exact opposite of Sam's.

"Talking with the Prices is a mistake," he said bluntly. "We don't have time for it."

He couldn't see her face. But the sudden bite in her voice was very clear. "Is that an order, Mr. Cotter?" she asked.

"It's a plain fact. Kelley, listen to me."

The ache that stabbed him from inside was sudden and fierce. *I want you to come out of this alive.* The words battered at him, demanding to be said. *I can't stand to see you hurt again . . . I can't stand the idea of losing you.*

I love you . . .

Sam closed his eyes, trying to hold back the torrent of feelings that was rising inside him.

This was exactly what he'd been trying to avoid. He couldn't afford to think of these things now—not now.

And he couldn't stop thinking about them.

He couldn't forget the way he'd lost himself in the sweet haven of Kelley's arms last night, the way his whole soul had come alive with visions of a happiness he'd thought had disappeared from his life for good.

He'd thought about waking up next to Kelley every morning for the rest of his life.

He'd thought about babies—their babies—chubby, uncertain new lives, tottering in to ease the pain of the child—and the happiness—they'd lost so cruelly.

He'd gone to sleep picturing babies with blue eyes just like Kelley's, wide and calm and beautiful.

He wanted to tell her that, but he couldn't.

He wanted to take her in his arms and never let her go.

He couldn't do that, either.

They were both hog-tied and helpless in the back of Harold and Helen Price's van. The time was all wrong for these thoughts, these longings.

And if Sam couldn't come up with a way to get them both through this safely, there never would be a right time.

Never had a lonely sound to it. Sam's throat hurt as he fought against it, and against the wave of panic that kept threatening him from deep in his gut.

"We're going to have one shot at this, when Wayland stops the van. I want you to—"

"Sam—"

He shook his head in frustration. "Just listen," he said, more forcefully now, as though by sheer strength of will he could make this come out the way he wanted it to.

But his voice caught Helen Price's ear. "That's enough talking back there," she said sharply, turning to look at them.

This was it, Sam thought. Their only chance, and it was about to slip through their fingers.

He started to roll himself back to a sitting position again, but just before he moved away from Kelley, he managed to mutter very quietly against her ear, "Launch yourself at Helen when the van stops. I'll do the same. Maybe Wayland will—"

"I said that's enough." Helen sounded irritated now. "Although what you think you stand to gain at this point, I really can't imagine. Wayland, look out for that pothole. The storm has made a wretched mess of these roads."

Sam had a sudden vision of what it must have been like to grow up under Harold and Helen Price's thumbs. He'd never encountered a pair so affable on the outside, yet so callous under their mask of gentility. No wonder Wayland had turned out to be so slick and shallow.

"Where did Harold go?" Kelley asked the question almost casually, as though she hadn't heard Helen's warning. She ignored Sam's glare, too, when he tried to warn her into silence.

Helen hesitated, and then, to Sam's surprise, seemed to decide it wouldn't do any harm to answer. "To the boat, of course," she said.

Sam didn't like the fact that she seemed willing to let them in on what was happening. Only very confident criminals felt it was safe to talk to their intended victims.

But Kelley's question, and Helen's answer, made something click in Sam's brain. "The boat," he echoed. "That's where you've got Steve Cormier stashed."

"That's right. Although Wayland didn't realize that when he went to secure things last night."

"I thought I was doing you a favor." Wayland sounded bitter about it.

His mother turned to look at him briefly. "And when you 'borrowed' those twenty-dollar bills from the kitchen drawer?" she said. "Did you think that was doing us a favor, too?"

Wayland shrugged defensively. "I needed a few bucks," he said. "I never thought—" He lifted his hands from the steering wheel, then grasped it again to turn the minivan.

From his position on the floor Sam could see the sign for the firing range, clear against the scudding clouds overhead. The memory of his own useless attempt to hit a target a couple of days ago assailed him suddenly. He could feel the frustration and the failure of it settling into him again, and he fought hard for the strength he knew he had to hang on to.

"Somehow it's hard to imagine your own parents turning out to be counterfeiters, isn't it?" Wayland continued.

"There's no need to be flippant, Wayland. This is a very serious business."

"I already figured that out." Wayland's bitterness spilled over as he spoke. "It's bad enough to find out the family fortune I'm supposed to inherit doesn't even exist any-more. But the idea of you getting yourselves deep in debt to the mob to build the Windspray Community, for God's sake—"

"That's enough." Helen cut him off. "Keep your eyes on the road. There are a lot of branches down after that storm."

Sam looked over at Kelley and saw her brow furrowed in thought.

Stay quiet, he warned her silently.

She frowned at him and ignored the clear message in his eyes.

"So building the Windspray Community was a last-ditch way to make enough money to rebuild the family fortunes," she said. "It must have been hard to imagine going bankrupt, when the Prices have always been so wealthy and prominent."

She was quick at putting ideas together, Sam had to hand it to her. If only she would stop prodding Helen Price—

Once again, though, Helen answered readily enough. Was it some magic in Kelley's voice that did it, Sam wondered, or was the older woman secretly glad to be getting the story off her chest?

"It was *impossible* to imagine going bankrupt," she corrected. "The sales of the Windspray cottages were supposed to bail us out. Harold never would have considered building a resort community on his family property otherwise. But when the bottom fell out of the real estate market—"

She shrugged. The motion was enough to give Sam a glimpse of Kelley's pistol in her right hand, loaded and at the ready. He groaned inwardly and clamped his teeth together.

"Mob financiers aren't terribly sympathetic about things like real-estate slumps," Kelley said. "Did they call in your loan?"

"Yes. With interest." Helen sounded grim now. "Thank goodness I had that old engraving talent I could parlay into a deal, or Harold and I would have been in a real jam." It didn't seem to bother her in the least that Sam and Kelley were now in just as serious a jam.

"So you agreed to turn out counterfeit money for the mob as a way of paying back your debt," Kelley said. "And everybody was happy until Wayland moved back home and stumbled on a few loose bills that he figured nobody would miss."

"None of this was my fault." Wayland sounded petulant. "I never made any counterfeit bills. I wish everybody would stop—"

"Of course it wasn't your fault." Kelley's smooth voice slid in over his. "It's obvious you didn't know what was going on—Sam and I can both testify how surprised you seemed when you came back from fastening down that sailboat last night."

"You bet I was surprised." For once Wayland sounded absolutely sincere. "Hell, I thought that guy Cormier was on *my* trail—thought my wife sicced him on me to see if she could get her hands on some of my family money. And now it turns out there's no family money anyway, and it's you two who are the private investigators, and my parents are the criminals. If I didn't—"

And then, suddenly, Kelley's words seemed to sink in. "Testify?" he repeated, more slowly now. "You mean you could—"

"Never mind, Wayland," Helen snapped. "There's the spot. Pull over the lip of the hill. We don't want anybody to see us, not that anybody's likely to be around at this hour on a Sunday morning."

Kelley hadn't given up. Sam clenched his teeth again and wondered if this meant she was sticking with her own plan and ignoring his. If he had to jump Helen alone—

"Until now, you haven't done anything wrong, Wayland." Kelley sounded so cool that Sam almost wanted to believe in the calmness she was projecting. "But now that you're actively helping Harold and Helen—"

The fury in Helen's once-gentle brown eyes as she turned to face the back of the van made Sam wince inside. "Just because Wayland acts like a half-wit, don't make the mistake of assuming that I'm one, too," she said. "I see what you're trying to do. It won't help."

Sam saw Wayland look over his shoulder, first at Kelley and then at his mother. He seemed to be deep in thought. Sam couldn't decide whether that was a good sign or not.

"Park," Helen commanded. "Here."

Wayland guided the van into a spot just over the crest of a hill. Sam could hear the wind slacken slightly as the vehicle pulled into the sheltered area. In the moment of silence just after Wayland shut off the engine, he managed to catch Kelley's eye, and was startled and relieved to see her almost imperceptible nod.

She hadn't ignored him. The thought made him exultant.

They were still partners, in spite of everything. She was going along with his plan.

And the time to put the plan into action was right now. Sam nodded in return, and the two of them scrambled upright in unison, fighting for balance, careening against each other as they launched themselves toward the front of the van and over the seat at Helen Price.

It was a crazy thing to do. Sam was aware of that. But i was the only chance he could see. If Helen was surprised enough to let go of the gun, and if Wayland was ambivalent enough not to pick it up—

That was already more ifs than Sam was comfortable with. But the situation was desperate enough that it was worth a desperate attempt to get out of it.

At first he thought they'd pulled it off. Helen gave an enraged shout as Kelley and Sam hit her, and Sam could hear the welcome sound of the pistol thudding against the carpeted floor at her feet.

"Wayland, don't get yourself into something you can't get out of!" Even with that streak of urgency cutting through it, Kelley's voice was still as sweet as honey, still hard to resist. "You deserve better than to spend time in jail for something your parents did."

Between the two of them, they had Helen pinned to the seat now. And Wayland was hesitating, refusing to jump in to his mother's rescue despite her angry demands that he help her.

Sam hauled his tied legs all the way over the seat, managing not to land a boot in Wayland's face. "Come on, pal," he said. "Listen to Kelley. Untie us and we'll make sure you get out of—"

He didn't get a chance to finish the sentence. The passenger door swung open without warning, and Kelley, who'd braced herself against it, lost her balance and collapsed on the grass outside the minivan at Harold Price's feet.

She wrestled herself to a sitting position almost immediately, but Harold ignored her, knowing—Sam had to admit it—that she had no chance of escaping now.

The whole plan had depended on getting to wherever they were going before Harold showed up to join them.

But it hadn't worked.

Harold reached in and picked up the pistol that had fallen from his wife's grip. He was glowering at his son, at Sam, at everything his bristling blue eyes touched on.

"Your brother assured me that his people were extremely persistent when we hired you," he said. "But surely, Mr. Cotter, even you can see that the time for persistence is over now."

Chapter 14

It's over now...

The words kept echoing in Kelley's head.

Harold had hauled her roughly to her feet and kept a firm hand on her elbow as he propelled her across the wet grass. Her low leather pumps kept skidding out from under her, and she protested against Harold's pace.

He paid no attention. His concentration, and Helen's, seemed to be directed wholly toward their son. "We'll go over this one last time," Harold said, "and so help me, boy, if you mess it up—"

"Stop bugging me, all right?" Wayland sounded like a sulky teenager, Kelley thought. It was still the single hopeful thing she could see about this whole ugly situation.

The firing range sloped down toward the beach on the other side of the hill they'd just crested. Kelley could see the huddled body of a man at one of the target markers ahead of them. When he lifted his head slightly, revealing wind-tossed red hair, she recognized Steve Cormier. Harold must have brought him here on the boat, she thought, and marched him from the shore. From the cautious way Cormier was holding himself, it appeared that Harold had been none too gentle about it.

"You do realize, of course, that that man is a federal agent." Sam's voice was hard and angry.

"Of course we realize it," Helen Price snapped.

"A federal—" Wayland sounded incredulous. "I don't believe this is actually happening."

"Well, you'd better believe it," Harold said. "And unless we can dispose of Cormier and these two in some plausible way, we're going to have no chance of this thing ever dying down."

"The boat is anchored just offshore," Helen said. "We'll be on it as soon as this is over. Do try to keep your head on straight, Wayland, for once in your life."

"Wayland." Kelley half turned and met Wayland's confused gaze. "You're smarter than they're giving you credit for, smart enough to see—"

"Shut up." Harold shook her arm roughly, and once again Kelley had to scramble to keep her footing. "You're wasting your time. Wayland is with us. He has no other choice."

"You're sure we have to leave the country?" Wayland sounded as though he was desperately trying to find another choice for himself. "Couldn't we just—"

"It's all settled." Harold came to an abrupt stop. "The people we owe money to aren't going to just forget about it. And neither is the federal government. We've got to get out of the country, the sooner the better. Now all we have to do—"

Out of the corner of her eye Kelley saw Sam move suddenly. His raincoat was a blur against the green grass and gray sky, and she knew he must have been waiting to take advantage of the fact that the Prices had untied Sam's and Kelley's feet so that they could walk across the broad field.

But once again, he was outmatched. She watched Wayland lunge for Sam's feet, and in no time at all Helen Price was standing over him, weapon pressing into the back of his neck.

"Don't shoot him!" The words felt as though they were ripped out of her. "Sam—"

Harold Price laughed. Kelley could feel the sound vibrating unpleasantly at the spot where Harold was gripping her arm. "I keep forgetting that true-lover act of yours wasn't just an act," he said. "I'm sorry, Ms. Landis, but we're going to have to shoot him—and you too."

"And Steve Cormier—or whatever his name really is." Helen nodded at the roped and tied FBI agent they were approaching.

Kelley's heart rate had slammed into high speed at the sight of Helen's gun—Kelley's own gun, the one Sam had helped her buy—at Sam's neck. It was impossible to keep her voice steady as she said, "How exactly are you planning to make this look plausible?"

"It's simple." Harold started walking again. "We're sticking with our original story—that Cormier is a bad-apple agent, and actually in league with the mob masterminding the whole counterfeit scheme."

It did happen, Kelley knew. Jack Cotter had told her tales of federal agents who'd crossed the line to become criminals.

"We'll make it look as though you found the equipment at his cottage, he ran and you tracked him down. Most of the evidence is already planted—that's why we were so late getting back to Cairo this morning. Once we move the heavy equipment from our basement, we'll be done. When the FBI traces you, they'll come to the conclusion that you spotted Cormier and trailed him back here when he came to pick up the rest of his stuff."

"And then we all accidentally happened to shoot each other." Sam's deep voice was hoarse with cynicism.

"No." Helen Price took over. "You fired at Cormier, but because your aim isn't what it once was—" Kelley saw Sam wince with the sudden realization of how his own old injury was playing into the Prices' hands "—you hit Ms. Landis instead."

"No." His voice was low, but the instinctive protest in it made Kelley flinch.

"She, meanwhile, also fired at Cormier—and hit him. But in remorse at the realization that you'd mortally wounded your girlfriend, you—what's the phrase the papers always use, Harold? You turned the gun on yourself. That's it."

She sounded crisp and businesslike. And they were all getting close enough to Steve Cormier now that Kelley knew there wasn't a lot of time left for talking—or for anything at all.

She looked over her shoulder again and saw Sam wrestling against Wayland's restraining grip. But Wayland was physically strong, even if he had the moral backbone of a pollywog, and Sam's struggles were doing him no good.

They never do, she wanted to say to him.

She thought of the way he'd reacted when she'd first mentioned the child they had lost.

And the way he'd bolted out of bed this morning, escaping back into the Windspray case because it was easier than dealing with all the feelings their lovemaking had conjured up during the night.

Pain did that to Sam, she thought—it drove him in on himself, into that empty place where he never allowed anyone to follow.

The thought that they probably weren't going to make it out of here alive—that Sam might go to his death still mired in that bleak, lonely landscape inside him—made Kelley want to cry.

Or fight.

Her relationship with Sam had been a struggle from the first day they'd met. This past week alone, she realized suddenly, she felt as though she'd been wrestling one giant after another—Sam's silence, her own fears, their shared losses, the hope that kept flaring up at all the wrong times.

Was all that struggle going to be for nothing?

For this?

For a brutal death on a windswept field, without one word of love being exchanged between them?

Her mind wouldn't accept it.

Her heart wouldn't accept it.

And when Sam raised his steely eyes to meet hers, she locked on to his gaze with a ferocity that seemed to startle him.

Good, she thought. *Now listen.*

She had to mouth the words quickly, while the Prices' attention was elsewhere.

What she wanted to say was *I love you.*

And, *I won't lose you like this.*

And, *We can start again.*

What she had to say—the only words she had time for—was very different.

"Work on Wayland."

She shaped the syllables as clearly as she could, and felt her neck jerk painfully as Harold started walking her closer to Steve Cormier. In a few minutes she would probably be dead. So would Cormier.

And once the Prices had had a chance to switch the guns to make things look authentic, Sam would be dead, too.

She tried to look back at him, but Harold Price was blocking her way. She felt a surge of panic so strong it made her knees buckle. She tried for speech, tried to find a way to convince Harold and Helen that they were only creating more trouble for themselves, but the words wouldn't form. She was simply too scared.

And she hadn't told Sam she loved him....

The tears came without warning, although she tried to fight them back.

"Sam..." She said his name, but it was too soft to carry over the gusty wind.

What was he thinking right now? She reached desperately for the kind of near-telepathic communication they had sometimes shared, but she felt no connection between them, nothing but empty air.

Was he thinking that this was the way all partnerships ended?

That it was no surprise his relationship with Kelley had come to this?

"No..." She couldn't hold back the soft protest as she thought of how sweetly they'd loved each other last night, how instinctively they'd been drawn back together this past week in spite of all their efforts to stay apart.

Was Sam thinking now that it would have been better if none of this had ever happened?

The thought that she hadn't told him how much she loved him was bad enough.

The thought that he might not want her love was a thousand times worse.

And none of it mattered anyway, because Harold Price was holding her steady now, and Helen was taking up a position several yards away, obviously getting ready to simulate the gun battle they were hoping the authorities would reconstruct when this was all over. Kelley closed her eyes and prayed it would be quick, and that neither she nor Sam would suffer for long.

And then she waited for the gunshot.

It didn't come.

Instead, she heard Wayland's voice, loud and insistent.

"Wait!" he called out. "Wait just a doggone minute here."

Kelley let out the breath she'd been holding in.

"Keep out of this, Wayland," Harold warned his son.

"I *won't* keep out of it."

Whatever Sam had been saying to Wayland, it seemed to have pumped the other man's voice full of an authority that Kelley had never heard there before. *Way to go, Sam,* she thought, and found herself holding her breath again, waiting.

"Being an accessory to counterfeiting is one thing," Wayland was telling his parents now. "But accessory to murder—that's different. Especially murdering a woman."

As far as Kelley was concerned, murder was murder. But if Wayland wanted to quibble about gender, she, for one, wasn't going to argue with him.

"Especially a woman like Kelley." He sounded downright belligerent now. "Damn it, I won't be a part of this."

"It's too late. You already are." Harold's voice was grim. He took a step away from Kelley, leaving her unguarded.

She was still bound hand and foot—Harold had retied the ropes on her ankles when they'd reached the far end of the field—but the senior Prices were paying enough attention to Wayland now that Kelley had a chance to lower herself to the grass and slide her ankles through the circle of her arms. It wasn't as good as being free, but with her hands in front of her she felt a little less helpless.

Steve Cormier was doing the same thing. The three Prices were arguing loudly now, and Cormier, who'd been lying silently on the ground next to the target marker, began to move, slowly heading toward Kelley.

"What are you going to do if I don't go along with this?" Wayland was demanding. "Shoot me too? Your own son?" He seemed confident that they wouldn't. Kelley hoped to God he was right.

She got to her feet again, cursing the tight knots that held her ankles firmly together. She'd only barely regained her balance when she saw what Cormier was up to. Harold had given his weapon to Wayland to use in guarding Sam, which left him empty-handed when Cormier stood up sud-

denly and hurtled himself at Helen Price. Helen went
sprawling, the gun skidded over the grass and Cormier
quickly rolled himself on top of it.

Kelley knew there wasn't time to waste. She saw a flurry
of motion to her left and wondered what kind of miracle
had occurred for Sam to be moving so quickly. He seemed
to be shouting, too, or maybe that was somebody else. She
thought she heard yelling from over the crest of the hill, but
she couldn't spare the concentration to try to figure out
who was causing it.

Her whole attention was focused on Harold Price, who
was lunging toward his son—and the gun. She hurled herself at him as hard as she could, and was rewarded with a
deep *oof* as she connected with the back of his knees,
knocking him down. The air whooshed out of her own
body, too, leaving her winded, but she fought her way upright again, gasping for breath.

"Give me that gun!" Harold was roaring at his son now,
scrambling unsteadily to his feet.

"I won't. You're both crazy—this whole thing is crazy."

Wayland held the gun away from Harold's outstretched
hands, backing up as his father approached him. Kelley saw
his finger pressing the trigger, and the sudden loud report
of the weapon made all of them jump, including Wayland.

And then he backed into Sam.

Sam's hands were still tied, but he, too, had managed to
bring them in front of his body. He captured Wayland from
behind, locking strong arms around Wayland's shoulders.

There *was* yelling now. It must be the owners of the firing range, Kelley thought. But would the sound of shooting have warned them that something was wrong? People
were supposed to fire weapons out here—that was doubt-
less why Harold and Helen had chosen the spot.

Once again, there wasn't time to sort it out. She heard
Harold's cruel chuckle as their former client said, "You
might as well let him have it, Wayland. We don't have to

worry about him hitting anything. From what I hear, his shooting arm is virtually crippled.''

To Kelley's right, Helen Price and Steve Cormier were still trying to gain possession of the second gun. She knew she should be helping Cormier out, but somehow she couldn't take her eyes off Sam's face as Wayland slowly lowered the gun and handed it over.

Sam looked pale, and drained.

All the struggling he'd been doing couldn't have been good for his shoulder, she knew. He must be in pain, serious pain.

And Harold's taunting was exactly the kind of thing that had always set Sam off, made him do crazy things.

She wanted to call out to him, but she couldn't. She felt drained herself, exhausted by the fear that had taken over her body and her mind. All she could do was watch as Sam took hold of the revolver in his tied hands and raised it to shoulder level.

She could see the muscles in his arms shaking.

She could see the sweat start on his brow, under that unruly fall of hair.

She could see the fury in his blue eyes. And the determination. His face was pale with pain or doubt or both.

And suddenly she knew what was in his mind. *I'm going to do this, you son of a bitch.* The words were as clear as if she'd heard him speak. *I'm not going to kill you, because I'm not a killer. But I am going to win this fight.*

Everything seemed to slow down as Sam squeezed the trigger. Kelley heard the blast from the muzzle and recoiled instinctively. The puff of smoke was as gray as the clouds above, and it quickly disappeared against the sky.

Harold Price howled and dropped to the ground, clutching his right knee. Helen gave up her attempt to grab the second gun and rushed toward her husband.

And then Jack Cotter appeared.

Kelley couldn't imagine how he'd gotten there. But it really was Jack, with four or five other people, shouting at Sam and Kelley to keep their heads down, and at the Prices to get their hands in the air.

Everything turned loud and chaotic. Kelley could hear the crackle of walkie-talkies, and somewhere in the distance the howl of a siren.

She felt someone untying her wrists and ankles and didn't even care who it was.

She heard Wayland protesting, and Harold moaning, and people demanding to know whether Steve Cormier was all right.

None of it really registered.

The only thing that really mattered was the glimpse of Sam's turbulent blue eyes through the sudden confusion of people and noise. She held on to his gaze like a lifeline and felt her heart starting to thud against her ribs as he moved toward her, pushing past a woman in a dark blue suit who seemed to be trying to talk to him.

He looked as though he'd run a marathon over rough terrain. His face was still white and shaken, and the way he was holding his upper body told her he was in a great deal of pain. But he reached for her anyway, clasping her arms so strongly that Kelley winced at the bite of his long fingers.

Sam winced, too. But before she could ask him if he was all right, he turned the same question on her.

"Are you okay?" he demanded roughly. "You're not hurt?"

"I'm okay."

She wanted to move closer into his arms, to feel herself surrounded by the hard strength of his body. She needed the reassurance that he was alive, that he was as stubborn, as hardheaded as ever, that their chance at love hadn't vanished in a bleak moment in an empty field.

But Sam wasn't saying anything about love. He was looking fiercely into her eyes as though he wasn't sure he could trust her words. She could feel his arms shaking as he held on to her.

"Your shoulder—" She reached toward it. "Sam, you must have—"

"It doesn't matter." He shook his head tightly. "The only thing that matters is that we both got out of this alive. Thank God."

His last words were hoarse with relief. The woman in the dark suit had approached him from behind again and was speaking to him. Someone was asking Kelley a question, too. The siren she'd heard earlier was getting closer, and she could see flashing lights coming over the crest of the hill.

Someone had alerted the local police, she thought. And the ambulance. She was glad—Sam needed help for that shoulder. Judging by the pallor of his face, he was covering up a lot more agony than he was letting on.

He didn't seem to be covering up any feelings of love, as far as Kelley could see. Relief, gratitude, triumph—those were the only emotions she'd glimpsed behind those blue eyes of his.

We both got out of this alive. Thank God. After everything they'd been through, this was still just a case to Sam.

Kelley felt something wrench inside her. Suddenly she wanted to be alone, away from all these people and their questions, until she could answer the painful question that was forcing itself into her thoughts.

Was her heart strong enough to survive losing Sam Cotter a second time?

Night was falling and she still had no good answer.

Kelley pulled on her warmest sweater, the yellow wool one, over her jeans, which were finally dry after last night's rainstorm. Her sneakers were still damp, but she didn't care. Cold feet were a small price to pay for the luxury of a little time by herself.

She'd spent the entire day with Jack Cotter and his superiors, and with Wiley and the local police. She hadn't seen Sam since this morning—he'd been carried off in the ambulance directly from the firing range, and although she'd asked about him repeatedly, it seemed that no one among the law-enforcement crowd knew the extent of his injuries, or when he might be back.

If he might be back.

The case here was nearly closed, as far as the FBI and Cotter Investigations were concerned. Things had started coming to a head last night, Jack had explained.

"Our agents have been keeping an eye on the Houston mob just as a matter of course," he said. "When Harold and Helen Price showed up out of the blue to meet with one of the mob's top financial people, bells started going off."

Jack hadn't heard the news until early this morning. He'd tried to call Sam and Kelley, only to discover the phones weren't working. Uneasy about the lack of communication and the Prices' newly discovered connection to organized crime, he'd enlisted some backup and come straight to Cairo.

"And it's a lucky thing you've got health-conscious neighbors," he said. Susan Gustaffson, on her way to an early-morning workout at the Windspray health club, had happened to notice the Prices' minivan leaving the community not long before Jack came looking for his brother and Kelley.

"And to think Susan was one of our leading suspects," Kelley replied. Their questions about the Gustaffsons had been answered—the unexplained income of the year before had been a gift from Susan's father, and the gun Sam had found in their cottage was one that Jon used for target shooting.

The other loose ends in the case had been tied up by now, too. It had become very clear how Harold and Helen Price had manipulated Sam and Kelley, substituting an obviously faked job application for the one Steve Cormier had actually given them when he'd started working at Windspray, and leading their hired investigators directly to Cormier's cottage after they'd captured and imprisoned the handyman.

Wayland had gladly backed up Cormier's account of being tied and gagged in the hold of the Prices' sailboat for two days. In fact, Wayland was happily filling in every blank he could, out of eagerness to distance himself from his parents' crimes.

It was ironic, Kelley thought, that their prime suspects were turning out to be the best sources of information now. Not only was Wayland supplying details about the Prices' financial affairs—including naming the tottering oil companies where Harold had lost most of his money—but Susan Gustaffson had been the one to put Jack on the trail of the Prices' vehicle early Sunday morning. It had taken a few false starts, but the federal agents had finally narrowed the search down to the road that led to the firing range.

"Although it looked as though you guys had things more or less under control by the time we arrived," Jack had said, sounding amazed. "How the hell three unarmed people managed to get the upper hand over the Prices still beats me."

"It was a little diplomacy," Kelley told him, recalling Wayland's role in their escape, "and a lot of guts."

She hadn't been able to forget the look on Sam's face as he'd leveled the gun and fired—with point-blank accuracy—at Harold Price. What had that effort cost him, physically and mentally? How many old demons had he had to overcome to make that perfect shot?

And where the hell was he now?

After a hasty meal in the Windspray restaurant, Kelley had decided that she needed to get away from the commotion at the Windspray Community. She walked by herself to the massive stone breakwater near the town pier. The tide was ebbing, and the surf at the base of the breakwater was slow and deliberate, as though it had spent all its fury in last night's storm and was retreating into calmer waters.

And what about me? Kelley asked herself as she perched on a long flat rock with her arms clasped around her knees. *Is there anywhere I can go to find peace, now that I've let Sam Cotter turn my life upside down again?*

She didn't find an answer in the waves. But the motion of the sea *was* calming, and she let herself be lulled by it, watching the water curl itself into a long roll and then splash along the edge of the breakwater in a motion that seemed quick and slow at the same time.

"Kelley."

At first the sound of her name seemed to blend with the hissing of the surf. She didn't turn around until Sam spoke a second time.

"Not thinking of taking off across the Gulf like the Prices were, I hope."

"Sam—" She turned suddenly and saw him standing at the base of the huge pile of stones.

"Don't come down." He shook his dark head and clambered—unsteadily, she noticed—onto the breakwater. "I'm not as infirm as they might have told you."

"Nobody told me anything." She got to her feet, holding out a hand to him as he stepped from one big rock to the next. "Have you been at the hospital all this time?"

He nodded. He looked exhausted, Kelley thought.

And pale.

And gorgeous.

The touch of his palm against hers was like coming alive again. It wasn't just the warmth of his skin or the familiar

grip of his fingers. It was the way he was reaching out fo
her, accepting her offer.

"Thanks," he said. "I may not be infirm, but I am tire
as hell."

"And not too stubborn to admit it, for once."

"Damn, woman, give me a break, would you?" He sa
down next to her, stretching long legs out in front of hin
toward the open sea. She watched him lean on one hip, star
to pat his back pocket, then grimace. "Smoked the last on
on the way back down here," he muttered. "Well, mayb
that means it's time to quit again."

"You seem to quit every time you finish a pack."

"I know." His grin was sardonic, and Kelley found her
self smiling back at him, responding instinctively to th
quick gleam in his blue eyes. "Just goes with my stubbor
personality, I guess," he added. "Quitting isn't one of m
strong points."

She thought about him following his dad into unknow
territory at the tender age of seven. She felt fairly confi
dent that Sam Cotter had been born into this world wit
strong opinions of his own already forming in that head o
his.

"It's a good thing you're so stubborn." Her voice wa
softer as she answered him. "Getting those ropes off you
ankles was probably what saved us this morning." He wa
leaning back on one long arm, but his other hand wa
splayed against his thigh. Kelley could see the faint re
abrasions on his fingers from his efforts in fighting th
knots around his ankles.

She looked up at his face again, and saw for the first tim
that there was a tan bandage showing at the neck of hi
navy blue sweatshirt. She frowned and raised a hand to it

"I heard a rumor at one point this afternoon that you'
dislocated that shoulder all over again," she told him. "I
that's true—"

"Shh." He shook his head at her and captured her hand before she could reach the elastic bandage. "You're changing the subject, sweetheart."

"No, I'm not. The subject was how stubborn you are, and it seems to me—"

"We were talking about my never knowing when to quit. That's what's important here."

Kelley met his eyes again and felt her whole body tremble with the longing to be closer to him, to see his face transformed by that slow, sexy smile she loved, to know she could hold and comfort him without wondering how long it would last this time.

But he was talking about quitting.

She swallowed, and said, "I don't understand."

Sam's gaze shifted, and for a long moment he seemed to be mesmerized by the slow sweep of the waves, just as Kelley had been a few minutes earlier. The light wind stirred his tangled dark hair, and the look in his eyes was pensive, even regretful.

As he turned back toward Kelley, he sighed.

And she felt her heart constrict into a small, painful knot, just as it had the first time he'd rejected her.

"Hell, I didn't understand, either, sweetheart, until I realized this morning how close we'd come to getting ourselves killed." He started to shove his free hand through his hair, but Kelley saw him flinch as he moved his shoulder.

Everything was reminding him of the old lessons he'd learned so well, she thought.

And suddenly she couldn't stand to hear him say the same words she'd heard three years ago. *It was never meant to be. You'll be better off without me.*

"I know," she said quickly, cutting off his next remark. "You think there's no good way for us to work together, and maybe you're right. Maybe I should look for a job with another agency once you take over from Wiley. But, Sam—"

"Damn it, Kelley, will you listen to me?"

"I *am* listening to you. You're trying to tell me this whole thing was a mistake, and it nearly cost us both our lives. But, Sam—" This time she overrode his objections. "We may have gotten each other into a lot of trouble, but we saved each other, too. If I hadn't softened Wayland up—"

"I know."

"And if you hadn't finally gotten through to him—although I don't know exactly how you managed to do that—"

"I told him I was in love with you."

That stopped her short. Sam was grinning at her again, although there was something hesitant in his expression, too.

"Say that again." She wasn't completely willing to believe she'd heard him correctly.

"I said I told Wayland I was in love with you. Completely, absolutely, head over heels in love."

Kelley couldn't speak this time. Part of her—the trained, professional, suspicious part—was telling her, *Of course that's what he told Wayland. He knew Wayland was susceptible to that sort of stuff.* But the look in Sam's eyes, half triumphant, half uncertain, made her think it had been no mere ruse.

"I also told him I'd been such a bullheaded fool that it hadn't occurred to me to tell you I loved you until that very moment, when it was almost too late."

"Sam—"

He held up a hand, wincing slightly again. "Wayland thought that was just about the saddest old thing he'd ever heard," he said. "I don't think he was wild about the idea of seeing you die in the first place, but the idea of breaking up a red-hot romance in the process—"

"Was it true?"

Sam paused and drew in a slow breath.

"What you told Wayland—was it true, Sam?"

The laughter was gone from his face now. So was the hesitation. In its place she saw a tenderness, an honesty, that shook her. She'd never seen Sam let himself look so vulnerable, so certain and so scared at the same time. The undiluted longing in his eyes made Kelley want to cry.

"It was true." His words were slow, a declaration Kelley had barely allowed herself to imagine hearing from him again. "I love you, Kelley. Damn it, I never stopped loving you. I just couldn't figure out a way to fix what went wrong."

She saw frustration creeping into his expression and smiled at the sight of it. Nothing with Sam Cotter had ever been easy—nothing ever would be easy. But as long as they were together—as long as the visions his words were opening up were real, and not just dreams this time—

"Love fixes what's wrong, Sam." The throatiness of her own voice surprised her. She sounded close to tears—maybe she was *in* tears. She didn't care, and didn't let it get in the way of her next words. "And I love you, too—I've loved you all along. It would have been easier if I'd stopped, but I just couldn't."

Something primitive flashed in his dark blue eyes, and Kelley caught her breath as she felt that old intuitive connection between them. "You're like a part of me," she murmured, and finally gave in to the temptation to run her fingers through his thick, wind-tossed hair. "You've always been a part of me. You always will be."

"Then you can forgive me for what happened three years ago?"

"Forgive you!" It came out on a laugh. "Sam, what happened then was my fault. I was inexperienced, I had too much confidence in my own abilities, I didn't listen to—"

"Kelley, *none* of it was your fault. If I'd been thinking straight—"

She laughed again. She couldn't help it. "Sam, stop," she said. "It doesn't matter now. Remember? We love each other. And that's enough to fix what went wrong."

Sam was leaning closer to her now, his forehead almost touching hers. Kelley was aching with the need for his kiss, for his touch, for the silent confirmation of the love that had been stirring such unmistakable responses in her ever since this case had started.

But she didn't miss the direction of his gaze, or the sudden pensiveness on his face as he said, "We lost a new life that night, Kelley. Is love strong enough to make up for that, too?"

He was looking at her belly as he spoke. He lifted his free hand now and rubbed his knuckles gently over the spot where their child had started to grow.

Kelley had never been able to think of her lost child without a stab of anguish. But now, as Sam's hand moved in a slow circle against the soft yellow wool of her sweater, she felt something new—something strong enough to withstand pain, vital enough to fill her with hope.

She felt her own eyes shining with tears—and happiness—as she looked up at Sam again. "Love—real love—is strong enough to make up for anything," she told him "I'm willing to try again—if you are."

"Willing!"

And there it was, that slow, sexy smile that Kelley would have given her life for. It creased the corners of Sam's eyes, erasing all the cynicism he'd stored up there, and made his face come alive with emotions he'd kept buried for so long.

"I'm more than willing, sweetheart. I've been having fantasies about little blue-eyed babies all day while they were poking me with needles at that hospital, and taping me back together, and telling me I should rest—"

"You're not going to have much chance to rest." She said the words pensively. "Wiley's going to be leaving Cotter

Investigations in two more weeks, in case you'd forgotten.''

''I hadn't forgotten. But the new owner is a guy who's getting too old for the rough stuff in this business. He's planning on bringing in some new people to take care of the shoot-'em-up cases, so he can stick with what he really wants to do.''

''Financial crime?''

''Mmm.'' His noncommittal answer vibrated at the spot where her forehead was leaning against his. He kissed her briefly, tantalizingly, and added, ''Actually, it was babies I was thinking about. I hear the new owner is also planning to implement a very liberal mat─ ─al leave policy for his female employees.''

Kelley felt herself drawn into his smile, into the happiness that merged with hers and threatened to overflow. ''I suppose they would be blue-eyed babies,'' she said.

''They'd better be. And I just know they're going to be as elegant as their mother—''

''What if they're not? What if they're stubborn little so-and-so's, like their father?''

''What if they're *both?*''

The sound of his laughter blending with hers was a sweet music Kelley had almost forgotten about. ''Then we don't stand a chance,'' she said. ''Think we'd better not risk it?''

Sam shook his head and got awkwardly to his feet, holding out his left hand toward her. ''We don't have a choice,'' he said. ''There's no way I'm driving back to Austin with Jack and Wiley tonight. I'm too bushed. And that means sleeping with you in the cottage one more night. And *that* means—'' He waggled his dark eyebrows at her to let her know very specifically what he meant.

''And cigarettes aren't the only things I ran out of, if you know what I mean.'' His unrepentant grin seemed to wrap itself right around Kelley, and she moved into his arms feeling almost light-headed with joy. ''So we're going to

start to work on those blue-eyed babies right away, whether
that's part of the plan or not. Got it?''

"I've got it. And I've got *you*." She didn't know where
the familiar scent of Sam's skin ended and the fresh sea air
began. After this week together—this unlikely honeymoon
that had somehow managed to lead them in a backward
and roundabout way into marriage—she couldn't separate
the two in her mind.

And she didn't even want to try.

*   *   *   *   *

FORTUNE'S Children™

In July, get to know the Fortune family....

Next month, don't miss the start of Fortune's Children, a
fabulous new twelve-book series from Silhouette Books.

Meet the Fortunes—a family whose legacy is greater than
riches. Because where there's a will...there's a wedding!

When Kate Fortune's plane crashes in the jungle, her family
believes that she's dead. And when her will is read, they
discover that Kate's plans for their lives are more interesting
than they'd ever suspected.

Look for the first book, *Hired Husband*, by *New York Times*
bestselling author **Rebecca Brandewyne**. PLUS, a stunning,
perforated bookmark is affixed to *Hired Husband* (and
selected other titles in the series), providing a convenient
checklist for all twelve titles!

FREE
Keepsake
Bookmark

Launching in July wherever books are sold.

Silhouette®

™

Alicia Scott's

Elizabeth, Mitch, Cagney, Garret and Jake:

Four brothers and a sister—though miles separated them, they would always be a family.

Don't miss a single, suspenseful—sexy—tale in Alicia Scott's family-based series, which features four rugged, untamable brothers and their spitfire sister:

THE QUIET ONE...IM #701, March 1996

THE ONE WORTH WAITING FOR...IM #713, May 1996

THE ONE WHO ALMOST GOT AWAY...IM #723, July 1996

Order the first two books in the series: AT THE MIDNIGHT HOUR, IM#658 and HIDING JESSICA, IM#668. Send your name, address, zip or postal code, along with a cheque or money order (please do not send cash) for $3.75 for each book ordered ($4.25 in Canada) plus 75¢ postage and handling ($1.00 in Canada) payable to Silhouette Books, to:

In the U.S.	In Canada
Silhouette Books	Silhouette Books
3010 Walden Ave.	P. O. Box 636
P. O. Box 9077	Fort Erie, Ontario
Buffalo, NY 14269-9077	L2A 5X3

Please specify book title(s) with your order.
Canadian residents add applicable federal and provincial taxes.

"The Guiness Gang," found only in—

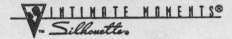

SILHOUETTE® Desire® CELEBRATION 1000

is on its way
in April, May and June 1996!

Join us for the celebration of Desire's 1000th book!
We'll have

- Book #1000, *Man of Ice* by Diana Palmer!
- Best-loved miniseries such as **Hawk's Way** by Joan Johnston, and **Daughters of Texas** by Annette Broadrick
- Fabulous new writers in our Debut author program

Plus you can enter our exciting Sweepstakes for a chance to win a beautiful piece of original Silhouette Desire cover art or one of many autographed Silhouette Desire books!

SILHOUETTE DESIRE CELEBRATION 1000
...because the best is yet to come!

DES1000TD

"Motherhood is full of love, laughter
and sweet surprises. Silhouette's collection
is every bit as much fun!"
—Bestselling author Ann Major

This May, treat yourself to...

WANTED: MOTHER

Silhouette's annual tribute to motherhood takes a
new twist in '96 as three sexy single men prepare for
fatherhood—and saying "I Do!" This collection makes
the perfect gift, not just for moms but for all romance
fiction lovers! Written by these captivating authors:

Annette Broadrick
Ginna Gray
Raye Morgan

BOOKS

THE
GREATEST
GIFT

"The Mother's Day anthology from Silhouette is the
highlight of any romance lover's spring!"
—Award-winning author **Dallas Schulze**

Silhouette®

™

MD96

Silhouette's recipe for a sizzling summer:

* Take the best-looking cowboy in South Dakota
* Mix in a brilliant bachelor
* Add a sexy, mysterious sheikh
* Combine their stories into one collection and you've got one sensational super-hot read!

Summer Sizzlers

MEN OF Summer

Three short stories by these favorite authors:

Kathleen Eagle
Joan Hohl
Barbara Faith

Available this July wherever Silhouette books are sold.

Look us up on-line at: http://www.romance.net

This July, watch for the delivery of...

An exciting new miniseries that appears in a different Silhouette series each month. It's about love, marriage—and Daddy's unexpected need for a baby carriage!

Daddy Knows Last unites five of your favorite authors as they weave five connected stories about baby fever in New Hope, Texas.

- **THE BABY NOTION** by Dixie Browning
  (SD#1011, 7/96)

- **BABY IN A BASKET** by Helen R. Myers
  (SR#1169, 8/96)

- **MARRIED...WITH TWINS!**
  by Jennifer Mikels
  (SSE#1054, 9/96)

- **HOW TO HOOK A HUSBAND (AND A BABY)**
  by Carolyn Zane
  (YT#29, 10/96)

- **DISCOVERED: DADDY** by Marilyn Pappano
  (IM#746, 11/96)

Daddy Knows Last arrives in July...only from

by
Cathryn Clare

The Cotter brothers—two private detectives and an
FBI agent—go wherever danger leads them...except
in matters of the heart!

But now they've just gotten the toughest assignments of
their lives....

Wiley Cotter has...
THE WEDDING ASSIGNMENT: March 1996
Intimate Moments #702

Sam Cotter takes on...
THE HONEYMOON ASSIGNMENT: May 1996
Intimate Moments #714

Jack Cotter is surprised by...
THE BABY ASSIGNMENT: July 1996
Intimate Moments #726

From Cathryn Clare—and only where
Silhouette Books are sold!

CCAR1